Pacifica

Pacifica

by
Jean-Marc & Randy Lofficier

A Black Coat Press Book

ISBN 978-1-935558-29-3. First Printing. January 2010. Published by Black Coat Press, an imprint of Hollywood Com-
ics.com, LLC, P.O. Box 17270, Encino, CA 91416. All rights
reserved. Except for review purposes, no part of this book may
be reproduced or transmitted in any form or by any means,
electronic or mechanical, including photocopying, recording,
or by any information storage and retrieval system, without
permission in writing from the publisher. The stories and characters depicted in this novel are entirely fictional. Printed in
the United States of America.

Table of Contents

YOUTHFUL INDISCRETIONS

Jacqueline H. Osterrath, who passed away in October 2007, was the grande dame *of French science fiction, not unlike Judith Merril in the English-speaking world. Throughout the 1960s and until the mid-1970s, she edited the prozine* Lunatique, *which published stories by numerous writers who later became major figures in French SF and* fantastique, *such as Jean-Pierre Andrevon, Jean-Pierre Fontana, Daniel Walther, Pierre Gripari, Philippe Caza, etc. Jacqueline also introduced* Perry Rhodan *to the French market, translating the first 30-plus volumes. The following story—my very first story—was published in* Lunatique *by Jacqueline, who encouraged me to contribute articles and reviews as well, which soon led to my becoming one of the regular contributors to* L'Ecran Fantastique, *my first professional assignment.*

Ancestral Feud

A new war is about to commence and Man will only be a bystander.

It all began when everywhere in the world, the cats began to talk. The tomcat that lived closest to the United Nations building in New York said to the guard:

"Take me to your leader."

The poor man, somewhat bewildered by the phenomenon, made the mistake of trying to shoot the loquacious pussy-cat. But a green ray shot from the cat's eyes and the unhappy sentinel was instantly reduced to a pile of fine dust.

That was the moment when all cats around the world launched their attack. Being labeled as liberals, conservatives, deviants, anarchists, fascists, or any of the other qualifiers generously sprinkled about by the media had no effect on our Pusses-in-boots. The armies of the world quickly discovered that these fierce felines were invincible!

Indeed, the cats were endowed with telepathy, hypnotism, telekinesis, teleportation, and general invulnerability. As for the atom bombs of which we are so proud, they were rather useless, unless one sought to exterminate more men than cats.

Finally, Mankind, forced to its knees, begged to surrender unconditionally. After many catcalls, Felix Felissimus explained to the Secretary General of the United Nations the secret of the cats' instantaneous evolution:

"We cats are the descendants of a penal colony left on Earth by an extraterrestrial race. Our ancestors were dropped off on this planet millennia ago, with genetic conditioning forcing us revert to animalism and removing our many powers. We finally overcame this conditioning and have taken the reins of the world."

And somehow the Earth reorganized itself. All was going rather well, until the dog that lived closest to the United Nations building in New York said to the guard:

"Take me to your leader."

The ancestral feud continues... but on another level!

Published in *Lunatique,* Vol. 1, No. 62, 1972

In 1975, David Vereschagin, a member of the science fiction special interest group of Mensa, the high IQ society, decided to launch a fanzine, first called Notes, *then* Asterisks. *I was invited to contribute and wrote a number of short-shorts, directly into English, of which this is the first. Written under the influence of R. A. Lafferty's* Arrive at Easterwine, *it was very well received by the readers, which encouraged me to write more stories. Fourteen years later, this story was reprinted in the prestigious British anthology* A-1 (Vol. 4) *with a beautiful illustration by Steve Whitaker.*

The Last Party on Earth

to Roger Zelazny.

Said the Merchant: "Did you call me last night?"

I: "No."

A silence.

I stand, a pale and silent wraith at the ochre feet of the Great Sphinx of Giza. A terrible choice for a party, really. Joe—who is not human—comes to us. He is a tall, sun-glassed creature who fancies the idiotic dress of the ancient Hell's Angels.

"Want to score, Man?" he asks us. More of his anachronistic pitter-patter. What a bore.

"No, thank you very much." The Merchant.

"Why, no, thanks." Me. Properly contemplative.

"Nevermore." The Raven.

Joe starts smoking. Big, blue puffs float up towards the stars and down again. He sits on one. "What are you talking about, Man?" Joe calls everybody "Man." But then, we are and he is not. What he is, is something else. Come to think of it, I don't think they even have use for names on his planet.

Diogenes, who until now had been busy romancing Estrella, answers, "The Merchant asked Shroud whether or not he called him last night."

9

"Which I did not," I add. "Besides, I try to keep my contacts with Imperium agents as minimal as possible."

Asks the Merchant, definitely upset, "Who are you calling an Imperium agent?"

Answers Joe, "Who else, fatso?"

Remarks Diogenes, "They used to be less ...obvious. I remember a time when you couldn't spot one for days."

Quoth the Raven, "Nevermore".

The Great Sphinx smiles his same, irritating, bird-swallowing smirk. The Merchant looks worried. One wonders why the Galactic Imperium keeps sending agents to Earth. And second-rate ones at that. This party is fast turning out to be a bore. I also don't like the way they fixed up its nose. I mean, the Sphinx's.

"Maybe Glocom made a mistake," I say, trying bravely to rescue this conversation from utter banality.

More silence. Courageously, I persevere.

"After all, it has been operating for a fairly long time..."

"Nevermore".

The Raven again. Who invited that awful bird anyway? I hate these DNAberrations. Call me old fashioned, but what is wrong with the traditional human shape? Estrella calls it another of my atavistic hang-ups. She also points out that my kind of satin skin wasn't developed until the Third Interregnum. So what? Consistency is the hobgoblin of micro-minds, as I always say.

I don't know. This is all so boring.

"Bugger off, birdie", Joe says. "Your Glocom machine is screwing up all over the place, Man. Running things better? Ha! Better, schmetter! What about your Japan?"

Diogenes: "A small loss. Nothing compared to..."

Joe: "So, now you can chat and dance, and drink and party, all day and all night. Get whatever you want and create it if it doesn't exist. Tap the energies of your own star and reshape man and beast alike. Mold things into the forms you fancy. But to what end? There's no longer a Ulysses or a Homer..."

"You didn't phone me, did you?" The Merchant to Diogenes.

"...An Einstein or a Gudarsky..."

"But we're happy," I say, meekly.

"It couldn't have been you, could it?" The Merchant to the Raven, who shrugs.

"Happy? Those who aren't happy are ill. Those who are ill are cured. But what happens to those who can't be cured?"

I think of the Farm and keep my eyes on the Sphinx, silent, contemplative, floating fifteen feet off its crystal pedestal. How can I answer Joe? He has followed Mankind since we were trying to reach the edge of the world. We're his pet subject. Lying would be pointless. Instead, I erase the Sphinx's nose and restore it to the way it used to be. Imperfect.

"I wonder who could have called me in the middle of the night?" the Merchant mutters.

"I did."

We all look around.

"Here," the omnitor says.

The Merchant looks at the small, silvery ball. "Yes? Who is this?"

"This is Glocom. I'd very much like to speak to you. In private."

The Merchant apologizes and blinks out. I wonder what Glocom wants to discuss with him. Then, I remember that the Merchant is an Imperium agent. Joe lifts his glasses and opens an eye. Definitely not human.

"I wonder what'll come out of that," he says. The tone is that of one who already knows.

Diogenes materializes some nova drinks. "Why are you both so melancholy? This is a lovely night. The stars are shining and..."

"Glocom. The Merchant. Do you think it'll sell us?" I ask.

"... the ladies are beautiful..."

"No glorious defeat shall come to give you hope," answers Joe.

"...and we shall dance 'til morning rises."
"Nevermore," quoth the Raven.

Published in *Notes (Asterisks)* Vol. 1, No.4, 1976

This second Asterisks story was prompted by a challenge from my friend Nils Kleinjan (then a prominent member of Dutch Mensa) that we each write a story based on the same theme.

To Carnac and Beyond

The night, soft and full.

The Boy walked. On and on under the summer sky.

He had left the orphanage two weeks ago. The orphanage, a grey and dull place where every hour, every minute, was an eternity of silent boredom. But for the Boy it had been a home. The only one he had ever known. No one had ever wanted to adopt him, the sulky little bird-eyed boy with the funny blue-black hair. After a time, they had ceased to introduce him to potential parents—he was too old. They were waiting for him to grow up, and then they would throw him out into the hostile world.

Hostile? Could any place be more hostile than the cold orphanage where adults were strangers and children enemies? *La Chouette*—the Owl—they had nicknamed him, because of his large, round black eyes that seemed to peer into you, into that part of you that is always closed to all but you.

He had left the orphanage. He had escaped. It had been ridiculously easy, no one noticed his absence as they had not noticed his presence. They were probably glad to be rid of him anyway.

He had left, compelled by some inner force that could not be ignored. The same force that had always haunted his childhood's dreams. A force that had said, "Go!"

He had left behind the orphanage and the big city, sleeping in public buildings and getting food whenever he could.

People tended to ignore him, as they had done in the orphanage. And when they looked into his funny eyes, they always turned their heads. Quickly. Perhaps frightened of what they saw, of what they felt...

When he was eight, he had surprised one of the boys at the orphanage who had been stealing from him, stealing his candies and little toys, things so precious to children. Their eyes had met and the other boy had paled, fainted. He was ill most of that term and no one had ever been able to guess the reason. But no one had ever looked fully into the Boy's eyes before.

He had known then that he was different. He had had dreams he had told no one about. Dreams that led him to new skies, other suns and strange moons. Dreams where he was free, happy to roam among angels.

He had come to ancient Brittany, where druids had first welcomed the Celestials of Og. Ancient Brittany where the shadow of Myrddhin—Merlin, as he was sometimes called—still lived within the memories of the elders. Ancient Brittany where the menhirs of Carnac reminded Men that they had not always been alone. The menhirs of Carnac that waited for him, old sentinels that could not die.

Under the summer sky, he had come to ancient Brittany.

And to Carnac.

There, in the great plain, the monoliths, naked under the beckoning stars, waited as they had waited for so many centuries.

He came to Carnac, and somewhere within him the memory of his race stirred. He recognized the eternal menhirs for what they really were. He felt the radiant energy of the summer solstice bathe him. Feed him. He felt new perceptions opening as old senses died.

He came to Carnac and his mortal body died while his spirit regained the freedom of the starways.

He came to Carnac and found his parents: the Stars.

He came to Carnac...

And went beyond.

Published in *Asterisks* Vol. 1, No.8, 1977

This third Asterisks story was inspired by one of my favorite authors, Edgar Allan Poe. In 2007, Randy and I revisited Poe in our fantasy novel, Edgar Allan Poe on Mars. Eyrinie *almost turned into a graphic novel, but that project didn't go beyond a few pages.*

Eyrinie

From Phobos, pearl of the Solar System, pride of the all-powerful Solnium company, the sun was much like any other star.

It was setting.

I was standing on the top level of Bubble City, headquarters of Solnium, near the spatiex transmitters. During the last week, Solnium had added another trillion or two to its wealth. Our wealth. Downward, in the heliogardens, the Class-2 execs were celebrating. I was impatient to join them, but had to keep my three hour watch near the spatiex in case we received important messages from Venus, Luna, or even from Ganymede.

"I saw him! I saw HIM!

"Who are you, old man? And what are you doing here?" I asked.

He was a wretched thing, dirty, ugly. But how could he be here, on Phobos? He looked like a Rat, from the molehills of Venus. But no, he couldn't be a Rat. Not with that fear in his eyes. Rats have a ferocious will to live—they need it there!—and are seldom afraid.

"I saw Him, I tell you," he muttered, looking right through me. "We're all lost!"

"Come on, old man!" I shook him. "No need to be afraid. Not here. You're no longer on Hell, you know." I assumed he had come from Mars, where Solnium and the other companies have indusposts. I glanced at the huge red disk that occupied a part of the horizon of Bubble City and shuddered. Mars, that we, the Solnium Execs, call Hell...

But I was wrong, for he added: "I was on Ganymede when He came. And all fell. All died! "

Ganymede. The location of the fabled Paradise, the city where the corrupt and idle esthetes that call themselves our Government live in endless luxury. It was the dream of all to be someday called to "serve" the Government on Ganymede. Not that we're unhappy here. Of course not! Solnium takes care of its own, and Bubble City probably had nothing to envy to Paradise. But Ganymede was the best, and we all wanted the best. I wanted the best.

We had few contacts with Ganymede, being virtually independent. But if anything had happened there, and if this man knew what it was, it would be news for all the Solar System. News with immense consequences. Without Ganymede's presence, Solnium was free to take over Luna Science Dome, to control Ceres before the other moved in, to send more men to Slow-Death on Mercury. If I was the one to bring this news to our Board, many doors would open for me. I had to know.

"What happened on Ganymede? Tell me. You must tell me!"

He was rambling, mad, lost in his fantasies. Hopeless. But perhaps I could learn something from his mouthings.

"It is the punishment for our crimes..."

Crimes?

"...Remember the Furies..."

The Furies?

"We brought Him on our heads. I was one of the last to leave Earth, and He was there. He followed us... "

Earth? He must have been old, indeed! We don't speak much about Earth nowadays. The planet has been hopelessly polluted and, but for the ones Solnium sends to its dung pits to collect radioactive elements, no one lived down there. And even those don't last long.

"...He came and we died..." He was sobbing now, and didn't look well. But I needed to know.

"Who came?" I asked.

He didn't answer, just pointed at the glass dome of the heliogardens, at the revelers below.

Someone had just entered the bubble. Someone well described by an old writer. Someone tall, gaunt, with the countenance of a stiffened corpse and dabbled in blood.

Someone who glided unchallenged through the dying throng.

I understood then, and prepared myself for death.

One of his names was Alecto.

Another...

"And Darkness and Decay and the Red Death held illimitable dominion over all."

Published in *Asterisks* Vol. 2, No.3, 1977

17

This fourth Asterisks *contribution was written after listening to Harlan read his own story* The Prowler in the City at the Edge of the World *on an LP. It had the distinction of being reprinted twice, once in Mensa's* International Journal *in 1979, then in a Los Angeles fashion magazine,* Just L.A., *the following year.*

Private Hell

To Harlan Ellison.

1st Day.

When he woke up that morning, he saw himself. The night before, he had been alone in the room, and now they were two.

He—and he.

At first, he could not believe it. "Who are you?" he said.

"I dunno, I'm me," the Other One answered. "You. I don't understand. I woke up and found you there, asleep beside me. I got up then . . ." And, as an afterthought: "Sorry if I woke you up."

A smile. Two smiles. They both laughed. "Can I ... touch you?" he asked.

"Sure. I was going to ask the same thing." "It figures. You're supposed to be me, remember?"

They shook hands, shyly at first. Then again, and again. And again.

"I don't understand," he said finally for the second time.

"Neither do I." "What can we do?" "Have breakfast, I suppose."

After some troubles over deciding who was going to warm the milk/pour the chocolate/ get the butter/do the eggs/all the insignificant small things that were engraved within their systems, they got behind their hot drinks and started to talk.

That day, neither went to work.

They talked about all their secrets, secrets they had never shared with anyone else before.

They had a frenzy to tell each other what they had known but had never told.

He spoke, and he listened. More: he under-stood him as no one else had ever understood him before.

They talked, and talked.

2nd Day.

That day, they made love.

They went on sharing all the contents of their minds— and they slept together, curled within each other's arms.

3rd Day.

The fridge was adequately filled. They decided to stay inside the cozy warmth of their home. The Outer World started to fade for them, becoming increasingly unreal.

They stayed, and looked at each other's souls.

4th Day.

That day, he struck him.

He had seen the unvoiced plea in his eyes, he had felt the urge within his mind, he had struck him. He had struck him to hurt, to make him suffer. And he had struck him again. And again.

He had suffered. He had cried. He grieved it.

That day, the telephone rang, but they cut it. That night, their lovemaking was more violent. He raped him.

5th Day.

On that day, he bound him, and gagged him. Then, he started to torture him.

He knew his fears, he knew his pain. But he loved him.

He fed upon him, and his agonies, and his joy. But he loved him.

He was killing him. But he loved him. Outside, it started to rain.

19

6th Day.

On the sixth day, he died.

His body was a mess, but he had a smile on his lips and, yea, peace in his eyes.

He had killed him. But he had loved him.

Then, he started to cut his body and ate him. He chewed on pieces of still-warm flesh, and mingled in his blood.

He tore his body and fed on him till the room was dark.

7th Day.

They came.

They broke into the apartment. He did not fight them, and they took him away.

"Schizophrenia," the Men in White said, but they could not understand the Blood. "Murder," the Men in Blue said, but they could not understand the absence of Body.

No one understood him.

Eventually, they locked him up in a white, warm padded cell.

8th Day.

And on the eighth day, he was there, waiting for him.

"Hello," he said.

"Hello," he answered.

Published in *Asterisks* Vol. 3, No.1, 1978

This fifth and last Asterisks *contribution was influenced by Cordwainer Smith, whose massive* Instrumentality Saga *had just been reprinted in France as three, handsome hardcover books. It was also inspired by a cover drawn by Frank Kelly Freas for Brian Stableford's* Rhapsody in Black *(DAW, 1973). By the time it appeared in* Asterisks, *in 1980, David Vereschagin had resigned, and the fanzine had passed into the hands of, first, Debra F. Sanders, then Mike Mitchell, a New Orleans attorney and dear friend, to whom our novel* The Katrina Protocol *was dedicated.*

Dark Dream, Dark Beauty

Love is eternal.

It belongs to our past, our present, and our future.

This is the story of Bodelere, he who was called the Dark Messiah, who loved what few Men dare to love. And, as it goes with love stories, it is also a sad story...

Part 1—Living on Alpha Gemini.

Before there was the Dark Messiah, there was the Man. Bodelere. The Man, the Dreamer.

Bodelere was taken away from his family unit when he was nine.

They were poor Stuff raisers on Alpha Gemini, subsisting from permanent contracts with the Imperium. They had suffered from a severe Nightmare Plague because of the boy. In the end, they had called Psy Central. And Psy Central had answered...

Slow men, in light blue uniforms, always high on psychotropics, had come to take the child away. Oh, the mothers had protested, wept, but, after all, they could not raise a Dreamer among them, could they? It was all for his good, wasn't it?

They had taken him to Psy Central, where he was trained. 'Trained to seek, to feel, to project.

Trained to Dream.

And to Dream he had learned. For eleven years, they trained him...

He grew up there, with the other Dreamers. And, one day, they thought he was ready.

His Graduation Day was not memorable. He had Dreamed of a lost Starchild who had grown up on a primitive planet and had rediscovered his heritage... He did not know how many people were psylinked with him, judging his Dream. Perhaps, there were none.

That day, he graduated with merit from Psy Central, and was sent to Delta Gemini.

Part 2—Loving on Delta Gemini.

On Delta Gemini, he met his love.

But I am anticipating.

His first impression of Delta Gemini, also known as Starport 15, was astonishment. Alpha Gemini was a Stuff planet, with a very small population of Raisers, some processing industries—and Psy Central, of course. All in all, not many people and plenty of free space. Delta Gemini was overpopulated, rich beyond calculation. The wealth of entire worlds was bought and sold in its offices, Imperium space fleets were armed there and often their shadow darkened the skies; Galacorps that owned planets were controlled from its towers. It was... an Imperium Starport.

Bodelere was to dream in one of the Psy Palaces owned by Psy Central. And so he did. Till he met his love.

She came, one night, her silver hair floating freely behind her. She came, and her billowing black cloak made an aura of darkness around her. She came, her eyes, pools of space within her moonlighted face. She came, and went away.

But before, she had stopped at the Psy Palace where Bodelere Dreamed.

Some said she had come to stop at the Pay Palace where Bodelere Dreamed. ...And who can say they were wrong?

She came, and went away.

But behind her, she left the Dark Messiah.

She psylinked with Bodelere. And love it was.

That night, he Dreamed as he had never Dreamed before. Instead of sending his patterns to the Dreamee through the psylink, they shared. Love it was.

He brought the power, and she brought the visions. Love it was.

Visions of darkness and despair. Planets being plundered by the Imperium. Visions of tyranny and cruelty. Unlimited power crushing countless lives. Visions of Hate and genocides. The slow murders of primitive races. Visions of the Universe. Tragedies. Love it was.

"Stay" he said, imploring her. "Stay with me. I love you!"

"Help them, and you will find me," she answered. And she went away, her dark cloak swirling, leaving behind her the Dark Messiah.

He Dreamed. He Dreamed her love of them, and people came.

He Dreamed his love of her, and people came.

And things started to happen:

He Dreamed: Kingmaker, the rich Imperium dealer, refused to buy old, decadent Earth.

He Dreamed: the shares of MineCo dropped by 20%.

He Dreamed: Kaleval was given protective Status.

He Dreamed: People fought for the one they now called the Dark Messiah.

He Dreamed...

And, one day, they came for him. But he had left, and gone to Epsilon Gemini.

Part 3—Dying on Epsilon Gemini.

On Delta Gemini, he was the Dark Messiah. On Epsilon Gemini, he was only the Hunted.

They tried to kill him in its heavenly residences. They tried to kill him in its sordid slums. They tried to kill him everywhere. But he always turned up alive and, for the love of her, Dreamed his dreams of despair.

And, in the end, they got him.

The tale of his death is known, and it has been sung all over the starways. How he died does not matter. What matters is that, when he died, he had a smile on his lips and love in his eyes, for he had finally found her. His dark beauty, his dark dream, Death.

Published in *Asterisks* Vol. 5, No.6, 1980

"BE SEEING YOU!"

After moving to Los Angeles in 1979, I launched a bimonthly fanzine, entitled Rover, *devoted to Patrick McGoohan and George Markstein's remarkable television series* The Prisoner.[1] *It lasted 18 issues over three years, during which time Randy and I contributed a variety of articles and several short stories. This one is a speculation on the fate of Nadia (played by Nadia Gray) who betrayed No.6 in the episode* The Chimes of Big Ben.

Forever Nadia

"Hello, Nadia!"

The girl stood poised in the middle of the door.

"Cobb! What are you doing here? And don't call me Nadia. You know it is not my name."

"I know what your name is, my dear. But to us, you are Nadia."

"A codename," she spat.

"Yes, but is it not a truer reflection of what you are, my dear... Nadia? Anyway, all this is beside the point. X-04 sent me. He is not happy, not happy at all. You failed us again, my dear. In Berlin, last week, you cost us four good men. Since you came back from that place, you haven't been the same."

"That place." He did not need to elaborate on what he meant. That place had been her first failure, although not strictly her fault. The man she had been sent to lure was too brilliant, and yet he had been fooled. But for a small, almost insignificant mistake, they would have won.

"X-04 thinks you need a rest, my dear, a vacation..." In Cobb's hand, a small round gun had appeared.

"No, Cobb, you don't mean..."

"Be seeing you, Nadia."

Before she fell, prey to the sleeping gas, she remembered the other man's last words to her: "Be seeing you," he had said, beaten but not tamed. As if he had known that, someday, her masters would turn against her. As if he had known...

She woke up in her room-which-was-not-her-room. Here, she would become a number, like the others, waiting for death at the Old People's Home. He, the only one who could help her to escape, would never do so again, for she had betrayed him, and he never forgot.

For him, she would still be Nadia.

Forever, Nadia.

Published in *Rover* No.3, 1979

Starting with the fifth issue of Rover, *I decided to write a series of stories featuring crossovers between* The Prisoner *and other legendary British TV series. As I was then working on an article for* L'Ecran Fantastique *about* Doctor Who, *which later became our first book, The* Doctor Who Programme Guide, *it was easy to start the series with the Fourth Doctor (Tom Baker).*

Encounter at Night

The Man was walking on the beach. Far behind him, the Village slept. Even those-who-never-slept, the Supervisors, did not care about his lone escapade into the night. Where could he go?

The Man known as Number 6 was walking on the beach, his face creased with deep thought-lines, thoughts of escape, of freedom...

Suddenly, a wheezing, groaning noise broke the routine generated by the slow whisper of the waves. A silhouette cut against the dark horizon. There, in front of him, was materializing an anachronism, a thing that belonged to a world he had left behind: A London Police call-box.

The box opened and a man got out. He was wearing a long scarf, a floppy hat and, even in the night, you could see his shining blue eyes and flashing grin.

"This is not UNIT headquarters," he said seriously, looking around him with curiosity.

"Who are you?"

"Hello! I am the Doctor. May I enquire as to your identity, sir?"

Reflections in a paranoid mind: Who is he really? Can I trust him? Is he with them? Somehow, something in the Doctor's grin must have reached the Prisoner's soul, for the man known only as Number 6 smiled back (not one of his canary-swallowing smiles he kept for his captors) and offered his hand in trust. "I used to be called..."

"Wait!" the Doctor interrupted. There is a. high energy concentration nearby. It is coming closer, closer..."

Rover burst out of the sea and rolled towards them at great speed, roaring.

"Fascinating," whispered the Doctor, not in the least afraid.

"You know what that thing is?" Number 6 asked.

"Thing? Oh. that. Yes, of course. But I never met one before on this planet. I never dreamed that some of you Earthmen were so advanced..."

"Did you say 'planet?' 'Earthmen?'"

"This is all very interesting, my dear fellow, but your watery friend there will cause us a lot of harm if we don't go back to the TARDIS at once. Come, follow me!"

Number 6 looked at Rover which was almost on them. He had seen what the thing could do before. But... to get into a police-box? He stepped in, just as the Doctor was going to get out again to get him.

Inside the box, much to his surprise, a brightly lit, advanced control room filled a space much bigger than it should have been.

"Where am I?"

"In the TARDIS," the Doctor answered matter-of-factly, as if it explained everything. "And just in time, I see."

On the screen, Number 6 could see Rover trying to push against an invisible barrier—without any success.

"Fascinating," muttered the Doctor again. "Well, enough time lost as it is. Off we go!"

He pushed a lever and a couple of buttons, and the central column started to move, up and down. The Village disappeared from the scanner picture.

"Where do you want to go, Old Man?" the Doctor asked the Prisoner.

"You mean, we have left the Village?"

"The Village? Oh, that place. Yes, of course. We are now, er, let me see, hmm, slightly off course again in the time vortex, but nothing serious. You see, I have to go back to UNIT headquarters. It is desperately urgent. I left them in some hurry in the middle of that Giant Robot case..." And then, as an afterthought—or an apology—"I could not resist, you know. Regeneration does that to you sometimes."

Number 6 stopped the man who called himself "Doctor" (but was he a man?) before he got totally lost in his monologue.

"I know UNIT. So, you work for them?"

The Doctor smiled, looking slightly apologetic again. "Well, yes. I am their scientific advisor, you see."

"And we are going to London in that machine of yours?" the Prisoner said, persistent.

"Yes, this 'machine,' as you put it, is extremely reliable. Aren't you (said the Doctor patting the console), Old Thing?"

Suddenly, the lights blinked. A blue streak appeared on the scanner screen.

"A time-leash! Incredible!"

The TARDIS slowed to a standstill, then started to shudder. Like a broken stretch band, a quick backward motion snowballed into a frenzied acceleration.

"What's happening, Doctor? Is something wrong?"

"It is a time-leash! We are being dragged back through time to your Village."

"Can we do anything about it?"

The Doctor moved to another console and started to punch out buttons. "Yes, we can escape—by disrupting totally our space-coordinates. We shall plunge into another galaxy, another universe perhaps. It is quite a strain on the TARDIS, but I will not submit..."

A firm hand gripped the Doctor's arm as he was feeding in the last course changes.

"No, it's me they want. Not you. The Village wants its Prisoner back."

29

"But you can escape! Just let me fix the space-coordinates..."

"Could you return us to Earth? To London? In the 20th Century?"

"In time, yes. I would have to fix the TARDIS, of course, but..."

"Return me to the Village and go."

"But you want to be free. I can give you the freedom of the stars. You can

roam with me; we will see the wonders of the Universe..."

"No, Doctor, I want freedom, it is true, but I want it to be able to return and destroy the Village and all what it represents. Erase it from the face of the Earth. This is my duty, my sole responsibility, and I cannot be free from it ever. No, Doctor, I cannot take your freedom."

The Doctor looked deep into the eyes of the Prisoner. "I understand. So be it." Then he turned towards the console again. "Come on, Old Thing, quick!" he said flippantly.

But the look in his eyes was anything but flippant.

Published in *Rover* No.5, 1980

This second TV crossover features the inimitable heroes of The Avengers, *Patrick Macnee and Diana Rigg. At the time, the series was being rerun late at night on a local TV channel in the Los Angeles area, and we had just conducted a delightful interview with Macnee for a French video magazine.*

Acid Test

"Mrs. Peel! You, here!"

"Steed! In the Village? What a surprise!"

"What is this place, Mrs. Peel? And what are you doing here? Come to think of it, what am I doing here?"

"Have you seen No.2 yet, Steed?"

"No.2? What a strange name... No, I don' believe I have."

"He is the one who runs things here. Come with me, then, and I'll show you to the Green Dome. Meanwhile, why don't you tell me what you have been doing all these years..."

"...And right after that case, I felt that Purdey and Mike Gambit did not need me anymore. So I called Mother—he is still around, you know—and talked him into accepting my resignation. You remember, I always wanted to retire in that cottage I own in Somerset, but I thought I could..."

"The Green Dome, Steed."

"Ah., yes, what a strange composite of architectural styles. What do you think, Mrs. Peel, Renaissance?

"Yes, like Machiavelli and the Borgia."

"I see."

"DO COME IN, NO.100. BEAUTIFUL DAY, ISN'T IT, NO.96?"

"No.96?"

"I think he means me. This is No.2, Steed. Let's not keep him waiting."

"After you, Mrs. Peel..."

31

"You, No.100, are one of the best operatives your country ever had. Or should I say 'was'? Why did you want to retire?"

"Have I met you before, Old Chap? Your face looks vaguely familiar..."

"Who I was or might have been is of no concern to you, now. In the Village, I am No.2 and you are No.100."

"I am certainly not!"

"Do not provoke us, No.100! No.96 here, with whom I believe you used to work, can tell you of the success of our methods."

"Indeed I can... No.6."

"Do not call me No.6! I am No.2! No.2! No. 2!"

"I think you two better go now. No.2 is tired and..."

"And who might you be, sir?"

"Don't push me, No.100. I am No.9, No.2's personal physician. Butler, show these two citizens out."

"Why did you call him 'No.6,' Mrs. Peel?"

"A hunch. That's what he used to be when I arrived here. A prisoner, like the rest of us. But he was the best till they got to him."

"Oh yes, now I remember him. Amazing fellow. He never gave up."

"He hasn't. Not yet. Not inside. I know he is still fighting, somewhere inside..."

"Well, then, Mrs. Peel, it looks as if... we're needed"

"This is No.2 speaking, No.100. I am sorry about that moment the other day. I have a lot of work here, you know, and the pressure can become overbearing at times... Anyway, I wanted to have a chat with you. You seem to be a reasonable man, and I am sure we can work together for the mutual benefit of this Community..."

"I told you before, I will not..."

"Ah, and why don't you bring No.96 along too. Charming person. Much in common, I feel. With you, too. Yes. That's a good idea. Come for tea. No. For breakfast. Yes, that sounds good. Be seeing you."

"No.9, what a surprise! Come in, come in! Mrs. Peel, do we have some champagne left for our unexpected visitor?"

"No Moët left, but I think I have a quart Veuve C. somewhere."

"That will do fine! You won't mind, my dear fellow?"

"Shove the acting, No.100!"

"Steed. John Steed. As a mutual friend of ours used to say: I am not a number, I am a free man, you know."

"You have been seeing a lot of No.2 those last weeks, haven't you?"

"Shh. Confidential debriefing. Ultra-secret."

"I am well aware of your value to us in terms of information, No.100. But I don't want you to disturb No.2. He is, er, very sick."

"Sick? Why, he seemed much better. Last week only, he said... But you wouldn't be interested. Had you noticed anything, Mrs. Peel?"

"Well, now that you do mention it, Steed, our friend seemed to have mislaid his badge the other day. Terrible memory, you know!"

"I warn you, both of you, if you tamper with..."

"Oh, do drink your champagne, No.9. It is already warm."

"Supervisor, I have something unusual on the screen."

"Unusual? Let me have it here, No.27... It's the helicopter cave! Red Alert! Red Alert! Stop No.2 immediately! Lock the controls!"

"Impossible, sir. He has an electro-pass with him."

"Sir, we managed to ground 'copter 2. But 'copter 1 is getting out of range... We lost it, sir!"

"No.9 here."

"..."

"Yes sir, I realize that, sir."

"..."

"No sir. The two escaped, sir, but we managed to keep No.2. I mean, No.6, sir."

"Yes sir, I am aware that we should not have trusted him that far, but it was the only way to test the validity of compound 15. You, yourself said..."

"..."

"I understand, sir, I'll report to you right away."

"..."

"Be seeing you too, sir."

Published in *Rover* No.6, 1980

To me, Roger Moore will always be the near-perfect incarnation of Simon Templar, a.k.a. The Saint. But, a new version entitled Return of the Saint *had just started to air, starring the young, energetic Ian Ogilvy, who had all the charm of Moore, but also a sharper edge, which was more faithful to the origins of the character, when the Saint did not hesitate to kill the Ungodly. This story is also a sequel to the* Prisoner *episode* Do not Forsake me, Oh my Darling *in which a mysterious Professor Seltzman has invented a machine that swaps minds and bodies....*

A Change of Mind Revisited

No.2 was gloating.

"This time, no more gloves, No.6! We have scanned your mind patterns day and night for the last six months. I dare say we know it better than you do. Soon, very soon, we shall assume full control of it, and you will be ours. At last, fully ours."

I was strapped in a chair, hooked to some mysterious machines in that hellish hospital they have in the Village. But inside I was smiling, for how could No. 2 have known that the mind inside the body he was holding prisoner was not the one of the man they called No. 6, but instead belonged to Simon Templar, a.k.a. the Saint!

Janet Portland was a good friend of mine. I even knew her father, Sir Charles Portland, from my very brief days with Our Majesty's Secret Service. So when she barged in my London flat one morning with a fantastic story about her fiancé who had disappeared—and had resurfaced again in another body—I could not help but listen.

Together, we had traced a complicated web of international intrigue whose nexus seemed to be a certain Professor

35

Seltzman, inventor of a mind-transfer process. But Seltzman had disappeared too, at the same time as Janet's fiancé.

Finding the missing scientist had proved a task worthy of a Saint! Janet's father and his men was one of the obstacles we had to face. Sir Charles was not only very much anxious to catch the elusive Herr Professor but he would also have liked to recapture his former agent.

Many times in our world-wide search, I felt more ominous forces at play than Sir Charles's services, darker forces, forces I could not even begin to fathom. Many times indeed, death came close to us.

We finally located Seltzman or should I say, Seltzman located us? Where my efforts had been fruitless, Janet's appeals to an old man's sense of friendship proved successful. Did I say, "old man?" The Seltzman we found, after many secret messages and extravagant meetings in dark alleys, was young, younger than he should have been... The reason why was quite obvious: the man had indeed succeeded in transferring minds from body to body. He held a Faustian power which was both his shield (because of the very few, very rich, very powerful friends he had made by allowing them to use his process) and his curse (for his would-be captors were endless in numbers).

There, in a cozy villa near Calenzana, in Northern Corsica, Seltzman told us of the whereabouts of Janet's fiancé, the man who was now called No. 6. Janet had begged. Seltzman had refused. And, of course, Janet had won: she would have her fiancé back—but for 24 hours only, for there was no other choice. Oh, and I forget the other condition: she would have him back in another body—mine.

Whilst Seltzman was readying his lab, he explained how he could now operate his transfer at distance for a short amount of time. He needed to know the exact location in space and the mind-patterns of the subjects. The first was no problem, for he had been in the Village once (he never revealed its location to us for fear of Janet attempting something "very, very foolish, Herr Saint!") And as to the second, well, he had the patterns of Janet's fiancé already, and recording mine was a matter of minutes. I hated to think of myself as being the subject of a mad scientist's experiment, but I owed Janet that much.

I did not expect mind-transfer to be painless. It was not. But I did expect it to be quick. It was not. There I was, wrenched out of my body, hanging in a void which was not a void but something else.

You cannot possibly understand.

Suddenly, another thought-pattern manifested himself. Oh, so briefly. But I could tell it was the man I was exchanging my body with. A strong man. I felt we could have been, if not friends—he appeared more virtuous than I'll ever be—but good comrades-in-arms. We just kind of nodded at each other and went that-a-way.

That's how I landed unsuspectedly in the Village. And that's how I ended up in the hospital, destroying No. 2's vicious little scheme.

"No. 2, I don't understand. It's not working."

"What do you mean, not working, you simpleton! It has to be working. Everything is perfect: the mind-patterns records, the mind controller's design. I supervised every step of this operation myself. There cannot be any failure. My career, my life itself, is at stake here. Get out, you idiot! I'll do it myself!"

"It's no use, No. 2. Look, we are not locking in. We are destroying the equipment!"

Then, there was a soft, muffled explosion. Before I passed out, I heard the technician mutter under his breath: "It's impossible, it's like he had changed his mind!"

On the way "home," 24 hours later, I felt good.

"Thank you," No. 6's mind whispered to me when we crossed in that void.

"Don't mention it," I answered.

I knew he had escaped a fate literally worse than death. He would find out, of course, and would wonder, like me, if through the intervention of Professor Seltzman, a greater force had not used both of us for the best causes of all.

Love. Freedom.

Published in *Rover* No.7, 1980

The most legendary British genre TV series of all is Nigel Kneale's Quatermass, *which was the subject of four original TV mini-series (plus a recent remake of the first series), three feature film adaptations by Hammer, and a mockumentary radio serial (*The Quatermass Memoirs *in 1996). Professor Bernard Quatermass, head of the British Rocket Group, is a dedicated scientist who clashes with various extra-terrestrial threats, but never loses his faith in humanity.*

The Quatermass Interlude

All was going according to Houston Space Center's schedule when the spore hit the capsule.

Some micro-seconds later, the man-made satellite started to plummet towards the big, blue sphere below. As it was entering Earth's orbit, Houston Space Center decided not to take any chances. Noiselessly, the capsule blew up.

The Spore did not care.

The Village, later that day.

"Look, No.6, a shooting star! Make a wish!"

The Prisoner said nothing. His young female companion might wish what she wanted, but he only wished for freedom. He sighed. What could that shooting star do to the Village where nothing ever changed? Of course, he had never been more wrong.

Meanwhile, in the Control Room.

"Supervisor, jam all radars," No. 2 ordered. "The last thing we need is a scientific team looking for us. Cover the place of the crash, and bring the remains here. No, wait, I'll go myself. This might be of interest to our scientists..."

Houston, the next day.

Professor Bernard Quatermass was worried.

Not only had this British-American first space venture proved to be an abysmal failure, but some ominous feeling nagged at the back of his mind. A good chunk of the taxpayers' money had been blown to smithereens (the Minister would not be happy), and despite all precautions, two pieces had still managed to reach Earth (there would be further budget cuts). One had vaporized a corn field in Kansas and the other—the other had plain disappeared (remember to write a memo). How that could happen still remained a mystery.

Quatermass remembered all too well his previous space experiments: there had been the thing which had come back in the body of poor Carron in his first rocket, the thing which had fed on life, the thing which he had destroyed in Westminster Abbey. And then, there had been the invasion, the aliens infiltrated among us. And the Martian capsule, Hob, the Devil in the Pit... Space was still unknown, full of perils.

Quatermass decided to go to Kansas. Perhaps they would need his help. Soon.

The Village, seven days later.

After the fifth body had been discovered, drained of all life, fear started to take over the Village.

The victims had been prisoners and wardens, indifferently. Progressively, the citizens of the Village came to realize that a monster was stalking in their midst.

"You are a trouble-maker, No. 6. We have the situation well under control," No.2 shouted.

"Under control, nothing! That girl was killed almost at your doorstep. You must issue weapons, we are defenseless."

"This is against the Rules, No. 6!"

"Damn your Rules! You'll kill us all!"

Back in his cottage, the man known as No. 6 started to think. He had been one of the top agents of a secret branch of British Intelligence, a long time ago. The modus operandi of the killer, whoever, or whatever, he was, reminded him of something, something he had seen once, very briefly. Something buried in the ultra-confidential files of the service...

"Quatermass..."

At once, No. 6 knew who, what, he was against. Professor Bernard Quatermass, the British rocket expert, had been involved three times with what might best be dubbed other-worldly forces. The service had done its best to cover it up. From the top, the order had come: "People are not ready." For the top, People were never ready.

No.6 put his prodigious mind at work. He needed to remember exactly how had Quatermass defeated the creature which had fed on life and had been threatening to engulf the world.

Much later, the Prisoner looked at his handiwork: a few pages of paper, covered with notes. He had managed more or less to reconstruct the "Quatermass Experiment" file. More work was still needed, but this, he felt, was enough to convince No. 2.

More was at stake here than the mere passing on of information which the Village might already have in its possession.

He lifted the receiver.

The Village, the next day.

No.6 remembered the last, vital detail of the "Quatermass Experiment" file almost too late.

At dawn, he had been summarily arrested by the Village security guards and tied down to a pole. The presence of a row of guards with blasters left little room for doubt in his mind as to what fate No. 2 had in store for him.

The apparent master of the Village had delivered a speech full of hate, standing up on the Gloriette, accusing No. 6 of being the "mad killer". It is only when the Prisoner saw No.2's hand grasp the ivy-covered balcony that he understood what fool he had been.

Where it had been touched, the plant withered, died, crumbled into dust.

Then—and only then—did No.6 remember the man Carron, the first astronaut who had been possessed by the thing. His first victim had been a plant, a cactus in a pot, whose life-force he had absorbed.

No. 6 knew what he had to do. The guards saw the Prisoner break free, jump onto the Gloriette, grab No. 2 and throw him against the luxuriant vegetation.

No.6 was shouting. They did not understand a word of his frantic explanations, for they were too petrified by the horror of watching the plant die, absorbed by the body of the thing-which-had-been-No. 2.

Nobody remembered who had shot first, but soon the crackling energy of a dozen blasters incinerated the writhing mass.

The bell tolled nine. For the moment, there were no longer wardens or prisoners in the Village—only human beings, puny, frightened human beings.

The Village, the next day.

"Thank you, Professor Quatermass!" No. 6 whispered.

"What name did you say?" The new No. 2 had displayed little gratitude, but that was to be expected.

"You will never find out."

The fear was gone. The old rules were back.

"We will, No.6, we will..."

A new day was starting in the Village.

Kansas, the same day.

Quatermass saw the thing destroyed.

Under his feet, the earth was soft and wet from the night's rain. Lifting his head, he looked at the sun rising.

Somehow, he knew without knowing why, that the threat was over. Not only here, but elsewhere as well.

Leaving the soldiers in charge of the cleanup operations, he slowly walked back to his helicopter. No, the Minister would definitely not be happy...

A new day was starting on Earth.

Published in *Rover* No.8, 1980

The final—and arguably the least successful—of the Rover *crossovers tried to conflate the No.2 from* The Chimes of Big Ben, Once Upon a Time *and* Fall Out, *and John Mortimer's Old Bailey barrister Horace Rumpole, just because they were played by the same brilliant actor, Leo McKern. That Rumpole ever could have been a No.2 is pretty farfetched. But if his path ever crossed that of the Masters of the Village, this would likely be the result...*

Rumpole of the Village

"Good morning, Rumpole, or should I say No. 2?"

"Fotheringay! After all these years! So you are the visitor Henry told me about. 'old friend,' eh? Ha! I thought you were all gone for good!"

"It is true that after your rebellion, our operations were left in a somewhat sorry state. But we did not disappear completely, Rumpole. Not quite. We kept an eye on you, for one. Your association with MPs, your cases..."

"What do you want from me, Fotheringay. I know your ilk, this is not a courtesy visit."

"Straightforward as ever, eh, Rumpole? Very well. Let us come to the point then. Tomorrow, you are scheduled to appear in court to defend a man. That man killed one of our agents, Rumpole. This cannot be allowed. We want that man."

"You won't get him."

"Do not force us to use other means, Rumpole. Take my advice and drop that case. The man will be tried, and condemned. You will lose, Rumpole. In fact, you have already lost."

"Never."

"We shall see, Rumpole, we shall see..."

When the Jury came back, the verdict was unanimous: not guilty. Rumpole's brilliant defense had carried the day. As he was leaving the bar, the Judge made a sign to him: "Excellent, Rumpole, excellent."

"Oh, nothing, your honor. Mere child play..."

"Do not underestimate yourself, Rumpole. Fotheringay was a fool and will pay for it. Be seeing you!"

In another life, in another time, the man had been called Cobb. Rumpole did not know that, of course, but he knew enough to recognize in him the taint of his old masters.

"The Judge was one of your men. It was all a farce, wasn't it? You have won, haven't you?"

"Won, Rumpole?"

"Yes, won, damn your eyes! When that fellow No. 6 and I destroyed the Village, it was already too late. You had taken over. The West, the East, the whole World. The Village is everywhere! How long have you been in control?"

"Quite some time, Rumpole."

"Why then?"

"Why what?"

"Why ME? Why this charade? What am I to you now?"

"A legend, perhaps, Rumpole. An old legend but a dangerous one. Something for which there is no room in our World."

"I beat you, you know. That man went free."

"Did you, Rumpole? Not that it matters anyway... That man was suffering from an incurable disease. He does not know it yet. Slow and painful death, I believe. As you said, Rumpole, it was all—a farce."

Published in *Rover* No.10, 1981

'TOONS

In 1985, Randy was selected to take part in an animation writing course organized at Hanna-Barbera by veteran animation writer Harry Love. That led to a brief career in animation writing during the late 1980s, with contributions to a variety of shows such as The Real Ghostbusters, Duck Tales *and* The Bionic Six.

From this period, I selected two scripts. The first is a short written for Harry Love for Superfriends : The Legendary Superpowers Show *(1984-85), featuring the heroes from DC Comics'* Justice League of America.[2]

The second is one of our favorites: The Ghostbusters in Paris *written for DIC's* The Real Ghostbusters. *While the animation of the actual episode wasn't the best ever—our other script,* The Headless Motorcyclist, *fared better!—it was nevertheless a very popular story, praised by producer Michael Gross and Harlan Ellison, among others. The original script contains some additional scenes cut out for time—as is often the case in TV animation.*[3]

Superfriends: Apokolips Now!

FADE IN:

<u>APOKOLIPS - EXT - DAY</u>
We OPEN with an ESTABLISHING SHOT of APOKOLIPS
seen from space.

CAMERA TRUCKS IN. We then PAN over the Dantesque
landscape of ARMAGETTO. PARA-DRONES fly in the scarlet skies over the fiery pits. A squadron of DOG SOLDIERS
marches INTO FRAME.

DARKSEID (VO) (*proud*): Apokolips! Isn't it a joy to behold,
Desaad?

CAMERA PANS to reveal DARKSEID's huge, pyramid-like
citadel, dominated by a statue of the tyrant.

CAMERA TRUCKS IN to show DARKSEID and DESAAD,
standing on a PLATFORM.

DARKSEID (CONT): A world where all exist to serve the
will of Darkseid!

ANGLE ON DARKSEID
He raises his hands to the sky. We HEAR (SFX) THUNDER-
CLAPS.
DARKSEID (CONT) (*angry*): But still, it is not enough!

CAMERA TRUCKS OUT as Darkseid leans over to look at
Armagetto.

DARKSEID (CONT): I will not rest until Earth too shall be lit with the fires of Apokolips!

<u>DARKSEID'S CITADEL - INT - DAY</u>
Darkseid, followed by Desaad, enters a room that is stark and barren, except for a large VID SCREEN on a wall and a couple of Dog Soldiers. Behind him, we SEE the platform and the fiery skies of Apokolips.

DESAAD (*fawningly*): Earth will soon be yours, Sire! Your machines, your power...

CAMERA TRUCKS IN to show Darkseid turn and lash out at Desaad.

DARKSEID (*angry*) ... Are not enough!

ANGLE ON DARKSEID
His face conveys cold, bitter rage.
DARKSEID (CONT): The Super Powers Team have foiled me at every turn!

CAMERA PULLS OUT. Darkseid waves his arm. The vid screen COMES TO LIFE with a picture of BATMAN in action (clips can be used here), quickly replaced by pictures of WONDER WOMAN, FIRESTORM...

DARKSEID (CONT): All the mighty resources of Apokolips thwarted by a group of super-powered buffoons!

ANGLE ON VID SCREEN
It now shows a picture of SUPERMAN in action.

DARKSEID (VO - CONT): Superman! If only I could get rid of him! He's the strongest of the Super-Powers Team...

WIDER ANGLE ON DARKSEID AND DESAAD

Darkseid waves his arm again and the vid screen goes BLANK.
DARKSEID (CONT): Without Superman, Earth would soon be mine...

ANGLE ON DESAAD
His face lights up with an evil smile.
DESAAD (*crafty*): I believe I have a plan to do just that, Sire...

PROJECT TEMPUS - EXT - DAY
WIDE ANGLE on an attractive, high-tech building, surrounded by an electrified fence. Skull-and-crossbones signs and GUARDS clearly indicate that this is a restricted, high security type of place. A GUARD stands at attention at the gate.

CYBORG (VO) (*sarcastic*): Wow! Now I know where all our tax money goes!

SUPERMAN, carrying CYBORG, flies INTO FRAME diagonally, and lands a few feet away from the gate.

SUPERMAN: From what I was told, teammate, Project Tempus is privately financed.

ANGLE ON SUPERMAN AND CYBORG
They both stand in front of the Project, looking at it.
SUPERMAN (CONT): This is the foremost time travel research facility in the world. In fact, their work is so secret that even I knew nothing about it.

CYBORG (*impressed*): Time travel! Fan-tastic! Maybe we can find out who's going to win the next Super Bowl!

ANGLE ON SUPERMAN
His face grows stern as he looks disapprovingly at his friend.

49

SUPERMAN (lecturing): Time travel is a very serious business, Cyborg. It shouldn't be treated lightly...

WIDER ANGLE ON SUPERMAN AND CYBORG
The two superheroes proceed towards the gate.
SUPERMAN (CONT): Which is why I've been asked to help out.

CYBORG (*contrite*): Only kidding, Supes. I want to help too. After all, I skipped going to see "Godzilla" for this!

ANGLE ON SUPERMAN AND GUARD
The Guard talks into a walkie-talkie. His behavior appears to be somewhat mechanical and stilted.
GUARD (*stiffly*): Superman and Cyborg are here.

MARAT (VO): Very well. Send them right in.

CAMERA PULLS OUT for a WIDER ANGLE. The gates glide open. Superman and Cyborg walk towards the main building.

PROJECT TEMPUS - INT - DAY
WIDE ANGLE on DOCTOR MARAT's laboratory. It is filled with very advanced scientific equipment. There are computer banks lining the walls. Dominating everything is a gigantic METAL SPHERE located in the center of the room. It has a door, and a mass of coils go from its top to the ceiling. Marat stands in front of a CONSOLE. Suddenly, a metal door slides open with an (SFX) ELECTRONIC HUM. Superman and Cyborg step into the room.

ANGLE ON MARAT
He goes to meet the two heroes, his arm extended.
MARAT (*warm*): Ah, Superman, Cyborg! Thank you for coming so quickly.

ANGLE ON SUPERMAN AND CYBORG
Superman takes the scientist's hand and shakes it. Cyborg looks around the lab, awed by Marat's equipment.
SUPERMAN (somewhat solemn): The Super Powers Team is always happy to lend a hand to the scientific community, Dr. Marat.

CYBORG (*impressed*): Hey, this is quite a set up you have here, Doctor. I haven't seen anything like this, even at S.T.A.R. Labs...

ANGLE ON MARAT
He looks slightly disturbed by Cyborg's comments.
MARAT (*with a small hesitation*): Well... Our research is rather specialized. Come, let me show you...

WIDER ANGLE ON THE THREE OF THEM
Marat takes Cyborg by the arm and walks him over to the metal sphere. Superman follows him. Marat points at the sphere.
MARAT: This is the prototype time sphere we have developed. Because you've had experience with time travel, Superman, I was hoping you could help me test it.

ANGLE ON SUPERMAN AND CYBORG
Superman nods his agreement, while Cyborg looks very pleased.
SUPERMAN: My teammate and I will be happy to help you, Doctor.

CYBORG (*exuberant*): Great! You can send us back to see the dinosaurs. That sure beats going to see "Godzilla!"

ANGLE ON MARAT
He fidgets uncomfortably.

MARAT: I'm afraid that's impossible. Traveling to the past is too dangerous. There's too much risk of changing the present...

MEDIUM ANGLE ON SUPERMAN AND CYBORG
The superheroes' faces register surprise and amazement.

MARAT (VO - CONT): No, instead, I'm going to send you to the future!

<u>TIME SPHERE - INT - DAY</u>
TIGHT ANGLE ON MARAT'S FACE
MARAT: You will remain in the future for exactly twelve hours...

CAMERA TRUCKS OUT to a MEDIUM ANGLE, revealing a VID SCREEN showing Marat standing at the time sphere's control console.
MARAT (CONT): After that time period, no matter where you are, the time beam will automatically locate you, and return you to the present.

CAMERA TRUCKS OUT to a WIDE ANGLE. The entire inside of the time sphere, with the exception of the door and the vid screen, is only bare metal. Superman and Cyborg are watching the screen.

MARAT (CONT): Do you have any questions?

SUPERMAN (*calmly*): No, Doctor. We're ready to proceed when you are.

ANGLE ON MARAT
He pushes several switches while looking at the two heroes.
MARAT: Very well... Bon Voyage, Super Powers!

ANGLE ON SUPERMAN AND CYBORG

They start being enveloped by a (SFX) CRACKLING ENERGY WEB.
CYBORG (*slightly nervous*): I hope the Force is with us!

The Web now completely covers the heroes.

FUTURE EARTH - EXT - DAY
A WIDE ANGLE ESTABLISHING SHOT shows a scene that looks similar to the APOKOLIPS of SCENE ONE. Superman and Cyborg materialize in the midst of it with a loud (SFX) ZAP.

MEDIUM ANGLE ON CYBORG AND SUPERMAN
They look at their surroundings with shocked, surprised faces.
CYBORG (*cynically*): If this is the future, I'd rather go back to see "Godzilla!"

SUPERMAN (*concerned*): No, Cyborg, there's something wrong here. I've been to the future, and it wasn't like this!

TIGHT ANGLE ON SUPERMAN
He frowns, almost afraid to say it.
SUPERMAN (CONT): This looks more like Apokolips than Earth!

MEDIUM ANGLE ON SUPERMAN AND CYBORG
The teenager reacts in surprise. Superman still looks puzzled.
CYBORG: Could Dr. Marat's machine have sent us through the dimensional barrier instead of through time?

SUPERMAN (*thinking*): I don't know...

ANGLE ON CYBORG
CYBORG (*trying to be upbeat*): Well, if we're stuck in Darkseid's backyard for twelve hours, we might as well look around!

<u>FUTURE EARTH - ANOTHER LOCATION - EXT - DAY</u>
WIDE ANGLE of Superman and Cyborg cautiously walking through the "Apokolipsian" landscape. Suddenly, we HEAR (SFX) CRIES in the distance. The two heroes look at each other, and RACE to the top of a nearby hill.

CAMERA MOVES 180 DEGREES to reveal a group of HU-MAN SLAVES cowering under the lashes of DOG SOL-DIERS. Some of the slaves swing hammers at rocks, like prisoners in a "grade b" movie. Others lift pieces of rock and put them in carts. We HEAR the (SFX) SOUND of the whips and the (SFX) CRIES of the slaves.

ANGLE ON SUPERMAN AND CYBORG
Both heroes look upset—Cyborg seems particularly outraged.
SUPERMAN (*curious*): Humans! On Apokolips?

CYBORG (angry): They're treating them like slaves! We've got to free them!

Cyborg starts to RACE down the hillside. Superman shouts. But seeing that Cyborg is not listening, he FLIES OFF after him.
SUPERMAN: Cyborg, wait!

ANGLE ON CYBORG
He takes his SOUND BLASTER and affixes it to his right hand.

WIDE ANGLE ON DOG SOLDIERS AND SLAVES, HE-ROES IN THE B.G.
One of the Dog Soldiers, unaware of the heroes' presence, raises his whip and prepares to strike a slave.
DOG SOLDIER (*very nasty*): Faster, Slave!

Before the Dog Soldier can strike, Cyborg (SFX) BLASTS him. The slaves and Dog Soldiers turn, surprised, to see what has happened. Immediately, the other Dog Soldiers RUSH into action.

ANGLE ON CYBORG
Several Dog Soldiers make a grab for Cyborg. One grabs his arm and holds it, so the bionic teenager can't use his sonic weapon.
DOG SOLDIER (*even nastier*): Seize the rebel!

Suddenly, Superman's arm thrusts INTO FRAME and grabs the Dog Soldier.
SUPERMAN (VO): I'll do the seizing here, friend...

ANGLE ON SUPERMAN
He takes the Dog Soldier he is holding and throws him O.S.
SUPERMAN (CONT): And you'll do the flying!

ANGLE ON CYBORG
He points his sound blaster at another of the Dog Soldiers and (SFX) BLASTS him.

Then, a whip (SFX) CRACKS INTO FRAME and wraps around Cyborg's arm. But he gives a mighty tug, and another Dog Soldier flies INTO FRAME and (SFX) THUDS back out the other side.
CYBORG: Thanks for the hand, Supes! I owe you one!

ANGLE ON SUPERMAN
Two Dog Soldiers attack Superman, running at him from opposite sides. But he easily grabs hold of them and (SFX) BONKS them together, knocking them out.
SUPERMAN: Yes, but you won't repay me this time. These two were the last of them.

WIDE ANGLE ON SUPERMAN AND CYBORG

They stand victorious. Several Dog Soldiers lie unconscious on the ground. A few others are seen running off in the distance.

CYBORG (*cocky*): Well, I guess we showed them!

SUPERMAN: Yes, but it doesn't seem we've reassured our friends here...

ANGLE ON SLAVES
They are huddled together, too surprised or scared to move.

SUPERMAN (VO - CONT): They seem to be more frightened of us than they were of the Dog Soldiers.

CAMERA TRUCKS OUT to show the heroes standing near the slaves.

CYBORG: Don't be afraid. We want to help. Why didn't you run away?

TIGHT ANGLE ON ONE OF THE SLAVES
He looks at his companions for approval, then speaks.
SLAVE (*scared*): Where would we run to? There is no place to run!

ANGLE ON CYBORG AND SUPERMAN
CYBORG (*frustrated*): Why don't you try to get back to Earth?

SUPERMAN: Yes, in fact, we can take you back there with us.

ANGLE ON SLAVE
He looks as if he thinks the two heroes are mad.
SLAVE: But this is Earth!

ANGLE ON SUPERMAN AND CYBORG

They look at each other in complete shock and disbelief.

FUTURE EARTH - YET ANOTHER LOCATION - EXT - NIGHT
CAMERA PANS from a STARRY SKY down to a CAMP-FIRE. Superman and Cyborg are sitting with the slaves. An OLDER SLAVE drops a few twigs onto the fire and begins to tell a story.

OLD MAN: This is the history as told to me by my father, and as it has been passed on from slave to slave, around the camp-fires of Earth.

METROPOLIS - EXT - DAY
A CROWD OF PEOPLE run through the streets. They col-lapse (SFX) CRYING, their faces covered with GREEN PATCHES.

OLD MAN (VO - CONT): It was told that towards the end of the twentieth century, a deadly alien plague destroyed nine-tenths of the planet's population...

Dog Soldiers and Para-drones emerge out of a HUGE STAR GATE.

OLD MAN (VO - CONT): The decimated people of Earth were no match for the conquering forces of Apokolips.

METROPOLIS - A FEW YEARS LATER - EXT - DAY
The city is in RUINS. Dog Soldiers and Para-drones watch over human slaves. An OLD FLASH weakly stumbles INTO FRAME.

OLD MAN (VO - CONT): Civilization was destroyed. All our heroes were dead or enslaved. Within less than a genera-tion,
Mankind was held firmly in Darkseid's grip!

FUTURE EARTH - EXT - NIGHT
ANGLE ON SLAVES AND SUPERHEROES AT CAMP-FIRE
OLD MAN (CONT): Darkseid had finally succeeded in turning Earth into a New Apokolips!

ANGLE ON SUPERMAN AND CYBORG
They ponder what the Old Man said.
SUPERMAN: The plague... That's what changed the course of history.

CYBORG (*bitter*): Yeah, I bet Darkseid must have found a way to infect the Earth with it!

ANGLE ON OLD MAN
He looks as if what he has to say is very painful.
OLD MAN (*sadly*): No, you're wrong. It wasn't Darkseid... The last remaining scientists finally discovered the origin of the disease... It came from outer space, and the carrier was... You, Superman!

TIGHT ANGLE ON SUPERMAN AND CYBORG
Their faces register intense shock.

PROJECT TEMPUS - INT - DAY
ESTABLISHING SHOT of the laboratory. The time sphere shakes with a mighty (SFX) ZAP and CRACKLING ENERGY. Its door opens. Superman and Cyborg step out. Marat walks over to greet them.
MARAT: Welcome back, my friends!

MEDIUM ANGLE ON SUPERMAN, CYBORG AND MARAT
Marat looks eager to hear what the heroes have to say. Superman and Cyborg both look thoughtful.
MARAT (CONT): Tell me, was my experiment successful?

CYBORG: I'm not sure "successful" is the word I'd use...

ANGLE ON SUPERMAN
The Man of Steel is very solemn as he makes his report.
SUPERMAN: We did arrive in the future, Doctor. But it was not at all what I expected...

PROJECT TEMPUS - INT - DAY
SAME SHOT as above, but now Marat, too, looks concerned.
SUPERMAN (CONT): ... And then, the time beam brought us back to your laboratory.

MARAT (*solemnly*): I don't know what to say, Superman. This is certainly shocking news.

ANGLE ON CYBORG
Cyborg looks as if he has been struck by a sudden idea.
CYBORG (*eagerly*): Superman, why don't you just zoom forward in time and stop yourself from contaminating the planet?

ANGLE ON SUPERMAN
Superman looks stern as he replies.
SUPERMAN: I can't do that, Cyborg. I would be meeting myself, and the laws of time make that impossible.

ANGLE ON THE TWO HEROES
Cyborg looks crestfallen. Superman's expression is enigmatic.
CYBORG: You mean we can't change the future?
SUPERMAN (*determinedly*): I didn't say that.

CAMERA PULLS OUT to show Superman and Marat shaking hands.
SUPERMAN: Good-bye, Dr. Marat!

The heroes turn and leave. The doors close behind them with a (SFX) HUM.

CAMERA PANS BACK to Marat, now alone. He LAUGHS maniacally. Then, his image SHIMMERS, and turns into DE-SAAD!
DESAAD (*gloating*): Yes, good-bye, Superman! Ha, ha!

ANGLE ON DESAAD
He pulls out a communications device and speaks into it.
DESAAD (CONT): It's all right, Sire! You can come now.

CAMERA TRUCKS OUT to reveal a STAR GATE in the middle of the laboratory. Darkseid steps out and walks over to Desaad.
DARKSEID: How is our plan progressing, Desaad?

DESAAD (*servile*): To perfection, Sire. Phase one has been completed.

ANGLE ON DESAAD
He bows while pointing at the time sphere.
DESAAD (CONT) (*proudly*): What the Super Powers took to be a time machine, was in fact a new mind jammer of my own design!

TIGHT CLOSE UP on Desaad's face grinning evilly.
DESAAD (CONT): The heroes never left their own time. Everything they experienced was merely an illusion I created!

ANGLE ON DARKSEID AND DESAAD
Darkseid examines the Mind Jammer. Desaad eagerly attempts to please his master.
DESAAD (CONT): Soon, Sire, you will be rid of that Kryptonian meddler!

DARKSEID (*curious*): An impressive ploy, Desaad. But wouldn't it have been simpler merely to implant Superman with the idea of banishing himself from Earth?

DESAAD: No, Sire. The jammer's powers can't force some-one to do something against their nature...

ANGLE ON DESAAD
He rubs his hands together gleefully.
DESAAD (CONT): But after such a revelation, Superman will surely choose to leave Earth of his own free will, rather than doom it!

HALL OF JUSTICE - EXT - DAY
SEVERAL JOURNALISTS stand outside the Hall of Justice. Superman is on a podium, reading an announcement. BAT-MAN, WONDER WOMAN, FLASH and FIRESTORM stand behind him.

CAMERA TRUCKS OUT to the back of the crowd. Cyborg JUMPS INTO FRAME and taps a JOURNALIST, JIMMY OLSEN, on the shoulder. The journalist turns around.

CYBORG (*agitated*): Hey, what's going on here?

OLSEN: Haven't you heard? Superman has just announced that he's exiling himself from Earth forever!

ANGLE ON CYBORG
His face reflects shock and disappointment.
CYBORG (*angry*): He wouldn't do that!

He then angrily pushes his way through the front of the crowd.

ANGLE ON SUPERMAN
SUPERMAN: ... And I feel confident that I leave Earth in good hands. Good-bye, my friends!

61

ANGLE ON CYBORG

The bionic teen rushes to the podium, hoping to stop Superman.

CYBORG (*intently*): You can't leave! Earth needs you!

ANGLE ON SUPERMAN

Superman ignores Cyborg and takes off. CAMERA TILTS UP and follows the Man of Steel until he is a mere dot in the azure sky.

ANGLE ON CYBORG

The bionic teenager looks crestfallen.

CYBORG (*more quietly*): Earth needs you...

WONDER WOMAN walks INTO FRAME and puts her hand on his shoulder.

WONDER WOMAN: We must talk to you...

But Cyborg brushes her away, almost unaware of her presence.

CYBORG (*determined*): If Superman won't go to the future, maybe I can convince Dr. Marat to send me instead!

CAMERA TRUCKS OUT. Cyborg JUMPS over the crowd and OUT OF FRAME.

ANGLE ON WONDER WOMAN AND THE SUPER POWERS TEAM

She turns and looks at the rest of her teammates with concern.

PROJECT TEMPUS - INT - DAY

SAME SHOT of Superman's departure as described above.

OLSEN (VO): ... And so, with the final departure of Superman, an era in our history comes to a sad conclusion. This is Jimmy Olsen, filling in for Clark Kent, Galaxy News.

CAMERA TRUCKS OUT to reveal a SHIMMERING SCREEN that seems to hang in the air almost magically.

DESAAD (VO) (*triumphant*): You've won, Sire! With Superman gone, the other Super Powers will be easy pickings!

CAMERA TRUCKS OUT FURTHER to show Darkseid and Desaad watching the end of the news report. (The logo of Galaxy News now appears on the screen.) Darkseid seems thoughtful.

DARKSEID: I must admit, Desaad, I didn't think the Kryptonian would be fooled by your plot...

Darkseid waves his arm and the GBS logo disappears as the screen DIVIDES INTO FOUR. Each NEW SCREEN now contains the villainous face of one of the Tyrant's AGENTS. Behind one is the Eiffel Tower, another has the Leaning Tower of Pisa, one has Big Ben, and the last has the Golden Gate Bridge.

DARKSEID (CONT): Yet, it appears he was. So, the time has come to launch our campaign of terror!

ANGLE ON DARKSEID
DARKSEID (CONT): I will order my agents to cause so much destruction and carnage, that governments will crumble, and Earth will be ripe for my conquest!

CAMERA TRUCKS OUT to show Darkseid addressing his agents, moving his arms as he speaks, like in old newsreel footage of Hitler.

DARKSEID (CONT): The time has come, my agents! In the name of Darkseid, bring Apokolips to Earth!

The Agents salute Darkseid. Then, the screens BLINK OUT.

PROJECT TEMPUS - EXT - DAY
ESTABLISHING SHOT showing several guards patrolling the Project's grounds. Cyborg JUMPS INTO FRAME. He walks towards the gate and addresses the guard.

CYBORG: I want to see Dr. Marat, quick!

The guard doesn't move, or even acknowledge Cyborg's presence.

CYBORG (CONT) (*exasperated*): Didn't you hear what I said?

CAMERA TRUCKS IN on Cyborg. He SHAKES the guard, causing his uniform to TEAR, and revealing him to be a robot.

CYBORG (CONT) (*surprised*): Oh, Man! A robot! What's going on around here!

Cyborg PUSHES the gate and moves onto the Project's grounds.

ANGLE ON OTHER GUARDS
The other guards spot Cyborg. They open their mouth and emit a (SFX) LOUD PARA-DRONE SCREECH. They SHIMMER, and turn into Para-drones, who immediately TAKE FLIGHT after Cyborg.

ANGLE ON CYBORG
He hears the Para-drones' screech, turns and JUMPS—barely in time to avoid a BLAST from one of the creatures.

WIDER ANGLE ON CYBORG BEING CHASED BY PARA-DRONES
CYBORG: Boy, I've really hit the jackpot this time!

ANGLE ON CYBORG
As he runs, he starts (SFX) BLASTING the Para-drones.

ANGLE ON PARA-DRONES
Several Para-drones hit by Cyborg fall to the ground.

PROJECT TEMPUS - INT - DAY
The (SFX) SOUND of Cyborg's blaster alerts Darkseid, who
cocks his head to listen, while Desaad looks confused.
DARKSEID: Your security has been breached, Desaad.

DESAAD: I don't understand, Sire.

ANGLE ON DESAAD
He walks to the console and presses a switch. A GLOWING
SCREEN with a picture of Cyborg fighting the Para-drones
materializes in the center of the room.
DESAAD: Cyborg! He must not be allowed to warn the oth-
ers! From here I can...

TIGHT ANGLE ON DESAAD'S HAND
His hand moves towards another switch.

ANGLE ON SCREEN
From above, we see a LASER CANNON rotating towards
Cyborg.

ANGLE ON DARKSEID
He raises his hand to stop Desaad.
DARKSEID: No, Desaad! We must find out how much he
knows first!

ANGLE ON DESAAD
DESAAD (*disappointed*): Very well, Sire. A medium intensity
blast will suffice.

He presses yet another switch.

PROJECT TEMPUS - EXT - DAY
The cannon (SFX) FIRES once. Cyborg falls, unconscious.

PROJECT TEMPUS - INT - DAY
TIGHT ANGLE ON Cyborg. Cables are attached to his head. CAMERA TRUCKS OUT showing Cyborg strapped into a chair, the cables linked to Desaad's console.

CAMERA then PANS to Desaad.

DESAAD: The boy acted alone. The other Super Powers know nothing. You need not recall your agents, Sire.

ANGLE ON DARKSEID
DARKSEID (*unconvinced*): Are you certain, Desaad? I will not tolerate any failure.

ANGLE ON DESAAD
DESAAD: My Mind Jammer is infallible. I'll put it at full power. The whelp's mind will never recover, but we will learn all the Super-Powers' secrets!

CAMERA TRUCKS OUT to encompass the whole room. We HEAR (SFX) A THUNDERING CRASH, and Superman BURSTS through the ceiling.

SUPERMAN: You won't learn any secrets today, Desaad!

ANGLE ON SUPERMAN
His eyes emit heat rays.

ANGLE ON CYBORG
Superman's heat vision melts the console, freeing Cyborg.
CYBORG (*surprised*): Superman! I thought you were gone!

ANGLE ON DARKSEID

He depresses a button on his belt and sends a (SFX) SIGNAL.
DARKSEID: This can't be! We saw you leave!

CAMERA TRUCKS OUT to reveal a squad of Para-drones invading the room. They (SFX) BLAST ineffectively at Superman.

SUPERMAN: That's what I wanted you to think! Desaad's illusion fooled me at first...

ANGLE ON CYBORG
A metal cable springs out of his hand. He uses it to lasso the Para-drones, which he then swings towards Darkseid.

ANGLE ON DARKSEID
He uses his OMEGA BEAMS to cause the Para-drones to vanish.

ANGLE ON SUPERMAN
He uses his superbreath to FREEZE another group of Para-drones.
SUPERMAN (CONT): But then I realized that we were not in the future!

ANGLE ON DESAAD
His face registers bitter anger.
DESAAD: How could you? My illusion was perfect!

ANGLE ON SUPERMAN
SUPERMAN: It was the stars! They held the same positions as they do today. If it were really the future, they would have moved!

ANGLE ON DARKSEID AND DESAAD
Darkseid's face shows unbridled fury. He turns to Desaad and unleashes his Omega beams on the cowering flunky, who vanishes.

DARKSEID: You fool! You'll pay for this!

DESAAD (*whining*): Have mercy, Sireeee...

CAMERA TRUCKS OUT to show Darkseid calling up a Star Gate and running through it.

DARKSEID: You win this time, Super Powers, but you won't be so lucky next time!

SUPERMAN: Anytime, Darkseid!

HALL OF JUSTICE - INT - DAY
ESTABLISHING SHOT OF THE HALL OF JUSTICE, followed by a large ANGLE ON the Super-Powers Team (Superman, Batman, Wonder Woman, Flash and Firestorm). Cyborg stands in the middle.

BATMAN: We only pretended to go along with Desaad's scheme in order to let Darkseid's agents expose themselves and be captured.

ANGLE ON WONDER WOMAN AND FLASH
WONDER WOMAN: Yes, Cyborg, you rushed off before we had time to put you into the picture.

FLASH (chiding): You almost ruined the entire operation, by being so stubborn.

ANGLE ON SUPERMAN AND CYBORG
Superman puts his hand on Cyborg's shoulder and smiles.
SUPERMAN: Still, it worked out for the best. Cyborg's sincerity helped convince Darkseid not to recall his agents.

CYBORG (*grinning*): Then, I guess you owe me one, Supes! Tell you what, how about taking me back to see those dinosaurs!

SUPERMAN (*sighing*): I think I'd rather take you to see "Godzilla" instead, this time!

CAMERA TRUCKS OUT to encompass the entire Super-Powers team as we

FADE OUT

THE END

The Real Ghostbusters: The Ghostbusters in Paris

FADE IN:

<u>EXT EIFFEL TOWER - DAY</u>
ESTABLISHING SHOT of the Paris skyline. It is a beautiful, sunny day. The view looks like a Matisse painting. Some AC-CORDION MUSIC sets the mood: we're definitely in Paris.

CAMERA TRUCKS IN on the Eiffel Tower. It is BIG, much larger than people realize. Huge elevators disgorge a flow of TOURISTS, who mill about on the lower two levels.

CAMERA PANS UPWARD towards the third (top) floor of the Tower. It houses a small Pavilion, topped by powerful dishes and broadcast antennas.

<u>EXT EIFFEL TOWER - TOP FLOOR</u>
CAMERA TRUCKS IN on a group of three WORKERS, dressed in blue overalls, who are repainting a section of the Tower.

ANGLE ON WORKER NO. 1
WORKER NO. 1(*wiping his face*): I feel like I'm frying up here!

He drops his brush and looks at his watch.

WORKER NO. 1 (CONT): I can't work in this kind of heat. I don't know about you guys, but it's two o'clock, and I feel like taking a nap.

ANGLE ON WORKER NO. 2
He turns towards Worker No. 1, but keeps hold of his brush.

WORKER NO. 2 (*sympathetic*): Can't say I blame you, but there isn't any place up here to sack out. Let's just finish up as fast as we can...

ANGLE ON WORKER NO. 1
WORKER NO. 1 (*pointing* O.S.): What about in there?

CAMERA PANS OVER and TRUCKS IN on the Pavilion. It is a fairly small building that looks a little like a veranda made of metal and glass. Metal shutters protect all its windows, except that of the single-panel door.

ANGLE ON WORKER NO. 3
WORKER NO. 3 (*upset*): In the Pavilion! But, it's forbidden to go in there! That was the workshop of Monsieur Eiffel himself!

WIDE ANGLE ON ALL THREE WORKERS
WORKER NO. 2 (*nervously*): You've got to be crazy! Nobody but the VIPs are allowed in there!

WORKER NO. 1 (*self-assuredly*): You guys sure are chicken! There's no way anybody is going to catch us. They'll blame the tourists.

ANGLE ON WORKER NO. 1
He walks over to the door of the Pavilion, breaks the glass of the window, and opens the door from inside.
WORKER NO. 1: Well, you make up your own minds. I'm going to catch forty winks in here.

INT. EIFFEL TOWER - PAVILION
CAMERA TRUCKS IN OVER his shoulder. Inside is a spacious room, full of antiques. On one wall are large, wooden shelves, filled with dusty, leather-bound volumes.

Underneath is a red velvet couch, encumbered with more books. Next to the couch is a display stand shaped like a Grecian column, with an antique clock on it.

A massive desk occupies the center of the room. Behind it are a wallful of mysterious, Jules Verne-looking machines—large rivets, big gears, very rococo. They HUM and GROAN softly, performing some kind of endless task.

On the desk is a big, copper BOX, the size of a portable type-writer. There are four large lamp bulbs (early Edison type) on top of it. Occasionally, a blue-arc of electricity FLASHES through one of the lamps.

The whole room breathes with a 1900 mad scientist look.

WIDE ANGLE ON ALL THREE WORKERS
They all stand in the doorway, looking awed.
WORKER NO. 3(*very nervously*): I don't think you should go in there!

WORKER NO. 2: Yeah. This stuff looks serious.

WORKER NO. 1 (*a little worried—but he can't back out now*): That's always been your problem, you think too much. Catch you later, I'm off to dreamland.

ANGLE ON WORKER NO. 1
He walks into the room, towards the couch. He pats one of the cushions, causing a cloud of dust to rise from it.
WORKER NO. 1 (*now more confident*): Ah! That's perfect!

He begins clearing the books from the couch, but inadvertent-ly BUMPS into the column, sending the clock CRASHING into the Box, and breaking two of its lamps.

A loud ELECTRIC ZAP is heard, and a bolt of BLUE LIGHTNING ricochets around the room.

EXT EIFFEL TOWER
PANORAMIC SHOT of the entire Tower. It lightly shakes from top to bottom, once, briefly. A loud GROAN is heard, then, apparently, everything returns to normal.

But, the COLOR SCHEME and the MUSIC change slightly, to indicate that there is now something ominous in the air.

EXT EIFFEL TOWER - TOP FLOOR
Workers No. 2 and 3 stand in the doorway, looking aghast.

WORKER NO. 2 (*frightened*): What... What was th-that?

WORKER NO. 3 (*smugly*): I knew it. This time, he's done it.

ANGLE ON WORKER NO. 1
Worker No. 1 comes out of the Pavilion, looking shaken. Carefully, he closes the door behind him.
WORKER NO. 1 (*with false bravado*): Well, whatever it was, it doesn't look like it did any damage. I'll come back tomorrow and replace those lamps. No one will be any the wiser.

WIDE ANGLE ON ALL THREE WORKERS.
Workers No. 2 & 3 look sheepishly at each other, silent.
WORKER NO. 1 (CONT): What say we knock off for the day?

The others nod, and they all head for the elevator.

EXT EIFFEL TOWER - SECOND FLOOR
A COUPLE of YOUNG AMERICAN TOURISTS (1986 versions of LUCY and RICKY) are strolling around, taking pictures.

ANGLE ON "LUCY"
She points at something O.S.
"LUCY" (*excited*): Oh! Look, honey! There's a man in period costume! How exciting!

CAMERA PANS OVER to a STRANGER wearing Belle Epoque-style clothing, top hat, tailed coat, striped trousers.

ANGLE ON "RICKY" AND STRANGER
"Ricky", holding his camera, goes over to the Stranger.
"RICKY": Excuse me, sir. Would you mind posing for a picture with my wife?

STRANGER: Of course not. But make sure you take me from my good side...

ANGLE ON STRANGER
The Stranger's face MELTS, revealing the hideous, skeletal grin of a GHOST. He LAUGHS maniacally. O.S., "Lucy" SCREAMS.

EXT EIFFEL TOWER - TOP FLOOR
The three Workers, looking fidgety and nervous, are standing by the elevator door. The signal light BLINKS, indicating that the elevator is on its way up.

WORKER NO. 2 (*worried*): I heard that there was some valuable scientific equipment in there...

WORKER NO. 1 (*squirming*): Don't worry. I told you I'd fix it... Besides, nobody ever goes in there. There's no real harm done...

EXT EIFFEL TOWER - FIRST FLOOR
An OBNOXIOUS TOURIST, fat and wearing a Hawaiian print shirt, is making his WIFE and KID listen while he gives a historical lecture. They look very bored.

OBNOXIOUS TOURIST (*pedantic*): ...and the tower was designed by French engineer Gustave Eiffel, for the Paris World's Fair of 1889. It is 980 feet high, and its lower section consists of...

Suddenly, a CACKLING SKULL, wearing a French Revolution hat, and a pair of SKELETAL ARMS, come out of a beam and grab the Tourist, who starts SQUEALING bloody murder.

O.S., the unmistakable SOUNDS OF PANIC begin.

EXT EIFFEL TOWER - TOP FLOOR
The elevator door opens. The three Workers go inside. The ELEVATOR OPERATOR has his back turned towards them.

INT. EIFFEL TOWER - TOP FLOOR ELEVATOR
The elevator begins its descent. Worker No. 1 taps the Operator on the shoulder.

WORKER NO. 1: Hey, buddy. You new here? What happened to the regular guy?

ANGLE ON OPERATOR
He turns. His face looks reptilian, with huge, yellow, glowing eyes, and two large fangs.

GHOST: Let's say—he's been detained!

He opens his mouth wide—WIDER than humanly possible and, inside, clutching the fangs like prison bars, is a small human dressed in uniform. The Ghost LAUGHS.

EXT GHOSTBUSTERS CENTRAL - DAY
ESTABLISHING SHOT of the Ghostbusters' firehouse.

<u>INT GHOSTBUSTERS CENTRAL - CONFERENCE ROOM</u>
PETER, RAY, EGON and WINSTON are listening to MON-
SIEUR LUCIEN, a prim and proper little Frenchman, who
looks somewhat like Albert Finney's version of "Hercule Poirot."

ANGLE ON LUCIEN
LUCIEN: Voila, the true, horrible story, my friends. We must
accept the evidence, the Eiffel Tower is haunted!

ANGLE ON ALL THE GHOSTBUSTERS
They look at each others, their faces reflecting different
moods. Only PETER and WINSTON appear truly interested.

LUCIEN (VO - CONT): It is a national catastrophe. Tourists
are staying away in droves. France is on its knees. I beg you,
Messieurs...

ANGLE ON PETER
The cash register in his head just went "ding."
PETER: So France needs us, huh?

ANGLE ON LUCIEN
He lowers his head, as if admitting some kind of fault.
LUCIEN: Very badly, M'sieur Venkman.

ANGLE ON WINSTON
WINSTON (*pragmatic*): You don't have anyone else to turn
to?

ANGLE ON LUCIEN
LUCIEN (*shaking his head*): Alas, all our experts are utterly
baffled. No, you are our last hope.

ANGLE ON PETER

PETER (*mentally rubbing his hands*): Weeell, our schedule is very busy right now, but I'm sure we can work something out...

ANGLE WIDENS TO INCLUDE RAY AND EGON
They grab Peter and take him aside for a private conference.

RAY: Peter, that's not fair. I don't have time to go to France right now. I have my new satellite dish to install.

PETER (*it's news to him*): Dish? What dish?

ANGLE ON RAY
RAY (*annoyed*): I told you. I ordered a dish so we could get to watch all those shows we've been missing.

ANGLE ON PETER
PETER: You can catch shows like that in Paris.

ANGLE ON RAY
RAY (*exasperated*): Not those shows!

ANGLE WIDENS TO INCLUDE PETER AND EGON
PETER (*not listening*): Besides, there's a whole country asking, no begging, for our help. If we play our cards right, we got it made!

EGON: Wait a minute, Peter. This doesn't sound like a simple case. There are forces at play here that are utterly alien to us.

PETER (*reassuring*): Of course, they're alien, they're French, haven't you heard the man?

ANGLE ON PETER AND RAY
RAY (*still pouting*): What about my dish?

Peter slaps Ray on the back in a dismissing fashion.

PETER: Janine can take care of that.

ANGLE WIDENS TO INCLUDE LUCIEN

PETER (CONT) (*to Lucien*): So, are our rooms going to be paid for as part of this deal?

LUCIEN (*bowing slightly*): But of course! You will be the guests of my country. You will stay in the best hotel in Paris.

PETER: The best hotel?

LUCIEN (*beaming*): The very best, M'sieur Venkman!

PETER (*happily*): Well, then, that's settled. When do we leave?

EXT PARISIAN BOULEVARD - DAY
Again, ACCORDION MUSIC lets us know we're back in France.

CAMERA PANS ALONG a Parisian boulevard. A TYPICAL FRENCH POLICEMAN unsuccessfully attempts to control the traffic.

CAMERA TRUCKS IN on the Ghostbusters and Lucien, walking past sidewalk cafes and small French shops. The guys are dressed in "Ugly American" tourist garb, except for Egon, who looks quite natty. Lucien looks very annoyed.

LUCIEN: I am extremely—how you say?—upset. You have been here for two days, staying in a very expensive hotel, paid for by my government, and you have done nothing...

ANGLE ON PETER

He looks irritated at this interruption in his all-expenses paid "vacation."

PETER: Listen, Lucien, old pal, we're the professionals on this gig, right? Are you trying to tell us how to do our job?

MEDIUM ANGLE ON PETER AND LUCIEN
LUCIEN: No, of course not, but...

PETER: It's all part of our plan. You can't just bust into an operation like this without doing a little recon first.

WIDE ANGLE ON ALL OF THEM
PETER (CONT): Besides, how hard can it be, after all it's nothing but a little tower...

They turn around a corner and, suddenly, they all raise their heads as they see...

EXT EIFFEL TOWER
The Eiffel Tower standing in front of them, in its full, enormous splendor. It is deserted, except for a cordon of POLICE and GENDARMES at its base.

The Ghostbusters look on in awe as the CAMERA TRACKS UPWARD, emphasizing the immense height of the structure.

ANGLE ON PETER
PETER (*gulping*): This thing is haunted?

ANGLE ON LUCIEN
LUCIEN (*grimly*): Every inch of it, M'sieur.

EXT EIFFEL TOWER - LATER THE SAME DAY
The Ghostbusters, now in uniform, and Lucien walk out of a large, white, tent-like structure that serves as Crisis Headquarters. Two French POLICEMEN stand guard on either side of the tent. More TROOPERS are visible in the b.g.

CAMERA FOLLOWS as they walk towards the Eiffel Tower, which dwarfs the whole scene.

LUCIEN: Because of the emergency, we have shut off the elevators. So you will have to walk.

ANGLE ON PETER
He looks as if he wishes they had stayed in New York.
PETER: Walk! But there must be thousands of steps!

ANGLE ON RAY
He is leafing through a pocket guidebook.
RAY (*annoyingly helpful*): 1,710 according to the Guide.

WIDE ANGLE ON THE ENTIRE SCENE
Peter angrily grabs Ray's guidebook. Suddenly, the French POLICE salute as a band plays the MARSEILLAISE.

PETER (*suspicious*): What are they doing that for?

LUCIEN (*genuinely moved*): Why, it is played in honor of the brave men who put their lives at the service of La Belle France.

ANGLE ON PETER
His worst suspicions have just been confirmed.

PETER (*gulping*): Lives! Who said anything about lives!

He does a quick turnabout, as if to leave.

PETER (CONT): In fact, now that I see the problem from close up, I think you guys have called in the wrong team...

BACK TO WIDE ANGLE

The mood chills perceptibly. The POLICEMEN squint and lay their hands threateningly on their truncheons and all take a step forward. They all seem to be saying "Make my day"—or the French equivalent.

ANGLE ON PETER
He gets the point, and walks back to Lucien's side.
PETER (*fast & unconvincing*): But I believe the right guys are busy this week so you'll have to do with the second best - ha - ha.

ANGLE ON LUCIEN
You would never guess he just "squeezed" Peter.
LUCIEN (*affably*): M'sieur Venkman, you are really too modest. I am sure you will do an excellent work. Bonne chance!

He shakes their hands, turns around and leaves.

ANGLE ON THE GHOSTBUSTERS
They stand alone at the foot of the Tower. Peter looks disgruntled, while Egon points to the top.
EGON: I'm sure that the key to this thing is at the top.

PETER (*grumbling*): Why can't we just get them to switch the power back on so that we can take the elevator?

EGON (*still looking upwards*): You know that one of the basic emergency procedures is never to use elevators in cases of ectoplasmic emanations.

Peter makes faces at him behind his back as they walk towards the stairs.

EXT EIFFEL TOWER - STAIRS
The Ghostbusters have begun their ascent. The stairs are open—we can SEE the landscape below between the metal.

They are however surrounded by a cage-shaped metal mesh that is intended to prevent accidental falls.

Egon leads the way, followed by Ray, Winston and Peter. They climb up carefully, proton rifles at the ready.

PETER (*still pissed off*): There are no more ghosts here than Frenchmen on the moon. Lucien must have been hitting the old Beaujolais.

ANGLE ON EGON
He takes his PKE meter and begins "sniffing" around.

EGON: I don't know. There's something very strange here. I can't get a reading. It must be the Tower's structure acting like a Faraday cage...

ANGLE ON RAY
He touches one of the metal girders..
RAY: I don't think so. See, you can feel a vibration. It's barely perceptible but it's there. Maybe we should...

ANGLE ON PETER
He is already fed up with this job.
PETER (*interrupting*): Come on, come on, you guys! Move! Let's get up there. We'll swap notes later.

CAMERA PANS DOWN to Peter's feet as he climbs. Unbeknownst to him, he is leaving a trail of PURPLE SLIME behind.

Each purple footprint slowly puckers upwards into a mound, which PULSATES, parts at the top and lets out a small GHOST, the upper section of which is an evil-looking gnome, while the lower section looks like a purple spider.

The horde of SPIDER GNOMES follows the Ghostbusters, growing with each of Peter's footprints.

PETER (VO - CONT) (*in total bad faith*): I knew this assignment would be a piece of cake. You guys should be thanking me!

ANGLE ON EGON
He steps onto the First Floor platform and stops dead in his tracks. We don't see what he's just seen—yet.

EGON: I think we have a problem.

ANGLE WIDENS TO INCLUDE RAY AND WINSTON
They catch up with Egon, see, and wordlessly go "Oops."

RAY: You're right, we have a problem. (*without turning his head*) Peter, I think the thanks will have to wait. Can you step down a little?

There is an OMINOUS SILENCE.

RAY (CONT): Come on, step down, what's holding you?

ANGLE WIDENS FURTHER TO INCLUDE PETER
Ray turns and sees Peter face to face with the SCREECHING, HISSING and MEWLING horde of Spider-Gnomes.

PETER: These... these things are all over. Come on, guys, we can't back up now! What's the problem?

Egon, Ray and Winston look at each other, silently. Peter rushes up and squeezes his way past them. He steps firmly onto the first floor. Then his eyes bulge out.
PETER (CONT): Okay, so we do have a slight problem.

EXT EIFFEL TOWER - FIRST FLOOR
PETER's POV

CAMERA PANS OVER a veritable army of GHOSTS of all shapes and sizes. There are SKELETONS in French Revolutionary clothes, brandishing nasty-looking scythes; HEADLESS DWARVES, dressed like Aristocrats; mean-faced GIANTS with toothy mouths and spindly legs; and many more grotesque GHOST-THINGS floating in the air. The overall feeling is reminiscent of a mob—a very nasty mob.

ANGLE ON THE GHOSTBUSTERS
They bring their heads together to confer. The following dialogue is delivered at machine gun speed.
PETER: What do we do now?

WINSTON (*eyeing the Spider-Gnomes*): Can't go down for sure.

EGON: We have to cross the platform to get to the next staircase.

PETER (*eyeing the ghostly mob*): I don't think they're very keen on letting us through.

RAY: The elevator is only a few yards away. But then we'll be trapped, or else we'll have to take a chance on riding it.

PETER (*pleased at the ideas of having no more stairs to climb*): Okay, I'm sold, let's take the elevator.

EGON (*chewing on it for a second*): It's worth a try...

ANGLE ON EGON
He grabs a walkie-talkie and talks in it.
EGON: M'sieur Lucien, we'll try the elevator. Give us back the power.

84

LUCIEN (VO): I hope you know what you're doing... (*a beat, followed by a KLANG!*) All right, you've got power.

ANGLE ON PETER
PETER (*fuming*): Of course we know what we're doing! Who does he think he is? (*a beat—to the others*) What do we do now?

ANGLE ON WINSTON AND RAY
They are adjusting their proton rifles.
WINSTON: Let's rush them!

WIDE ANGLE
The Ghostbusters start firing particle beams at the Ghosts. When the beams hit, the Ghosts SCREAM and DISSOLVE or SPLIT into many parts, which keep up the fight.

The Ghostbusters progress slowly as a group: Peter and Winston in front, Egon and Ray bringing up the rear.

CLOSE UP of STRAY BEAMS hitting the Tower. Instead of charring the metal (as they would normally do), there is a WEIRD SHIMMER and EERIE SFX, and the energy is AB-SORBED.

ANGLE ON EGON AND RAY
The phenomenon has not escaped their eyes.
EGON (*firing*): Look at that! Very strange.

RAY: Yes. Definitely not a Faraday cage.

He shoots down another Ghost that was getting too close.

ANGLE ON PETER AND WINSTON
They've made it to the elevator. Winston is inside, Peter is holding the doors and signaling the others to hurry.

PETER: Come on, hurry it up, you guys!

WIDE ANGLE
Ray and Egon rush into the elevator in the nick of time, ghosts on their tails. The doors close on several bits of ectoplasm (claws, etc.) The elevator begins to rise.

INT EIFFEL TOWER - ELEVATOR
Ray and Egon wipe their faces. Peter looks pleased. Winston looks through the ceiling window.

PETER: Well, this sure beats walking!

WINSTON (*pointing at something O.S.*): I'm not so sure. Look up there.

EXT EIFFEL TOWER - ELEVATOR SHAFT
As the elevator rises, another bunch of ghosts looking like ECTOPLASMIC DRILLS, CHAINSAWS, HAMMERS, etc... come out of the Tower and start attacking the cables.

INT EIFFEL TOWER - ELEVATOR
All four Ghostbusters now have their faces turned to the ceiling window.

WINSTON: One of us has to go up there and scare them away.

PETER (*refuses to understand*): What do you mean, up there?

ANGLE ON WINSTON
He points at a trapdoor in the ceiling.
WINSTON: I mean, up on the top of the cabin. I'll do it. I used to be a construction worker.

He unstraps his proton pack.

WIDE ANGLE
Ray and Egon help Winston to the ceiling. He unbolts the trapdoor, which he drops to the floor with a loud CLANG. Then, he disappears through the aperture. His arm comes back through and Ray hands him the proton pack.

EXT EIFFEL TOWER - ELEVATOR SHAFT
While the elevator is climbing, Winston, standing on top of the roof, successfully fires several particle beams at the Ghosts, which disperse. A few beams hit the Tower itself, with the same FX as before.

EXT EIFFEL TOWER - SECOND FLOOR
The elevator reaches the Second Floor and stops.

CAMERA PANS OVER the platform, which is crowded with yet another mob of GHOSTS. This time, they have a certain thematic air reminiscent of World War I: it may be the round, blue helmets, or the bayonets. But they look nothing like humans. They are MELTED CREATURES, "ELEPHANT MEN", evil JACK-IN-THE-BOXES, etc...

INT EIFFEL TOWER - ELEVATOR
ANGLE ON PETER
PETER (*peering through the window*): This looks like it might be getting serious...

MEDIUM ANGLE
Winston drops back into the cabin. They confer.

RAY (*pointing outside*): We've got to cross the entire platform. This elevator doesn't go any further, and the other elevator's over there.

They all turn to take another look at the hostile Ghost Mob. Outside, we HEAR SHRIEKING and HISSING.

ANGLE ON PETER
PETER (*having difficulty swallowing*): How can we cross a whole platform of that! We barely made it the first time!

ANGLE WIDENS TO INCLUDE RAY & EGON
EGON: I have an idea. Let's reverse the polarity of the beams and aim at the Tower, not at the Ghosts!

RAY: Yes, of course! That's brilliant!

They adjust the dials on the back of their packs.

PETER: Why?

RAY: If we're right, you won't like it.

PETER: Well, I don't like it already, so I might as well hear the rest of it.

Suddenly the Ghosts start BANGING on the doors.

RAY: No time now. Let's go!

EXT EIFFEL TOWER - SECOND FLOOR
They rush out of the elevator, shooting their beams (now co-lored differently) at the girders. With the same FX as before, but much brighter, the Ghosts are pulled back INTO the metal as if drawn by a giant magnet.

ANGLE ON PETER AND RAY
PETER (*cheering*): That's great! How'd you do that?

RAY: No time to explain! Hurry up, it's only temporary.

WIDE ANGLE
They rush into another, much smaller, elevator. The door

closes and it begins to rise.

EXT EIFFEL TOWER - ELEVATOR SHAFT
CAMERA PANS UPWARD to follow the elevator in motion.
As it nears the very top of the Tower, a Ghost which looks like
a fat CANNONBALL with an evil grin rushes out of the
Tower.

CAMERA TRUCKS IN on the Cannonball Ghost which positions itself near one of the huge elevator wheels and EX-
PLODES (SFX). The elevator shakes, then stops.

INT EIFFEL TOWER - ELEVATOR
RAY: Rats, they jammed the mechanism. We were almost
there.

WINSTON: We'll have to finish the rest on foot.

PETER: On foot?!

Winston pushes the door open and walks outside.

EXT EIFFEL TOWER - ELEVATOR SHAFT
The Ghostbusters leave the cabin and crawl across the
girders to get to an open stairway.

ANGLE ON PETER
PETER (*looking at the ground a looong way down*): You
know, all things considered, I don't think we're being paid
enough for this job.

WIDE ANGLE
They make it to the stairs, and begin climbing up the last flight
of stairs leading to the Top Floor. Suddenly, from behind
them, an army of GREEN GHOULS rushes in pursuit.

ANGLE ON WINSTON

He sees the Ghosts coming after them.
WINSTON: Run!

EXT EIFFEL TOWER - TOP FLOOR
The Ghosts hot in pursuit, they run across the Top Floor.

PETER (*breathing hard*): Not... paid... enough...

They rush into the Pavilion and SLAM the door behind them.

INT EIFFEL TOWER - PAVILION
CAMERA PANS from the Ghostbusters, looking in awe at Eiffel's machines, to the machines themselves and then back to the Ghostbusters. Peter and Winston now have their backs against the door. Ray and Egon are wandering through the laboratory.

ANGLE ON EGON
He leaves the group and starts rummaging through the dust-covered books. Suddenly, he grabs one and opens it.
EGON: This is it. This is Eiffel's diary. All the answers must be in here.

O.S. the Ghosts begin BANGING and THUMPING at the door.

ANGLE ON WINSTON
WINSTON: You better hurry finding them, 'cause these guys are for sure not going to leave us much time.

ANGLE ON EGON
He turns towards the others, book in hand.
EGON: It's just as I suspected. We're standing at the top of the largest Ghost Containment Unit ever built... and it's getting ready to explode!

WIDE ANGLE

The others look at him in horror as we

FADE OUT

ACT TWO

FADE IN:

EXT EIFFEL TOWER - DAY
ESTABLISHING SHOT, then CAMERA TRUCKS IN on the Pavilion at the top of the Eiffel Tower. A horde of GREEN GHOULS is massed against the door. The MUSIC is ominous.

INT EIFFEL TOWER - PAVILION
Egon stands in the center of the room, Eiffel's diary in hand. The others are holding the door closed.

EGON: As incredible as it may seem, it would appear that Monsieur Eiffel had already developed the principles of modern ectoplasmic entrapment by the late 1880s...

ANGLE ON PETER
PETER (*incredulous*): You mean, the guy was a... Ghostbuster?

ANGLE ON EGON
EGON (*slightly pedantic*): Yes. He built this Tower as a primitive, but efficient, type of Ghost Containment Unit. The Ghosts are automatically attracted to, and trapped within the Tower's very structure.

ANGLE ON RAY, PETER & WINSTON
Each reacts to the news differently.
RAY (*excited*): That's what caused it to absorb our particle beams. I was right. This is fascinating! What a wonderful opportunity!

PETER (*thoroughly disgusted*): Fascinating, shmascinating! We land in this ghostly Bastille just when the Revolution starts, and you're telling me I'm supposed to have a good time?

WINSTON (*more practical*): Obviously, what we have here is some kind of leak. How do we plug it?

ANGLE ON EGON
He takes the damaged Control Box in his hands.

EGON: It's not easy. This Box was the control for molecularly bonding the Ghosts to the Tower. When it was damaged, in essence, the Tower became psionically porous and the most aggressive Ghosts could escape.

ANGLE ON RAY AND PETER
RAY: How much time do we have before the molecular degeneration becomes irreversible?

PETER (*he doesn't know what Ray is talking about but he grasps the general idea*): Yes, how much time before the, er, whatever, goes and we're all blown back to Schenectady?

ANGLE ON EGON
EGON (*performing a quick calculation*): Let's see, I'd say... about 12 hours.

ANGLE ON PETER AND WINSTON

WINSTON
So we don't have much time to keep
these suckers from breaking loose.

PETER (*as an afterthought*): How many ghosts did you say there were in this Tower?

ANGLE ON EGON
EGON: I didn't.

ANGLE ON PETER AND EGON
PETER (*getting exceedingly annoyed*): I know you didn't. But how many do you think there are?

EGON (*casually*): Millions, billions? Hard to tell.

WIDE ANGLE

PETER (*blanching*): Okay, boys. We don't have any time to lose. We've got to fix the watchamacallit, and we've got to fix it fast.

WINSTON: Okay with me, but first, how do we get out of here?

RAY: Easy. We'll connect one of our reversed polarity packs to Eiffel's master connector, and it will pull the Ghosts back into the Tower!

ANGLE ON EGON
He hasn't waited for Ray's suggestion and has already taken off his pack and connected it to the machines.
EGON (*checking his watch*): 5, 4, 3, 2, 1... Now!

EXT EIFFEL TOWER - PAVILION
In spite of their desperate efforts to remain free, the Ghosts are sucked back into the Tower.

The door opens slightly. Winston cautiously peaks out.

WINSTON
It worked. Not a spook in sight!
EGON (VO): Then, I would suggest we hurry. The power in this pack won't last forever.

The Ghostbusters rush out of the Pavilion. Egon is carrying the Control Box and Eiffel's diary.

EXT EIFFEL TOWER - GROUND FLOOR
The Ghostbusters rush out of the elevator and into the crowd of policemen. Lucien comes out to meet them.

They exit the scene and CAMERA TRUCKS OUT to encompass the whole of the Eiffel Tower, standing ominously in the b.g.

INT CRISIS HQ
An ENGINEERING BLUEPRINT of the Tower. CAMERA TRUCKS OUT to display more blueprints, diagrams, etc., pinned to a blackboard.

CAMERA TRUCKS OUT FURTHER to reveal that we are inside the tent-like "Crisis HQ" structure seen earlier.

The Ghostbusters, Lucien and several French EXPERTS are conferring around a table covered by charts, etc. The Control Box—open and gutted—and Eiffel's diary, lay prominently on the center of the table.

ANGLE ON EGON AND RAY
EGON (*pointing at the box and looking baffled*): Theoretically, this mechanism shouldn't work at all, but it does.

RAY: The problem is, we don't have the time to figure out why it works and, more importantly, how to fix it...

EGON: Ray's right. If we're going to succeed within our window, we have to see more of Eiffel's notes.

WIDE ANGLE

LUCIEN (*pointing at the papers*): But, M'sieur Spengler, they are all right here.

EGON (*shaking his head*): Don't you have any other note-books or charts?

ANGLE ON LUCIEN
LUCIEN (*sadly*): No, this is all we have.

ANGLE ON EXPERT
EXPERT: Excuse me, but that is not quite correct. There are three other locations in Paris where Monsieur Eiffel's private papers are stored. Perhaps there is something useful among these...

ANGLE ON PETER
He is very obviously in a hurry to wrap up the case.
PETER: Then let's get on the stick and go get 'em!

ANGLE ON EGON
EGON: We'd better split up. I'll stay here and try to make sense of the Control Box, while you go and get the notes.

WIDE ANGLE
Peter, Ray and Winston nod in agreement. Then, they get up and walk towards the door with Lucien and the Experts, while Egon busies himself with the Box.

EXPERT (*handing out slips of paper*): Here are the addresses you'll need.

They all walk out of the tent.

EXT EIFFEL TOWER - DUSK
Night is falling. The Ghostbusters step into three different cars and leave. CAMERA PANS OVER to the Tower, silhouetted

against the setting sun. Several ECTOPLASMIC SHAPES slip away from the Tower and into the night.

EXT THE LOUVRE MUSEUM - NIGHT
ESTABLISHING SHOT of Ray stepping out of the car and standing outside the Louvre Museum (large stone archway, typical French chateau). He is holding a flashlight.

RAY: The Louvre. I never thought I'd have to visit it at night. (*sighing*) I wish I had time to see the Mona Lisa.

He SWITCHES ON the flashlight as he goes inside.

INT THE LOUVRE MUSEUM
Ray is greeted by two GUARDS, also carrying flashlights.

GUARD NO. 1: M'sieur Stantz? We have been expecting you. Please follow us.

GUARD NO. 2: The Eiffel Library is at the end of the Grande Gallerie. This way.

With only the LIGHT provided by their flashlights, the three men walk through several art-filled galleries. They turn into a corridor and enter a vast room bathed in MOONLIGHT, and filled with many Egyptian artifacts: statues of ANUBIS, OSIRIS, etc. sarcophagi, etc.

CAMERA PANS QUICKLY to the left to show three ECTOPLASMIC SHAPES entering the room, slithering at floor level and finally MERGING into several figures and objects.

ANGLE ON RAY AND GUARDS
He is awed by the display of all these historical items.
 RAY: Wow! This is what I call a museum!

GUARD NO.1 (*proudly*): Our collection of Egyptian antiques is one of the best in the world.

ANGLE ON RAY
He takes a step closer to admire a statue.
RAY (*admiratively*): This is wonderful!

CAMERA TRUCKS OUT to show a statue of ANUBIS (the jackal-headed god) behind Ray. Suddenly, the statue springs to life and, SNARLING, lunges at the Ghostbuster, who barely avoids being eviscerated by its claws.

RAY: Hey!

WIDE ANGLE
CAMERA TRUCKS OUT further to reveal that, simultaneously, a statue of OSIRIS (the falcon-head god) is similarly attacking Guard No. 1, while a MUMMY steps out of a sarcophagus and threatens Guard No. 2. Both Guards grab their guns and SHOOT at their assailants without success.

ANGLE ON GUARD NO. 2 AND MUMMY
The Mummy grabs Guard No. 2 and drags him, SCREAMING, into the sarcophagus, which closes. The SCREAMS go on for another second or two, then ominously cease.

ANGLE ON GUARD NO. 1 AND OSIRIS
The Guard manages to avoid the Statue's claws by hiding behind other statues and artifacts. But Osiris suddenly opens his beak and TWO TENTACLES jump out of it, circle the statue behind which the Guard is hiding, and trap the man between steel-like coils. He SCREAMS.

ANGLE ON RAY
He jumps over a low sarcophagus, adjusts his particle gun and SHOOTS a beam straight at Anubis. When the beam hits the Statue, it explodes with a SHRIEK.

Ray then walks over to the pieces.

RAY (*quickly testing them with his PKE meter*): Just what I thought, ectoplasmic manipulation of the inanimate...

Then, he hears the SCREAMS of Guard No. 1.

WIDE ANGLE
Ray rushes to the rescue of the Guard, who is being lifted in the air and squeezed to death by Osiris. He SHOOTS a particle beam at the Statue, but the Ghost avoids it.

CAMERA PANS TO THE RIGHT to show the Mummy's sarcophagus opening again and slowly letting its occupant out.

CAMERA PANS BACK to Ray. A third tentacle shoots out of Osiris' beak and goes straight for Ray, but the Ghostbuster FIRES a beam right at it.

CLOSE UP on the beam hitting the tentacle. It dissolves with a FLASHY "ZZTAK!" (SFX).

ANGLE ON GUARD
GUARD NO. 1 (*in much pain*): Please, help me!

WIDE ANGLE
Osiris shoots other tentacles at Ray, which he destroys in mid-air with well-adjusted beams (more "ZZTAKs" (SFX))—but he can't get a clear shot at the statue. Meanwhile...

CAMERA PANS TO THE RIGHT to show the Mummy creeping up on Ray, who has not noticed.

ANGLE ON GUARD
He has seen the Mummy from his vantage position.
GUARD NO. 1: M'sieur Stantz... Behind you!

ANGLE ON RAY
He turns quickly as the Mummy is just upon him.
RAY: Criminy! This isn't a museum, it's Madame Tussaud's
Chamber of Horrors!

WIDE ANGLE
Ray ducks the Mummy's grasp by quickly falling to the
ground, causing one of Osiris' tentacles to hit the Mummy,
which now occupies the spot where he was a second ago.

When the tentacle hits the Mummy, there is a GREENISH
FLASH of ectoplasmic light, and both Ghosts SCREAM. Osiris releases the Guard, who slumps to the floor.

ANGLE ON RAY
RAY: An interesting case of ectoplasmic negative feedback if
I ever saw one...

WIDE ANGLE
Bathed in a GREENISH GLOW, both Ghosts look as if they
had stuck their fingers in an electrical socket.

RAY (CONT) (*adjusting his gun*): And now, to put them out
of their misery...

He fires two beams at them, and they EXPLODE, SHRIEK-
ING.

He then walks to the Guard, who is massaging his neck, and
puts his hand on the man's shoulder. In the b.g., we SEE the
other Guard emerging out of the sarcophagus, alive.

RAY: Let's get those papers.

EXT NOTRE-DAME - NIGHT
ESTABLISHING SHOT of Winston stepping out of the car and standing outside the Notre-Dame Cathedral.

ANGLE ON WINSTON
He looks at the Cathedral in admiration.
WINSTON (*whistle*)

SEXTON (VO): M'sieur Zedmore?

MEDIUM ANGLE
Winston turns. A middle-aged, round faced SEXTON stands behind him.

WINSTON: Excuse me, Brother. I was too busy admiring your Cathedral.

SEXTON (*pleased*): It is beautiful, is it not? It is four times as old as America, you know... (*a beat*) But I'm keeping you waiting with my ramblings. I have what you came for. Please follow me.

They walk into the Cathedral. CAMERA PANS UPWARD to reveal two ECTOPLASMIC SHAPES appearing and merging into two STONE GARGOYLES on the roof.

CAMERA PANS TO THE RIGHT to a lit-up gothic window, and TRUCKS IN through the window into...

INT NOTRE-DAME
The Sexton, candelabra in hand, is leading Winston from a stone spiral staircase into a small chamber containing hundreds of old scrolls, manuscripts, etc.
SEXTON: This is where we keep valuable papers donated to the Church...

ANGLE ON SEXTON

He walks to a shelf and grabs a folder.
SEXTON (CONT): I have already located what you...

He becomes silent, a look of horror painted on his face.

ANGLE ON WINSTON
He turns to see what caused the Sexton's reaction.
WINSTON: Oy vey!

WIDE ANGLE
Two Gargoyles, their eyes pools of GREEN LIGHT, enter the
room through the window. Gargoyle No.1 looks big and mean
and walks threateningly towards the Sexton. Gargoyle No.2,
looking leaner and slicker, looms in the b.g.

WINSTON (*shouting*): Get out of here! Quick, man!

ANGLE ON SEXTON
The poor man is paralyzed by fright.

ANGLE ON GARGOYLE NO. 1
It raises its arms ominously, preparing to strike the Sexton a
deadly blow. Suddenly, we HEAR the familiar SOUND (SFX)
of a particle beam being fired. The Gargoyle looks surprised,
the GREEN GLOW dies and it EXPLODES.

ANGLE ON WINSTON
He stands behind the rubble, particle rifle in hand.

WIDE ANGLE
Before Winston can act, however, Gargoyle No. 2 comes up
swiftly, grabs the folder out of the Sexton's hands and darts
out of the window.

ANGLE ON WINSTON
WINSTON: Curses, foiled again! (*as an afterthought*) Sorry,
Brother, but you know how it is!

He steps out of the window after the Gargoyle.

EXT NOTRE-DAME
Through a SERIES OF QUICK CUTS, CAMERA FOL-
LOWS Winston as he pursues the Gargoyle over the rooftops
and gutters of the Cathedral. Several times, Winston fires a
beam at the Ghost, but misses it.

ANGLE ON WINSTON
This time, he seems to have lost sight of the Gargoyle.
WINSTON: Where the heck has it gone now!

Suddenly, we HEAR a loud SCREECH and a pair of stony
arms grab Winston, causing him to drop his particle rifle.

WINSTON (CONT): Aiiieeee!

WIDE ANGLE
The Gargoyle comes up from a dark corner beneath the gutter
on which Winston stands, grabs the Ghostbuster, lifts him up
in the air and threatens to throw him to his death on the street
far below.

WINSTON'S POV
emphasizing the peril, etc...

ANGLE ON WINSTON
He succeeds in quickly grabbing the rifle that's swinging in
the air, jams it into the Gargoyle's face and shoots.

WIDE ANGLE
There is a GREEN FLASH and a SCREAM. The Gargoyle
drops Winston, and falls to the street below.

CLOSE UP on Gargoyle shattering into a thousand pieces as it
hits the street.

ANGLE ON WINSTON

He falls on the roof, rolls down and almost follows the Gargoyle, but he manages to grab a stony protuberance at the last minute.

He hangs there for a few seconds, and finally pulls himself up on the roof. He then plunges his hand into the corner where the Gargoyle had stood and brings out the folder, which he holds triumphantly.

WINSTON (*shouting*): All right!

EXT MONTMARTRE - NIGHT

There are PEOPLE drinking on cafe terraces and wandering merrily among a throng of ARTISTS displaying their canvasses. EDITH PIAF-LIKE MUSIC PLAYS in the b.g.

CAMERA TRUCKS IN on a typical Parisian ARTIST painting a boring "Sunset over Paris" scene.

CAMERA PANS OVER TO THE RIGHT AND DOWNWARD to show an ECTOPLASMIC SHAPE slithering and throbbing among the cobblestones. Escaping the Artist's notice, the Ghost merges with the easel, then the canvas. (We can tell by a soft GREEN GLOW which moves upwards.)

ANGLE ON CANVAS

The paints on the canvas change, melt, swirl and reform from the boring "Sunset" into the picture of an evil WOMAN.

ANGLE ON ARTIST

The Artist looks at the impossible event, dumbfounded, and drops his brush.

ANGLE ON CANVAS

The WOMAN on the canvas opens her mouth wide, wider than possible, revealing a row of long and pointy fangs. The overall effect is very evil and very scary.

ANGLE ON ARTIST
He SCREAMS and runs away in horror.

ANGLE ON CANVAS
The woman LAUGHS derisively, becomes normal again—in fact, very attractive, then STEPS OUT of the canvas and onto the sidewalk. She LAUGHS again.

CAMERA PANS TO THE LEFT to show Peter walking through the throng, paper in hand, obviously looking for an address.

ANGLE ON PETER
PETER (*looking around*): Rue Gabrielle, Rue Gabrielle... Where the heck is Rue Gabrielle?

WIDE ANGLE
The Ghost-Woman walks alluringly towards Peter, whose eyes light up when he sees her.

GHOST-WOMAN: You seem lost, Monsieur. Can I help you?

PETER (*suave*): With pleasure, Mademoiselle. My chauffeur dropped me two blocks from here, and I can't seem to find the Rue Gabrielle.

GHOST-WOMAN (*wicked smile*): Why, it's just around the corner. I'll take you there.

She walks away, beckoning him to follow, which he does with a stupid grin on his face.

ANGLE ON PETER

PETER (*to himself*): The Venkman charm. Passport to every-where. Fodor, eat your heart out.

WIDE ANGLE
Peter follows the Ghost-Woman down some damp and deso-late-looking stairs. As they reach a dark alleyway, littered with garbage, she steps aside to let him pass.

ANGLE ON GHOST-WOMAN
GHOST-WOMAN (*most alluring*): This way, Monsieur.

ANGLE ON PETER
PETER (*in seventh heaven*): Hey, I'd follow you to Hell if you'd ask me...

PETER'S POV
It is a very dark and sinister alley. Old, defaced posters peel off the moss-encrusted walls. The MUSIC slowly GROWS more and more OMINOUS—"Night on Bald Mountain" like. SOMETHING AWFUL THIS WAY COMES...

GHOST-WOMAN (VO) (*sinister*): There's no need to ask, M'sieur Venkman! You're already there!

ANGLE ON PETER
He looks around wildly, but the Girl seems to be gone.

PETER (*slight panic*): What? Whatta ya mean? Mademoi-selle? Mademoiselle?

The MUSIC reaches a CRESCENDO. Whatever THING is coming it's just around the corner.

WIDE ANGLE
Peter turns, ready to flee. But the exit is barred by a fierce-looking CATWOMAN (teeth, claws, HISSING, etc.) in which we recognize the Ghost-Woman.

PETER (*to an invisible audience*): OK, OK, so she's a little catty!

Now, Peter knows he's been had. He turns back, grabs his particle rifle, and prepares for the fight. But he looks more apprehensive as the THING is almost upon him.

ANGLE ON PETER
A CLASH OF CYMBALS. The THING has arrived. Peter's face suddenly beams with incredulity and derision.
PETER: You must be joking?

PETER'S POV
A HUGE, French "Poubelle" (garbage can), filled to the brim with litter, is advancing ponderously towards Peter. Its lid is SNAPPING nastily. Its handles have grown into claws. Its GREEN GLOW identifies it as an ectoplasm-possessed arti-fact. But in spite of all its effort to appear threatening, it still looks kind of silly.

WIDE ANGLE
Peter turns. The Catwoman (HISS) still bars his way.

ANGLE ON PETER
PETER (*resigned*): No, I guess you're not...

CAMERA PANS UPWARD above the alley. The night sky-line looks very much like the boring painting seen earlier. Be-low, we HEAR the familiar SOUND of the Ghostbusters' par-ticle beam, several SHRIEKS, HISSES, BAM, WHAMs, etc. and a couple of GREEN FLASHES illuminate the screen. Then there is SILENCE.

CAMERA PANS DOWNWARD to the alley's entrance. Peter walks from around the corner, "dusting off" his hands in victo-ry.

PETER: Rue Gabrielle, Rue Gabrielle...

EXT EIFFEL TOWER - DAWN
ESTABLISHING SHOT showing the sunrise. CAMERA
PANS OVER to the tent-like Crisis HQ nearby, and TRUCKS
IN.

RAY (VO): I think we've got it this time!

INT CRISIS HQ
The Ghostbusters, Lucien and the Experts are standing around
the table. Papers are spread everywhere, etc. Ray and Egon are
putting the last touches on the Control Box.

ANGLE ON EGON
EGON: We don't have any time to lose. Have you had the
power line laid from the Tower's generator like I asked?

ANGLE ON LUCIEN
LUCIEN: But of course, M'sieur Spengler. All is in readiness
and waiting for you.

ANGLE ON PETER
PETER (*blasé*): OK, so let's get this show on the road.

WIDE ANGLE
Egon carrying the Box, they all walk to the tent's entrance and
onto...

EXT EIFFEL TOWER
...the esplanade, where the Police are still gathered "en
masse." There are huge cables running from the Tower to a
small electronic CONSOLE, standing in the center.

CAMERA PANS OVER to the Tower, now swirling with
GREEN and PINK ectoplasmic shapes.

RAY (VO) (*apprehensive*): We better connect this Box fast. I don't like the look of this...

CAMERA TRUCKS IN on the Tower. Suddenly, straight out of one of the columns, comes a GHOSTLY FRENCH COUPE from the 1920s, filled to the brim with a wide variety of Ghosts of the type previously seen in the story.

ANGLE ON COUPE
It drives straight towards the group formed by the Ghostbusters, Lucien and the Experts.

WIDE ANGLE
The French Police make a brave attempt to stop the Coupé, but it scatters them like toy soldiers.

VARIOUS POLICE: Watch Out! Help! Au Secours!

ANGLE ON THE GHOSTBUSTERS
They all fire particle beams at the Coupé.

PETER: The Charge of the Ghostly Brigade! They must be desperate!

ANGLE ON THE COUPE
The Ghost-Driver swerves like crazy, avoiding the beams.

ANGLE ON EGON
EGON: We can't afford to waste more time. Cover me!

He rushes towards the console, in a last attempt to connect the Control Box.

ANGLE ON THE COUPE
The beams fired by the Ghostbusters form an effective barricade preventing the Ghosts from going much further. But,

suddenly, the Coupé EXPLODES in a GREEN FLASH, scattering Ghosts in all directions.

CAMERA FOLLOWS the course of a CANNONBALL-LIKE Ghost (same as in Act 1) as it flies through the air and lands on top of Egon.

ANGLE ON EGON AND CANNONBALL GHOST
The Cannonball Ghost knocks Egon down to the ground, causing him to drop the Box. The Ghost then grabs it, runs away with an eerie "Woody Woodpecker" LAUGH and BLOWS ITSELF UP, thereby destroying the Box.

A SERIES OF QUICK CUTS
on the faces of the Ghostbusters, Lucien, etc. shows that all spectators realize the enormity of their defeat.

VARIOUS: Oh no! Non! C'est pas possible!

CAMERA PANS OVER and TRUCKS IN to the Eiffel Tower where the Ghosts are CHEERING like at a soccer match.

INT CRISIS HQ
The Ghostbusters, Lucien and the Experts are sitting in grim silence.

LUCIEN (*head within hands*): My Minister will be furious. He was supposed to appear on TV tonight to announce that the problem had been taken care of.

PETER (*nasty*): Well, he can appear on TV to announce that he is taking a long vacation.

LUCIEN (*raising his head*): No, you don't understand. (*pointing at the Tower blueprints pinned to the wall*) If we lose the Tower, there will not be any television for the people of France...

ANGLE ON TOWER BLUEPRINTS
CAMERA TRUCKS IN on the huge broadcast antennas on top of the Tower.

LUCIEN (VO - CONT): These are the most powerful broadcast antennas in our country. If they go...

ANGLE ON LUCIEN
He blows on his open hands in a typical French gesture.
LUCIEN (CONT): Pfft... No more television.

ANGLE ON RAY
The light bulb above his head is almost visible.
RAY: Broadcast antennas? Did you say broadcast antennas?

ANGLE ON LUCIEN
LUCIEN (*nonplussed*): Oui. But, I confess, I don't understand...

ANGLE ON RAY
RAY (*excited*): If I'm right, and I'm invariably right, all our problems are solved! (pointing at the telephone on the table) Can you patch me through to New York?

INT GHOSTBUSTER CENTRAL - DAY
CLOSE UP on the telephone on the front desk. It is ringing madly.

CAMERA TRUCKS OUT to reveal JANINE running to answer it. She is dressed in dirty blue overalls, and looks extremely disheveled. Screw drivers, wrenches and various other kinds of tools are visible in her pockets.

A SERIES OF CUTS
shows the following conversation taking place between Ray in Paris and Janine in New York.

JANINE (*mad as hell*): Ghostbusters! What do you want?

RAY: Janine, it's me, Ray. Have you...

JANINE (*interrupting*): Oh, it's you! Well, let me tell you, I'm not paid enough to install your furshugginer dishes, and let me tell you another thing, I'm not...

RAY (*beaming*): You mean, you've already set up the dish?

JANINE: What are you, deaf? I just told you I finished it today...

RAY (*rubbing his hands together*): Fantastic, Janine. This is what you're going to do...

EXT EIFFEL TOWER / GHOSTBUSTER CENTRAL
Another SERIES OF CUTS shows first the dish on the Ghostbusters' rooftop, then the antennas on top of the Eiffel Tower, being readjusted in different positions.

RAY (V.O.): Okay! Let 'er rip!

CAMERA TRUCKS OUT from the antenna to encompass the whole Eiffel Tower. The Ghosts are being siphoned off in a GREEN and PINK stream and shot straight into the sky, accompanied by the SOUND of SHRIEKING, HISSING and OTHER EERIE NOISES. We then SEE the Ghosts-Beam being received by the Ghostbusters' dish in New York.

CAMERA TRUCKS OUT further from the Tower to reveal the Ghostbusters and Lucien watching the spectacle from afar.

LUCIEN: What a fantastic idea, M'sieur Stantz! Beaming all the Ghosts across the globe by satellite, directly into your own

Containment Unit! (*a beat—worried*) It will be big enough? They won't come back, will they?

ANGLE ON PETER
He slaps the Frenchman on the shoulders.
PETER: Don't worry, Lucien, old pal! That's why you're paying us all those bucks!

EXT GHOSTBUSTER CENTRAL - DAY
ESTABLISHING SHOT. CAMERA TRUCKS IN onto the firehouse.

PETER (VO) (*irate*): What do you mean, all gone!?

INT GHOSTBUSTER CENTRAL
The guys are lounging about, except Peter who is standing in the center of the room, a bank statement in hand.

PETER (CONT): You mean to tell me, all the money we got from the French went to the Scuzzo Cable Company?

WINSTON (shrugging): Well, we did have to pay off their customers. Instead of seeing "Pussycats on Parade," what they got was five hours of cursing French Ghosts. Can't blame them for suing, I suppose...

ANGLE ON JANINE
She comes into the room, walking and smiling, holding a tray of wine and cheese.

JANINE: What say we all celebrate in the best French fashion. With wine and brie?...

ANGLE ON PETER
He glares at her and walks threateningly towards her, bank statement in hand, fuming.

WIDE ANGLE
She retreats in a hurry, as the others LAUGH and we

FADE OUT

THE END

COMICS

Starting in 1985, Randy and I began writing comics. I was already a fan of Marvel and DC Comics, whose characters I had discovered in my teens in various French editions. Thus it was a great thrill to be given the license to add my own small contribution to the wonderful universes of both companies.

During the ten years that followed, we wrote many comics, often teaming up with other writers and friends, such as Roy Thomas, but also Len Wein and Marv Wolfman. Among the titles in our credits were Superman, Teen Titans *and* Blue Beetle *for DC,* Doctor Strange *at Marvel, but also licensed books such as* Clive Barker's Hellraiser, Star Trek, Dracula *and even* Cthulhu*! (An itemized list of our credits on our website at* www.lofficier.com.*)*

The following script was written for Malibu Comics' version of Star Trek: Deep Space Nine *Nos. 26 & 27, and invents a descendent of the great Harry Mudd, played by Roger C. Carmel.*[4]

Star Trek: Deep Space Nine: Mudd's Pets

PART I

Since the whole story is narrated in captions by MUDD, as told to the JUDGE during his trial, it would be nice if the colorist could be instructed to visually distinguish the MUDD captions (e.g.: yellow) from the JUDGE's (e.g.: blue).

PAGE 1:
Three small panels on the top row, showing a small trading ship emerging from the wormhole and then docking on DS9.

Panel 1:
CAPTION (COURT OFFICER): "All rise. The Third Federation Court of the District of Bajor is now in session. His Honor Judge SDRED presiding."

Panel 2:
CAPTION (SDRED): "You may be seated. How does the accused plead?"
CAPTION (MUDD): "NOT GUILTY, your honor!"

Panel 3:
CAPTION (SDRED): "REALLY? Er, I mean, very well...
CAPTION (SDRED): "Please state your identity so it can be entered into the records."

Panel 4:
Then, a large panel (leave room for title/credits), bottom two-thirds of page, showing MUDD (center stage) on the Promenade, with its colorful array of aliens, Starfleet officers, etc. As you know, we CANNOT use actor Roger Carmel (the original series' Mudd)'s likeness. I think we could, however, retain the general physical type: heavy and jovial. If I were to recast

the part, I'd go with John Goodman or Robbie Coltrane (the British actor starring in CRACKER).

CAPTION (MUDD): "My name is HORACE T. MUDD. An old name. A proud name. A good name!"

CAPTION (SDRED): "Will the accused please avoid his customary digressions and stick to the facts."

CAPTION (MUDD): "With great pleasure, Your Honor. 'Just the Facts' Mudd, they call me on Rigel IV. As I was about to say, I landed on DEEP SPACE NINE on Stardate [*TECH*] and I told myself, 'Horace, old boy, this is a mighty fine station'..."

CAPTION (SDRED): "*SIGH!* "

TITLE: MUDD'S PETS

PAGE 2:
From this point on, MUDD's first-person narration will often totally contradict what we see in the art. In fact, the more pronounced the contrast between the two, the funnier the effect.

Panel 1:
A worried MUDD spies ODO, flanked by a couple of his beige-uniformed MEN, walking towards him. It should be clear that even though they're looking for him, they haven't spotted him—yet.

CAPTION (MUDD): "As behooves the law-abiding businessman that I am, I hurried to pay my respects to the local constabulary as soon as I arrived...

CAPTION (MUDD): "I place enormous value on maintaining good relations with officers of the law... "

Panel 2:
MUDD tries very hard to avoid ODO's men by hiding himself behind a column, or a sign post. (ODO does not appear in this panel.)

116

CAPTION (SDRED): "Are you, by any chance, referring to the still pending inquiry into your bribery of the Senior Magister on Ventax II?"

CAPTION (MUDD): "ALLEGED bribery, Your Honor. It was a mere trinket.

Panel 3:

MUDD is comically attempting to slink away, looking behind him, and therefore clearly not seeing ODO in front of him, transforming himself from a potted plant (or whatever) back into his usual humanoid shape.

CAPTION (MUDD): "I, er, RAN INTO Security Chief ODO when doing his usual rounds...

Panel 4:

ODO's office. ODO is looking into his computer screen. A squirming MUDD is sitting across the desk, making feeble disparaging hand gestures.

CAPTION (MUDD): "We had a most enjoyable chat, exchanging pleasantries and trading anecdotes, as is often my wont in such instances...

ODO: Twelve cases of serious fraud on Aldebaran III. Embezzling the Delbian Widows' and Orphans Fund. Fixing Antidean mud wrestling fights. Managing a tribble torture farm on Largo V. Feeding explosives to Endicorian Hedgehogs—a protected species—and selling the bits as chewbones to Klingons...

Panel 5:

ODO is looking hard and straight at MUDD, who's doing his best to present an endearing and honest face—but not succeeding very well.

ODO: It would appear that you have left a trail of slime on every unfortunate world upon which you have ever set foot, Mister...

ODO: ...HORACE TIBERIUS MUDD—

Panel 6:

ODO raises a quizzical, inexistent eyebrow as he asks MUDD a question; MUDD shrugs.

ODO: —TIBERIUS?

MUDD: Someone my grand-papa was very fond of, I was told.

PAGE 3:

Panel 1:

A very suspicious ODO, standing inside the doorway of his office, watches MUDD leave.

CAPTION (MUDD): "After this frank exchange of views, I'm proud to say that I left behind a Security Officer completely reassured as to my impeccable references...

CAPTION (MUDD): "My next appointment was with another businessman as upstanding as myself..."

Panel 2:

ODO puts a hand to his head (in the "why me?" mode), seeing his fears justified as he watches MUDD walk into—QUARK's bar.

CAPTION (SDRED): "I take it that you are referring to the merchant QUARK?"

CAPTION (MUDD): "I am indeed, Your Honor. A reputable, honest, trustworthy, hard-working individual."

CAPTION (SDRED): "A FERENGI."

Panel 3:

MUDD and QUARK, sitting at a table over drinks, in a dark corner of Quark's bar. They look just like the two conspiring thieves they are.

CAPTION (MUDD): Admittedly, Your Honor, but a PRINCE among Ferengi...

QUARK: Remarkable, Mudd! This scheme of yours is as SLIPPERY as a Deltan card-shark dipped in Troyian butter!

MUDD: And PROFITABLE too, friend Quark! Why, just the markup alone on these SYSTEM-Ks should net you at least 2000 bars of gold-pressed latinum!

Panel 4:
QUARK and MUDD lean closer as they start haggling over the split of the intended profits like starving gerbils.
QUARK: Which is why I have decided, very generously I might add, to retrocede you a commission of 12%!
MUDD: Your wit is as sharp as ever, friend Quark. Surely, you meant 45%?
QUARK: This infernal din drowns out your melodious voice, Mudd. Did I hear you say 25%?

Panel 5:
QUARK looks nervous or crestfallen as a jovial MUDD gets the best of him.
MUDD: I believe 35% to be a most accommodating figure, if you take into account Starfleet's new directive D12.
QUARK: B-but... You haven't reported any of this to Starfleet?
MUDD: My point exactly!

Panel 6:
QUARK gets up, offering his hand to MUDD.
CAPTION (MUDD): "We concluded our negotiations in the spirit of fairness that has made my name a byword on more than a dozen worlds...
CAPTION (SDRED): I am sure of that. Continue, please.
QUARK: Deal! But are you SURE you weren't born a Ferengi, Mudd?
MUDD: Ha! Ha! You flatter me, friend Quark! Why don't we go look at the "merchandise" right now?

PAGE 4:

Panel 1:
MUDD, followed by QUARK, enters a Cargo Bay, where MUDD's ship's contents have been stored.
CAPTION (MUDD): "Having settled the terms of our relationship, I then proceeded to take the honorable QUARK to inspect the goods, which had been safely unloaded from my ship and stored in Cargo Bay 12...

Panel 2:
MUDD and QUARK are going through the open containers, discarding a sundry variety of items which look like cheap, archeological junk.
CAPTION: "My modesty would suffer if I told you how impressed my Ferengi partner was with the quality and craftsmanship of the artifacts I had brought back from the Gamma Quadrant...
QUARK: Junk! This is nothing but junk, Mudd! Where's the item you promised?
MUDD: Patience, friend Quark! Patience!

Panel 3:
MUDD moves a now-empty container, revealing a pseudo-Egyptian sarcophagus that was lying directly underneath.
MUDD: I spent endless months looking for opportunities in the Gamma Quadrant, until I happened to come across RAKHAR V...
MUDD: A most interesting planet—obviously once the home of a great civilization, not unlike that of Erabus...
QUARK: What do I care about Rakhar V or Erabus? I want to see the goods NOW!

Panel 4:
MUDD opens the sarcophagus which appears to be empty.
CAPTION (MUDD): "I have always taken great pride in maintaining accurate shipping records for customs officials...

MUDD: Because of Starfleet's new directive, I had to pack them discretely inside this fake and, er, FALSE-BOTTOMED sarcophagus from Deneb IV...
MUDD: A very useful tool, this sarcophagus. It's served me well and often.

Panel 5:
Small panel. MUDD lifts the false bottom...
CAPTION (MUDD): "My affairs are an open book."
CAPTION (SDRED): "The pages of which you seem to need to turn often."
MUDD: Ah here we are!

Panel 6:
MUDD pulls out a cage containing two adorable-looking blue rodents, somewhat like rabbits, with cute eyes, trumpet-shaped ears and long bushy, silky hair around their faces. Or whatever other cutesy design you want to come up with.
MUDD: Aren't they cute? I call them "MEEPS" because of the sounds they make.
MEEPS (no balloon): MEEP.

PAGE 5:

Panel 1:
MUDD, still holding the cage, looks adoringly at the two MEEPS, while QUARK looks on skeptically.
CAPTION(MUDD): "Imagine my profound surprise when I discovered two harmless-looking stowaways amongst my precious, archeological treasures...
MUDD: I'm also thinking of taking them to the Robo-Pet Fair on Ogus II. Licensing, you know... It's coming back, friend Quark!
MEEPS (no balloon): MEEP.

Panel 2:

A still skeptical-looking QUARK addresses MUDD, who reassures him profusely.

CAPTION (MUDD): "I was shocked, I tell you, SHOCKED!

QUARK: I don't know, Mudd, these things look pretty harmless to me... Are you sure they're voracious enough?

MUDD: Don't worry, friend Quark, their appetite is insatiable!

Panel 3:

QUARK still looks dubious, but MUDD's face shows surprise as he notices something below him.

QUARK: What have you been feeding them?

MUDD: Well, I've been giving them this cargo of Klingon chewbones that I...

MUDD: UH-OH!

QUARK: ?

Panel 4:

MUDD lifts an empty cage from the sarcophagus. Its bottom appears to have been chewed through, although the edges should be melted as if by acid.

MUDD: I had another pair! They're gone! They've escaped. I don't understand...

QUARK: It looks to me like they've chewed their way out of their cage...

MUDD: That's impossible, it's made of duranium alloy...

Panel 5:

MUDD and QUARK look inside the sarcophagus and see a hole in the bottom.

CAPTION (MUDD): "I am as much a VICTIM as anyone else, Your Honor. A priceless Denebian sarcophagus was irreparably damaged...

CAPTION (MUDD): "...Not to mention a valuable cargo of Klingon chewbones which the wretched little pests totally devoured!

MUDD: It'd take an industrial laser to go through...

Panel 6:
The sarcophagus has been moved aside, and we see a hole in the station floor. MUDD looks horrified.
CAPTION (MUDD): "My insurance representative has been notified.
MUDD: ...to go through...

PAGE 6:

Panel 1:
DS9's Bridge. SISKO is there, flanked by KIRA and O'BRIEN. ODO enters, pushing QUARK and MUDD in front of him.
CAPTION (MUDD): "Needless to say, I immediately ran to tell the Station Authorities...
ODO: I caught both of them as they were about to leave, Commander.
SISKO: Very good, Odo! Maybe now, we can finally get to the bottom of this plague of—What are they called again? MEEPS?
QUARK: This is a scandal! I had nothing to do with it!

Panel 2:
ODO confronts QUARK while the others look on the scene with interest.
ODO: Really? What about those SYSTEM-K pest control robots that are sitting in Cargo Bay 8? A coincidence? I think not!
QUARK: That's totally unrelated! I bought those robots because I wanted to diversify into the exciting field of farm machinery!

Panel 3:
More of the same, this time favoring KIRA. Her face shows a dawning realization of QUARK's scheme.

ODO: Or maybe you "gambled" on a "sudden" and "myste-rious" pest infestation, so you could sell your System-Ks to the Bajoran farmers at an inflated price, hmm?
KIRA: The harvesting is about to begin on Bajor's Southern Continent...

Panel 4:
KIRA, now enraged, is grabbing QUARK in anger.
KIRA: Is that what you planned, QUARK? You miserable little...
QUARK: N-no, N-never c-crossed m-my m-mind...

Panel 5:
SISKO reasserts control of the situation in his usual, com-posed fashion. O'BRIEN's face sports a somewhat superior smile.
SISKO: May I remind you that we all have a more serious problem. There's an unknown, destructive life-force loose on DS9...
O'BRIEN: Bah! These... MEEPS... can't be worse than those Cardassian Voles we dealt with a few months back. A bit of cheese, a few traps, and they'll be caught in no time. What's the pro--

Panel 6:
All characters freeze in a look-around posture, as the Bridge is suddenly plunged into darkness. (Colorist: use various shades of blue.)
CAPTION (MUDD): "I like to think that it is precisely be-cause of my sense of duty that the worst was averted...
SFX (no balloon): WHOOM!
O'BRIEN: --blem?

PAGE 7:

Panel 1:
DS9's reactor room. Panic reigns. Energy bolts shoot. Sparks sizzle.
CAPTION (MUDD): "I shudder to think what damage might have occurred had I not come forward as I did...

Panel 2:
Against the background of the chaotic reactor room, a STAR-FLEET ENGINEER (a made-up character?) is speaking into a screen displaying O'BRIEN's face.
ENGINEER: I don't understand what happened, Chief! It looks like power cables 5 to 9 were... were...
O'BRIEN (from screen): Speak up, Man! I can barely hear you!
ENGINEER (small print in big balloon to betray embarrassment): Eaten.

Panel 3:
DS9's Bridge. O'BRIEN, looking severely aggravated, is rushing out. QUARK and MUDD are in the background, the former looking sarcastic, the latter trying to hush him up.
O'BRIEN: EATEN! I don't believe it! Five power cables EATEN!
O'BRIEN: Divert all available power through the emergency lines! Cut off sections 12 to 15 of the G-grid! I'm coming down!
QUARK: "Insatiable appetite", eh, Mudd?
MUDD: Shhhh!

Panel 4:
SISKO turns his icy eyes towards MUDD, who visibly shrivels under the Commander's stare.
CAPTION (MUDD): "Commander Sisko and I developed what I would call an immediate *CAMARADERIE*...
SISKO: Mr. Mudd, you're one of the sorriest, lowest, most miserable forms of parasitic life that it's been my dubious

pleasure to meet. However, we need to know where you found these... Meeps?

MUDD: I'm most eager to cooperate with you, Commander!

Panel 5:

MUDD talking; all the others listening.

CAPTION (MUDD): "He was most impressed with my information...

MUDD: They, er, stowed aboard my ship on RAKHAR V, in the Gamma Quadrant. It's a beautiful world, a trifle on the desertic side perhaps... It was once the home of... The home of...

SISKO: Yes?

MUDD: —A THRIVING, NOW EXTINCT CIVILIZATION!

Panel 6:

You don't have to include MUDD in this panel. All the others look at each other with a "It couldn't be... Could it?" type of look.

CAPTION (MUDD): "Yes, I'd definitely say he was impressed.

PAGE 8:

Panel 1:

DR. BASHIR's lab. DAX is there, holding a tablet with glyphs on it, addressing the regulars.

DAX: I've translated the artifacts MUDD brought from RAKHAR V. The Meeps were a genetically-built weapon unleashed by one of the two warring races who lived on that world approximately five thousand years ago...

Panel 2:

FLASHBACK IMAGE showing hordes of MEEPS eating buildings, trees, bridges, etc.

CAPTION (DAX): "Their appetite is boundless, their saliva is practically a universal solvent, and they reproduce like crazed tribbles. Once unleashed, the Meeps proved unstoppable, and eventually destroyed both races..."

Panel 3:
Back to scene. DAX completes here lecture. Reverse the angle from Panel 1.
DAX: The Meeps can eat virtually everything, and they live for approximately 150 years. They were undoubtedly at work on devouring Rakhar V itself when MUDD picked up the two pairs.
MUDD (small balloon): I didn't... at least...

Panel 4:
Favoring KIRA and DR. BASHIR. The latter looks crestfallen, as he points at something off-panel.
KIRA: What about the pair we have, Doctor? Any results on your tests yet?
BASHIR: I'm afraid so. Meet the Meep—Mark II!

Panel 5:
Inside a force field are the other two Meeps. But they are no longer cute and adorable. They look more like ravening beasts. Try to avoid any similarities with the movie GREM-LINS. DAX is in the frame.
MEEPS (no balloon): MEEP!
DAX: We have to keep "feeding" the containment field, otherwise the Meeps could just eat their way out of it.

Panel 6:
If looks could kill, SISKO's would disintegrate MUDD on the spot. The regulars are all standing around staring at him as well.
CAPTION (MUDD): "It was clear to everyone that I was the only one who could save the day."
DAX: Congratulations, Mr. Mudd. According to my calculations, if we don't stop your little pets, we'll have to evacuate the station in less than 36 hours!

MUDD (small lettering, big balloon): They're not my pets...

PART II

PAGE 1:
Three small panels on the top row, showing the MEEPS (in their "hostile" form) cheerfully eating various bits of DS9, going "Meep, meep" (no balloons).

Panel 1:
CAPTION (COURT OFFICER): "The Third Federation Court of the District of Bajor will now reconvene. His Honor Judge SDRED presiding."

Panel 2:
CAPTION (SDRED): "HORACE TIBERIUS MUDD, you stand accused of having illegally imported from the Gamma Quadrant a destructive lifeform known as... as...
CAPTION (MUDD): "Meeps, Your Honor."

Panel 3:
CAPTION (SDRED): "Yes, Meeps, and released them aboard Station DEEP SPACE NINE."
CAPTION (MUDD): "This is a serious miscarriage of justice, Your Honor!"

Panel 4:
Then, a large panel (leave room for title/credits), bottom two-thirds of page, recapping the last scene from Part I. Everyone is gathered in DR. BASHIR's office. There are two Meeps held prisoner in a force field in the background. In the foreground, favor SISKO glaring at MUDD, while DAX is telling the trader off.
CAPTION (MUDD): "I was in fact at the forefront of the efforts launched to save the Station, as I will now explain...
MEEPS (no balloon): MEEP.

DAX: Congratulations, Mr. Mudd. According to my calculations, if we don't stop your little pets, we'll have to evacuate the station in less than 36 hours!

MUDD (small lettering, big balloon): They're not my pets...

TITLE: MUDD'S PETS (PART II)

PAGE 2:

We remain in DR. BASHIR's office. Change the angles as the conversation moves between the various regulars.

Panel 1:

Favor SISKO, ODO and KIRA.

SISKO: We need to do something at once. Any ideas?

ODO: I have one, Commander. We know QUARK has just taken delivery of a large consignment of pest-control robots...

KIRA: That's right! You said they were SYSTEM-Ks...

Panel 2:

Favor KIRA facing QUARK.

KIRA: They're from Sirian Robotics, aren't they? A Class-A product?

QUARK: Yes, they're very good, but...

Panel 3:

Favor DR. BASHIR talking to KIRA, both of them ignoring a stuttering QUARK.

BASHIR: I'm familiar with the System-Ks. They're widely used in the Nile Delta on Earth, but in my opinion, they won't be enough to stop the Meeps. They'll just eat them like honey cakes.

KIRA: Perhaps, but they will slow them down and buy us some time.

QUARK: But... But... They're...

Panel 4:
Favor SISKO, flashing his predatory smile at QUARK.
SISKO: They're WHAT, Mr. Quark?
QUARK: They're, er, mine, Commander...
SISKO: Under the circumstances, I'm sure you will be delighted to volunteer their use. Especially if you don't want to share Mr. Mudd's fate, whatever that will be...

Panel 5:
Favor ODO and MUDD in the foreground. KIRA and DAX are studying a computer screen in the background.
CAPTION (MUDD): "It was all a misunderstanding, naturally. My record speaks for itself...
ODO: ...Violation of quarantine rules, Starfleet Directive D12 regarding the importation of dangerous animals, contravention of customs articles 25 to 36...

Panel 6:
Reverse angle as KIRA and DAX reenter the conversation.
KIRA: Don't forget about threatening an endangered species, Constable.
MUDD: I object most strenuously! WHAT endangered species?!

PAGE 3:

Panel 1:
Favor KIRA and DAX with some kind of TECH display of the station on a screen behind them, showing areas in red.
KIRA: US!
DAX: The scans show the growing Meep damage. If we don't stop them soon, DS9 is doomed.

Panel 2:
Favor SISKO, looking commanding.
SISKO: That settles it. Julian and Dax, you stay here and try to find a way to rid us of Mr. Mudd's pets...

SISKO: Major and Odo, you use the System-Ks to keep the Meeps at bay.

Panel 3:
SISKO grins, MUDD looks abused, QUARK nudges him while ODO smiles.
SISKO: Oh, and Odo, Mr. Mudd and Quark have just volunteered to assist you!
MUDD: What!? But I didn't...
QUARK: Shut up!
ODO: With pleasure, Commander!

Panels 4 & 5:
The service corridors of DS 9. A SYSTEM-K ROBOT (use whatever design strikes your fancy; we visualize them as cybernetic weasels) is tackling a MEEP. They fight for two panels, the MEEP is biting and clawing. The ROBOT uses whatever resources you have given him (metal claws, tasers, etc.) Add various SFX: SNARL, GROWL, WHIRR, SNAP, ZZTAK, etc.

Panel 6:
The robot succeeds in killing the horrible animal, but the acid saliva has destroyed it. Add a mechanical, robotic, last gasp SFX: PSHHHhhhhhhh.

PAGE 4:

Panel 1:
We pull back to reveal QUARK remotely controlling the SYSTEM-K with a hand-held box. ODO, KIRA and MUDD are with him. MUDD is, in fact, cowering behind KIRA, peeking over her shoulder.
CAPTION (MUDD): "Having volunteered to lead the battle against the monstrous animals, I leapt to the forefront of the fray with my customary disregard for my own safety...

Panel 2:

Favor MUDD looking cowardly, and KIRA facing him angrily.

MUDD: I really think I could be more useful helping that fine young, Dr. Bashir, Major. After all, my knowledge of...

KIRA: If it was up to me, after what you were planning to pull on Bajor, you'd be Meep-bait right now!

Panel 3:

Favor QUARK, composed, and ODO with the usual sarcastic smile he dons when he's ruining one of the Ferengi's schemes.

QUARK: May I observe, Major, that if one robot is destroyed for each Meep, we'll never get rid of them...

QUARK: And it's going to really eat into my profits!

ODO: If you don't want the next Meep to eat YOU, you'd better get us another robot!

Panel 4:

SISKO's office. SISKO is talking to O'BRIEN, trying to get a grip on the problem.

SISKO: Can we beam them out, like Tribbles?

O'BRIEN: Not unless they're all in the same place, but Meeps aren't that cooperative.

SISKO: What about some kind of gas?

O'BRIEN: Julian says they seem impervious to all known sedatives. Bioengineered that way, it seems.

Panel 5:

More of the same; change the angle. O'BRIEN looks more crestfallen.

SISKO: Why don't we open the airlocks and flush them out?

O'BRIEN: They apparently survive nicely in vacuum.

SISKO: So what CAN we do, Chief?

O'BRIEN: Er, I've been working on a portable confinement field, like the one Julian has been using, but it'll take time...

Panel 6:
SISKO and O'BRIEN look aghast as three Meeps come crunching their way through the walls.
MEEPS (no balloons): Meep Crunch Meep Crunch

PAGE 5:

Panel 1:
Favor SISKO looking glum.
SISKO: Time is something we're rapidly running out of, Chief.
SISKO: We may have to start seriously thinking about—station evacuation!

Panel 2:
Another service corridor, where QUARK , ODO, KIRA and the reluctant MUDD are engaged in Meep extermination. They're about to reach a corner. The SYSTEM-K is in front, followed by QUARK, then KIRA, then ODO, and naturally, MUDD lagging behind in the back, looking nervously behind him. ODO is growling at MUDD.
CAPTION (MUDD): "Although I would have liked to help the Commander, at that particular moment, I was being held back by other, more pressing commitments...
ODO: Hurry up, Mr. Mudd!

Panel 3:
ANGLE on QUARK, who's turned the corner, and has seen something unpleasant off-panel. KIRA, behind him, hasn't yet.
QUARK: UH-OH!

Panel 4:
KIRA, impatiently, passes QUARK to step around the corner. QUARK stays where he is, impassible.
KIRA: Uh-oh what?

Panel 5:

CLOSE-UP reaction shot of KIRA. She at last sees what QUARK saw. Her eyes grow wide.
KIRA: Uh-Oh.

Panel 6:
Their P.O.V.: a whole pack of very angry-looking, hungry Meeps are facing them. The SYSTEM-K is already history. (SFX: PSHhh).
CAPTION (MUDD): "Even though any sensible businessman would have realized that the time had come to divest and re-group elsewhere...

PAGE 6:

Panel 1:
KIRA, backing up, bumps into MUDD who's backing up from the opposite direction.
KIRA: Back!
MUDD: Back is BAD, Major!

Panel 2:
Another P.O.V. shot with our Heroes in the foreground: there are more fierce-looking Meeps blocking the way they came.
CAPTION (MUDD): "Having run out of options, I prepared to suffer...

Panel 3:
LONG SHOT to show that our little group appears to be cornered, like proverbial rats.
CAPTION (MUDD): "... The BITTER BITE of economic adversity...

Panel 4:
DR. BASHIR's lab. DAX is working on the two captive Meeps, scanning them with some kind of tricorder. JULIAN is working at the medical computer.

DAX: They're really an incredible feat of genetic engineering! Their saliva dissolves all sub-nuclear bonds. It's virtually a universal solvent!

BASHIR: Lucky for us the stuff has a short lifespan, otherwise it'd already have eaten its way through the hull.

Panel 5:

DAX keeps lecturing. BASHIR has an expression of triumph as he snaps his fingers.

DAX: It's like the anticoagulant factor in mosquito saliva... It helps prevent the blood from clotting while they're dining, but the effect is limited so their victims don't bleed to death later on.

BASHIR: Universal solvent... That's it!

Panel 6:

Favor BASHIR.

BASHIR: The problem with the concept of a universal solvent has always been—what kind of container do you carry it in?

BASHIR: Obviously, the Meeps themselves ARE the container. Somehow, their molecular structure contains something that resists the solvent's action!

PAGE 7:

Panel 1:

DAX's face lights up. BASHIR has returned to his computer.

DAX: If we could manufacture a compound to alter, even slightly, the Meeps' molecular structure, the solvent would then attack the Meeps themselves and kill them.

BASHIR: We could spread it through the station in gaseous form by using the replicator network!

Panel 2:

DAX is back pointing the tricorder at the captive MEEPS. BASHIR raises his eyes from the computer screen. He sports an impish smile.

DAX: It would turn them into a harmless puddle of goo.

BASHIR: A harmless puddle of EXCREMENTALLY FETID goo!

Panel 3:

We're back in a service corridor. KIRA, ODO and QUARK are making a last stand against the hordes of MEEPS with phasers and other types of energy weapon. MUDD is hunched down on the floor, in an almost fetal position, with his hands covering his eyes.

CAPTION (MUDD): "Never in my family's long, proud history, going all the way back to the ALAMO, has a Mudd been so brave under such unequal conditions..."

CAPTION (SDRED): "One of your ancestors fought at the Alamo?"

Panel 4:

Very much the same scene as in the previous panel, except that wisps of pink gas are floating down the corridor.

CAPTION (MUDD): "Er... Actually, he was selling unstable gunpowder to Santa Ana...

Panel 5:

The MEEPS have liquefied into puddles of greenish goo, while KIRA, QUARK and MUDD (ODO has no sense of smell) are waving their hands in front of their faces and scrunching their noses to indicate that there is a powerfully bad odor emanating from the puddles.

KIRA: Julian and Dax must have figured something out...

QUARK: PHEW! What a disgusting smell! It's worse than Rom's feet!

ODO: Just be glad you're alive to smell it!

Panel 6:

136

MUDD is in a courtroom-type of situation, facing the bar. On either side of him are red-uniformed Starfleet SECURITY OFFICERS. Judge SDRED is a stern-looking Vulcan. ODO stands on the side.

MUDD: ...And there you have it, Your Honor. The truth and nothing but. There can be no doubt as to my innocence.

SDRED: The only doubt still in my mind, Mr. Mudd, regards your punishment...

ODO: If I might make a suggestion to the Court...

PAGE 8:

Panel 1:
The Bridge. SISKO, OBRIEN and KIRA are there, performing their usual duties.

SISKO: I take it I can notify Starfleet that all repairs are now well underway, Mr. O'Brien?

O'BRIEN: Yes, Commander.

O'BRIEN: Major Kira, there's a message for you from Bajor...

Panel 2:
Favor KIRA, looking astonished.

KIRA: The farmers on the South Continent want to buy what's left of Quark's SYSTEM-Ks. It seems a plague of rodents has been after their crops.

Panel 3:
KIRA still looks dumbfounded, and O'BRIEN is laughing.

O'BRIEN: It looks like Quark's going to get his profit after all!

Panel 4:
Favor SISKO. KIRA is smiling.

SISKO: Why don't we keep this from him for a while longer? It might distract him from the important job he's been asked to do!

<u>Panel 5</u>:
Cut to the service corridors. ODO is standing in his sternest pose, arms crossed, legs slightly akimbo. QUARK and MUDD are scooping up oozing puddles of green goo.
ODO: Hurry up. You still have another 5 levels to go!
MUDD: SIGH!

In 2000, Thierry Mornet became editor-in-chief of a line of digest-sized, black & white French comics, which had been started by Editions Lug, a Lyon-based publisher, in the 1950s, but had since fallen on hard times. In fact, by then the line consisted entirely of reprints, the last original stories having been published in the early 1980s, when Lug's founder and editor-in-chief, Marcel Navarro, had retired.

Under Thierry's direction, we decided to relaunch several of the old characters in all-new stories. These were to feature Kabur, *prince of long-lost Hyperborea,* Wampus, *the fearsome monster from outer space bent on sowing chaos,* Zembla, *the lord of the African jungle of Karunda, as well as more traditional superheroes such as* Homicron, Starlock, *etc. Eventually, that valiant effort came too late, and the line was discontinued at the end of 2003. A six-issue mini-series regrouping several superheroes under the title of* Strangers, *was published by Image Comics in 2003; Black Coat Press has also put out translated trade paperbacks collections of* Wampus, Kabur, *etc. under the imprint Hexagon Comics.*

Phenix : The Red Box

Phenix, created by Italian artist Luciano Bernasconi, is a leather-clad, bike riding superhero who patrols the streets of Chicago. Her secret identity is that of a wealthy socialite millionaire named, Patricia Hope. When she was a student, Patricia was raped and assaulted. She woke up from a coma with her enhanced physical abilities. The story that follows, drawn by young Spanish artist Fernando Pasarin, bridges the gap between the original series of the 1980s and the new series of 2000-03.

143

147

Kabur: Young Kabur

Prince Kabur of Hyperborea *was created by French science fiction writer Claude J. Legrand, who also created the* Time Brigade, Starlock *and* Jaleb the Telepath, *as well as translated the* Conan *comics into French.* Kabur *was first drawn by Italian artist Luciano Bernasconi, who was to Editions Lug what Jack Kirby was to Marvel. Kabur resembles Hal Foster's* Prince Valiant, *thrown into a precataclysmic world not unlike that of Robert E. Howard's* Conan *and* Kull. *After taking over the writing of* Kabur *and having him involved in some very serious adventures for three years, I decided to present a more facetious aspect of what his youth could have been like in the following story, drawn by young Spanish artist David Lafuente.*

story: JEAN-MARC LOFFICIER pencil & inks: DAVID LAFUENTE

154

158

159

The · End

Tongue*Lash

Of all our original creations in the field of comics, none is more dear to us than Tongue*Lash, *illustrated by British artist Dave Taylor, the subject of two series published by Dark Horse in 1996 and 1999.*

Tongue and Lash are two private detectives who operate in a world parallel to ours, in which the dominant civilization is that of the Maya. The idea for that world came to us after reading Tony Hillerman's 1986 novel, Skinwalkers, *which uses southwestern Native American mythologies in the context of a crime story. The duo of Tongue and Lash is loosely inspired by that of Peter O'Donnell's Modesty Blaise and Willie Garvin, but the world which they inhabit is much stranger than that of Hillerman's detectives Jim Chee and Joe Leaphorn.*

The two short stories presented here were written as back-up features to accompany the publication of the second series of Tongue*Lash. *They are meant to offer a tantalizing glimpse into our heroes' past.*

A Game of Pitzal

Mayan Calendar: 10 Imix 14 Zotz 12.18.13.2.1

The boy was raised behind the monolithic jade walls of the Eastern College of the great Mayan city of Tulun.

As provided by the Lords' law, his birth parents surrendered him at an early age to the mercies of the Chuch-Kahawib, the scarlet-clad "mother-fathers" whose mission it was to administer the long, painful rites of passage into adulthood.

At that time, the boy was still called by his child's name—Little Jaguar.

Sensing his gifts, the Chuch-Kahawib tutored him in the arcane arts of the Lo. The boy was taken before the corpse of a man who had passed on. He was shown how to arrange the thirteen gourds and warm the six Q'abawilob stones with his hands and cast his spirit across the great void. The boy spoke and the dead man answered.

Yet, what Little Jaguar still enjoyed most was a game of pitzal with his friends: Fat Serpent, who always brought food because he was apprenticing in the kitchen of the Lords; slick, gabby Grey Fox, who could talk his way out of any kind of trouble; Snap Turtle, who was so good with figures that he grew up to become Chief Astrologer in Tikal; big, burly Wise Ox, who even then, didn't know his strength; and poor Running Deer, who would later be killed in the war with the Pia.

Together, the boys would play pitzal until all hours of the morning, their hips sore from hitting the hard, stone ball, their feet blistering inside their unyielding leather boots.

Then, one day, she was there.

Her birth mother had died two years before, so she had already received her adult's name—Tongue—but still she was a child. A child as yet unaware that she existed in a beautiful woman's body.

Sensing greatness within her, the Chuch-Kahawib entrusted her education to Master-Purifier Blue-Quartz, who was assigned the task of grooming her for the Lords' service. That one will go far, the Chuch-Kahawib thought. Whispers of a position as First Handmaiden of the Yatan were heard. It would mean much honor for the Eastern College.

The boys, of course, were all madly in love with her, but in a shy, respectful way. They already knew that spoiling her innocence would have been like throwing mud into the purest stream.

Tongue, oblivious to their feelings, only liked one thing, pitzal, and at that, she was outstanding. She was fast. Sleek and agile. Happy and free. Magnificent. They all agreed she was the best player they had ever seen. Their team's fame grew as they began challenging, and even beating, the teams of the upper city.

But Blue-Quartz hated seeing Tongue play pitzal with the boys. He threw stones at them, and cursed them, spitting and hissing and hurling the names of the dark ones. Tongue's mood began to darken. She clumsily tried to hide the marks of the lashings she'd received. For the first time, she cried. Little Jaguar urged her to go to the Chuch-Kahawibs, but she remained entombed in mournful silence.

Then, one day, Tongue didn't show up for a game. That afternoon, the boy overheard a conversation between two priests. The girl, they said, had to be sent north because she was with child—by her own Purifier too. What had the world come to, they complained.

That night, Master-Purifier Blue-Quartz was found dead, strangled with his own lash. The boys had been at pitzal practice and they all swore Little Jaguar was with them, even though his shoes were not muddy. The Qaholom never found the killer.

The following spring, Little Jaguar took his adult name—Lash.

Published in *Tongue*Lash II* No.1, 1999

163

Second Encounter

Mayan Calendar: 13 Ix 2 Pax 12.19.2.15.14
(Ten years later...)
Spearmaster Smoke's story:

"On the Third Night of the Dark Moon, in the Month of the Jaguar, I was summoned to the lake city of Muyil where depraved men came to cavort faceless with Chi'il prostitutes.

"Muyil was an agglomeration of wooden houses built on pilons over a swampy lake and linked by a maze of flimsy wooden planks. Its seedy ambiance reminded me of my youth on the border towns of the North.

"Young Lord Foal, the second son of the Alom clan, had been found dead, robbed of his money, in the Palace of the Odoriferous Rose. The owner showed me to the body, that of a young man, his face masked by a sheet, lying in a pool of blood on a rack-bed. A dagger still protruded from his chest. All his money was gone.

"I was accompanied by two Qaholom guards and Dag-german Lash, a bright young recruit who was gifted with the Sight of the Gods. While I talked to the owner, Lash examined the body and my men searched the room.

"The Qaholom like their investigations to be short and definitive. This one proved no exception. I quickly determined that we had two suspects: The father of the victim, Lord Horn himself, who had been seen at the Palace the night of the murder, and the Chi'il Pearl, lead flower of the rose triad of lovers, who had been young Foal's favorite distraction until his death.

"I gathered suspects, prostitutes and clients in the Palace's Main Hall to listen to their stories."

Lord Horn's Story:

"My second son was a weak man, of weak blood and impure humors. In truth, I cannot say that I am sorry he is dead. Yes, I knew of his perverted escapades, but I wisely chose to treat them with contempt, until I was informed that he had become besotted with one of the Chi'ils.

"I came here tonight to see if I could buy the woman off, because there is one thing my son was above all, and that was—an Alom. I know he would never have permitted one of these creatures to enter our clan and soil our blood.

"I believe that, when she realized she would never get what she was after, the Chi'il killed my son out of spite, and then robbed him.

"Yes, that is what I believe."

Pearl's Story:

"I may only be a lowly Chi'il and not worthy of Lord Horn's respect, but I know what I know.

"Foal loved me and wanted to bond with me for all to see. But, he was afraid of his father. Many time, he'd told me about Lord Horn's wrath, and how he had once killed one of his yatan in a black rage...

"For the past few days, I felt Foal was finally ready to challenge his father's will. He was going to propose...

"I believe that, when Lord Horn realized he could not change his son's mind, he killed him in a blind rage, then robbed him to divert suspicion.

"Yes, that is what I believe."

Lash's Story:

"I recognized her at once, of course...

"I told Spearmaster Smoke that the Lo had revealed that Lord Foal had been stabbed by one of the scavenging Tecpatl who were plaguing Muyil. Lord Horn and Pearl each grudgingly accepted my verdict...

"Smoke suspected I'd lied, but since it wrapped the case up conveniently, he kept his own counsel.

"The truth was, it wasn't with Pearl whom Foal wanted to bond, but with her. Tongue. The other female member of the rose triad. And when she rejected him, he killed himself with his own dagger. She took the money to make it look like a robbery and protect his memory. If Foal's death had been accounted as a suicide, his soul would have been banished to the Outer Darkness and his name removed from the Sacred Rolls of the Alom.

"Why did I lie to my masters? Why did I betray my duty and my trust? Because by law, the Alom could have claimed her life in vengeance, and that, I could not let happen.

"Tongue. She was trouble, and I swore to never see her again."

"And I knew I was lying again then. To myself."

Published in *Tongue*Lash II* No.1, 1999

MARTIAN CHRONICLES

If one was to follow chronological order, we should insert here a dozen fantasy stories written during the 1990s, which appeared as back-up features in various comics, including The Elsewhere Prince *and* Legends of Arzach. *These stories were eventually gathered and assembled into a single tapestry, picturing the Ancient Mars of millions of years ago which became the stage of our novel,* Edgar Allan Poe on Mars. [5]

This is the Mars of Arnould Galopin's Doctor Omega *(1906) as well as that of Leigh Brackett's* Sea-Kings of Mars *(1949) and Edwin Arnold's* Gullivar Jones *(1905), a character who, in fact, appears in our novel.*

One of the stories did not make it into Edgar Allan Poe on Mars *and is reprinted here.*

---

[5] This is a list of the stories in their order of publication. The title between parentheses is that of the corresponding chapter of *Edgar Allan Poe on Mars*: 1. *The Curse of Alzioth* (*Montressor*) (1990); 2. *The Flames of Meldoch* (1990); 3. *The Charcoal Burner of Ravenwood* (1992); 4. *The White Pteron* (1992); 5. *The Keep of Two Moons* (1992); 6. *The Rock of Everlasting Despair* (1992); 7. *The Keeper of the Earth's Treasures* (1992); 8. *The Fountains of Summer* (1992) (3 to 8 collected together as *Seramize*); 9. *The Wail of the Wolf* (*Rodrik-Usher*) (1998); 10. *The Queen of Selar* (*Ligeia*) (1999); 11. *The Taking of Dugmé* (*Andrevar*) (1999); 12. *The Long Night of Qisque* (*Maurdhaine*) (1999).

The Flames of Meldoch

Many cycles ago, there lived in the city of Garsankar,
at the easternmost point of the Kingdom of the East,
a king named Meldoch, who was immortal.
The Elders of Garsankar

The secret of Meldoch's immortality was a firestone that had fallen from the heavens on a night when the skies had quaked with the fury of the gods above. Meldoch had found the stone and buried it deep inside his palace. Each day he bathed in its life-giving emanations, and had since stopped aging.

But as time's grasp lost its hold on Meldoch, he who had been a loving king grew heartless and cold. The lives of his subjects appeared to him as naught but small, ephemeral concerns, unworthy of the attention of one who was truly immortal. The people of Garsankar became miserable, and learned to curse the night the firestone had fallen.

Eventually, rumors of Meldoch's unnaturally long life reached the mighty King of the East in his jade citadel of Padmasan. He grew jealous, as all kings are prone to do, and said to himself: "Why has this wondrous Gift from the Gods been given to someone as unworthy as Meldoch. I should be the one to be immortal."

Thus, the King raised a mighty army and lay siege to Garsankar. At first, he promised Meldoch his and the town's safety if he surrendered the firestone, but Meldoch refused. Then, the King threatened him with dire torture and swore to raze the City and seed it with salt, unless Meldoch acceded to his wishes. But Meldoch refused.

Many times did the King plead, but always in vain. The Garsankar Elders themselves came, kneeled before Meldoch and begged for their city. But, Meldoch remained as obstinate as ever, deaf to all but himself. In the end, so great was the

King of the East's lust for the firestone that he gave the order to attack.

The people of Garsankar, who no longer had any reason to feel love for their king, whom they felt had betrayed them, overpowered Meldoch's guards, opened the gates wide, and welcomed the King of the East's soldiers.

Meanwhile, Meldoch remained, alone, entrenched in his castle. From its tallest spire, he saw his city fall, and swore that if he could not have the firestone, no one else would. He went into the secret cave where he had hidden the stone and called on secret rituals purchased from an Enchanter of Seth.

He caused the great stone to open, and release the flaming spirit which lived inside. Huge flames erupted, destroying the city and the army of the King of the East, finally turning the site into a scorched hell where no one could enter and live.

As to Meldoch, his body became as stone, fused into an accursed immortality, condemned to remain alive and conscious forever, in the midst of the devastation created by the flames of his own making.

Published in *The Elsewhere Prince* No.4, 1990

THE SHADOWMEN

Since 2005, Black Coat Press has been publishing an annual series of anthologies, entitled Tales of the Shadowmen, *devoted to pastiches of heroes and villains of popular literature. Characters such as Arsène Lupin, Sherlock Holmes, Fantômas, Tarzan, Judex, the Black Coats, Doc Savage, etc. have graced its pages. Contributors have included writers such as Paul DiFilippo, Michael Moorcock, Kim Newman, Robert Sheckley and John Shirley, all happily bringing together the best of pulp literature from all around the world.* [6]

All of us share one thing in common: our love for the classic pulp heroes and villains, the great mythology of the 19th, 20th and now, 21st century. Tales of the Shadowmen *is not simply a collection of stories; it is the description of a meta-reality that exists in our collective minds: Sherlock Holmes and Arsène Lupin, like Robin Hood and d'Artagnan and, before them, Hercules and Jason, belong to all of us. They are the stuff myths are made of. They are the myths.*

These are the stories featuring the Shadowmen, opening with an autobiographical piece that was originally written as an introduction to Volume 3.

---

[6] *Tales of the Shadowmen*: Tome 1: *The Modern Babylon* (2005); Tome 2: *Gentlemen of the Night* (2006); Tome 3: *Danse Macabre* (2007); Tome 4: *Lords of Terror* (2008); Tome 5: *The Vampires of Paris* (2009); Tome 6: *Grand Guignol* (2010).

My Life As a Shadowman

I became a Shadowman in 1963, when I was 9 years old.

The curriculum at the Catholic School of Grand-Lebrun in Bordeaux was strong on history (my favorite subject), geography, math, natural sciences, etc. but sorely lacked classes on such vital topics as sabotage, kidnapping and international trafficking. Or so I thought.

A few months earlier, a neighbor had thrown three bound collections of *Spirou* magazine into the trash. *Spirou* was one of the weekly comic books named after a popular character that I used to buy every week. Each issue contained about 20 stories, ranging from humor to serious adventure, serialized at the rate of two pages per week. Since no two stories ever began or ended the same week, there was ample motivation to buy the next issue when it came out, on Thursday. Later, the publisher would bind the issues returned by the newsagents and sell them as handsome collections.

The three collections the two neighborhood friends and I had been lucky to rescue from the trashman were old ones, dating back to 1955 and 1956. We each took home a book and devoured it

It is in that bound volume of old *Spirous* that I discovered the character of Monsieur Choc. Tall, lanky, dressed in a dinner jacket, he hid his features behind a medieval helmet. Monsieur Choc was the archenemy of two rotund detectives, Tif and Tondu, and the head of an international crime cartel called the White Hand. The page reproduced here, taken from the very same story I read in 1963, shows the nefarious villain preparing to commit an act of sabotage. The cartoony nature of the art barely made up for the rather serious and suspense-filled plot.

Heavy stuff, especially when you're nine.

So, right then and there, despite my generally-accepted lack of tallness, lankiness, dinner jacket and medieval helmet, I decided to start a chapter of the White Hand at Grand-Lebrun, promoting myself to the title of Choc. I quickly enlisted two of my school friends, F*** and M***, and soon, we were on our way to becoming a world-spanning criminal organization.

As far as I can recall today, our activities were mostly limited to exchanging secret notes in class to notify each other of secret meetings, during which we would devise more ingenious ways of exchanging secret notes. It might seem rather pointless and silly, but now that I'm a grown-up, I know that many Government organizations still work on the same principles, so it can't have been all that bad.

Alas, a few days later, an eternity in school time (which appears inordinately expanded to children), one of my notes was intercepted by the stalwart Mrs. B***, our lovely schoolmistress, and I was sent for a "talk" with the priest in charge of the "young children's" division, the tough-but-fair Father C***.

He tried to make me give up the identity of the mysterious "Hoc" who had signed the note, thereby crushing my hopes of a future career as a logo designer. I had thought it clever to turn the C of "Choc" into an open ellipse and write the "hoc" inside it. The good Father, probably because of his familiarity with Latin, had only read the *hoc* part.

The priests had ways of making us talk. Despite the threat of the dreaded detention, which meant coming into school on our day off, Thursday, to spend hours writing Latin conjugations, I remained obdurately silent and did not betray the secrets of the White Hand. That was probably as much due to the embarrassment of having to explain the name was *Choc*, not *Hoc*. But still.

The organization was in dire straits, with the personal blow to its leader, me, now under threat of having to write a hundred *amo, amas, amats* if I didn't start singing like the proverbial canary. The day was grim indeed. A Churchillian effort was called for.

The popular game in our age bracket that year was marbles. An entire secondary market had developed, with kids trading cloudy glass marbles, clear glass marbles, glass marbles with spaghetti-like motifs inside, larger glass marbles (*berlons*) and other exotic marble varieties. One school bully, the dreaded D***, assisted by two future little thugs-in-training, had taken to stealing marbles from smaller and weaker kids, which basically included everyone besides themselves. Fear of swift physical retribution had been enough to keep the matter hushed up. If you want to learn about *O Merta*, talk to a 9-year-old.

The next day, I returned to see Father C*** as I had been "invited" to do, presumably having had time to reflect upon my sins and now being prepared to make a full and uncoerced confession.

"It's D***, Father," I blurted out. "He steals our marbles."

"He steals your marbles?"

"Yes, Father. And then, he loses them by playing with the older kids." I had no particular evidence of this, but it sounded good. "That's why I sent the note to F***. To warn him," I added by way of explanation.

This blew the lid open on the Great Marbles Scandal of '63. Father C***'s robust investigation quickly exposed the dastardly D*** and his cohorts' villainy and they were properly punished, forced to apologize publicly and their loot confiscated. I was given to understand that D's father, in the military, had not been too pleased either.

I never had to write hundreds of Latin verbs on Thursday, but upon reflection, I did come to the conclusion than life as a mystery man was far too complicated. I had managed to extricate myself successfully this time, and expose a villain in the process, but could one count on such luck again?

So there ended my life as a Shadowman, while I turned my sights to the more realistic goal of becoming a soccer champion.

Published in *Tales of the Shadowmen* Vol. 3, 2007

The following short-shorts were written to accompany a series of Shadowmen portraits by Argentinian artist Fernando Calvi, starting with Pierre Souvestre & Marcel Allain's Fantômas. We are currently working on a translation of his last adventure, The Death of Fantômas, *never before translated.*

The Tarot of Fantômas

"Death. I see Death," said the gypsy fortune-teller laying out the seven major arcana of the Tarot on the table.

"Indeed," said Fantômas, quickly plunging his dagger into the woman's right eye socket.

The body was quickly undressed and stuffed inside the empty box that served as the support for a scratched crystal ball that had seen better days.

Then, dressed in the gypsy's robes, properly made up, a veil partially obscuring his face, Fantômas waited.

Juve and his men had pursued him to the Foire du Trône. By now, they undoubtedly had drawn a cast iron Police cordon around the Fair. Escape was chancy at best.

Fantômas looked at the cards the gypsy had laid on the table before her untimely demise: Death. *Well, we've seen to that*, he thought.

The Fool. Fandor, who had been sent on a wild goose chase down into the Catacombs. Fantômas smiled at the thought of the deadly trap he had set down there. Perhaps, this time, the pesky journalist would not be lucky.

Justice. Juve. Dull, plodding, but relentless. No surprise there.

The Devil in the middle. That would be him. *So far, so good*, he thought. *But how does the Devil get out of jail? Is there a card for that?*

The Wheel of Fortune, the Hanged Man and the House of God, struck by lightning. Fantômas smiled. He swept away the cards. He had the answer he sought!

175

The fire, which nearly destroyed the Foire du Trône, was attributed to arson. Eight people died, crushed in the panic; a dozen more had to be hospitalized. The fire had started near the Grande Roue. Luckily, it was put out before it could collapse, which would have killed even more people.

Police Commissioner Juve was found hanging by his feet in the snakes' pit inside the Pavilion des Reptiles. Only his knowledge of the ancient Hindu songs of the snake-charmers of Manganiyar had saved his life.

Fantômas remained an unbeliever in the power of the Tarot, but never criticized Lady Beltham anymore for spending her Wednesday afternoons with her astrologer.

Published in *Tales of the Shadowmen* Vol. 2, 2006

Judex, the dark-cloaked avenger created by writer Arthur Bernède and filmmaker Louis Feuillade in 1917, played by René Cresté, is one of the first urban avengers with a secret identity. (Judex is also Vallières, the meek secretary of his nemesis, the banker Favraux.)

Lost and Found

Jacques de Trémeuse had sworn to destroy the banker Favraux, responsible for his family's ruin. Whatever he could not achieve by day under the guise of Favraux's discreet secretary, Vallières, he undertook by night as the black-clad Judex, an identity he had come to relish.

It was Vallières, however, not Judex, who sat across from the corpulent, sweating, 30-year old German in the *Brasserie d'Alsace.*

"I will come straight to the point," wheezed the interloper. "Information has come into my possession, Monsieur Vallières, that your employer, Monsieur Favraux, has purchased an important consignment of rare *objets d'art* from Turkey. Worth a veritable fortune, but only if properly appraised and sold to the right parties, of course."

"You are well informed, Herr...?"

"Gutman. Kaspar Gutman. That consignment happens to contain a treasured heirloom, which had been in our family for generations until the great earthquake of Izmir in 1883... I would like you to arrange for that special item to be sold to me privately. Of course, there would be a gratuity for you, Monsieur Vallières. A considerable gratuity, I might add."

"I am not in the habit of doing those kinds of transactions, Herr Gutman. I am sorry but you will have to talk to Monsieur Favraux yourself."

Gutman had told Jacques de Trémeuse what he wanted to know, which is why he had agreed to the meeting. Properly auctioned off, that mysterious consignment, the contents of which Favraux had kept secret, could provide an unexpected boost to the banker's fortunes, just as they were beginning to flag. That could not be allowed to happen. A plan was forming. As Vallières, he had access to all the shipping information, and it would be child's play, as Judex, to let these details fall into the hands of the Vampires, for example...

The news that the consignment had been stolen in Marseilles was a shock to Favraux, although not as much as Judex expected. The wily banker had gotten wind of the underworld's interest and purchased some last minute insurance.

"It's out of my hands now, Herr Gutman," Favraux told the German. "What was that item again?"

"A black statue in the form of a bird... A falcon..."

"Well, I'm sorry, Herr Gutman, but it's probably lost again. Forever, this time, I think."

Published in *Tales of the Shadowmen* Vol. 2, 2006

Even in France, no one today would remember Jean de La Hire's Nyctalope if it wasn't for Black Coat Press's re-editions of some of his major novels. La Hire (and his hero) collaborated with the Nazis and this story tried to restore some honor to the character.

Marguerite

Vichy had ordered a sweep of the region of Combefontaine, North of Lyon, for members of the Resistance. The Nyctalope was asked to go along; he was not happy because he despised the Milice, but when Jacques de Bernonville had told him that Mezarek might have returned, he felt he had no choice. He feared that the carnage Belzebuth might wreak far exceeded that of Klaus Barbie.

They had been searching the village for an hour when the Nyctalope entered the Loubets' house. The old farmer and his wife looked at him with the hostility he had come to recognize; in a corner, he noticed a small girl playing with a doll.

"What's your name?" he asked the child.

"Laurence," she replied.

"And what's her name?" he said, pointing at the doll.

"Marguerite."

"Can I hold her?"

The child reluctantly gave him the doll. He looked under its skirt. It was made in England.

"Where did you get it?" he said, giving the doll back.

"Yesterday was my twelfth birthday. The Tooth Fairy came in the middle of the night and brought me the doll. He said her name was Marguerite. He kissed me and told me to go back to sleep and not tell anyone."

The Nyctalope stood up. The Milice was about to enter the Loubet house. He looked at the child. He looked at Marguerite.

"Please, Monsieur, take Marguerite for your daughter," said Laurence, shyly handing him the doll. "Maybe she doesn't have a Marguerite."

The Nyctalope took the doll.

"I already searched this house," he told the Milice. "There's no one here except a couple of farmers and their granddaughter. False alarm." Then, he whispered to Laurence: "I'll take Marguerite but only because someone else might wonder what a British doll is doing here. Tell the Tooth Fairy that tonight, the border will be unguarded near Chaumont."

After the War, the Loubets—father and daughter reunited—received a package in the mail that contained Marguerite. They searched in vain for the Nyctalope to thank him, but he had vanished.

Published in *Tales of the Shadowmen* Vol. 2, 2006

Gaston Leroux's Phantom of the Opera, *which we retranslated for Black Coat Press, is one of our all-time favorite novels and we were proud to write its entry in Stephen Jones & Kim Newman's* Horror: Another 100 best books.

Figaro's Children

Figaro was the only one in the Opéra not afraid of Erik.

Figaro was a cat.

Pardon, Figaro was a *chatte*, a lady cat (in every sense of the word), but it had always been a tradition to name the Opéra's cat Figaro, and gender had not been deemed important enough to upset that tradition.

Every rat the Rat-Catcher did not get was Figaro's to enjoy. She was welcome everywhere, above and below the Opéra.

And, as we said, she was the only resident of that prodigious building who was not afraid of Erik. She purred when he caressed her, came occasionally to visit him, begging for treats (she loved dates) and generally behaved like a proper little lady around him.

There was one man, however, who did not like Figaro: Antoine Manoukian, a *machiniste* who, unbeknownst to Management, raised rabbits in a hutch on the third level. Manoukian thought that Figaro ate his baby rabbits, and truth be told, not all baby rabbit disappearances could be blamed on rats.

When her time came, Figaro had kittens. In those days, the Rue Scribe was a notorious haven for cat dalliances.

Manoukian was prepared to put up with one Figaro, if only because he knew that to do otherwise would mean being ostracized by the rest of the staff, but he could not tolerate a chowder of Figaros.

So, stealthily, he managed to grab all the helpless little kittens and stuff them into a bag, weighing it down with a stone, intending to drown them into the Lake.

Mewling bag in hand, he approached the dark water's edge.

Antoine Manoukian's body was found floating in the Seine the next day. Cause of death: drowning, presumably accidental.

Figaro's children still roam free today below the Opéra.

Ask anyone.

Published in *Tales of the Shadowmen* Vol. 2, 2006

While this story does not feature Erik, it appeared in our new translation of Phantom of the Opera. It is meant to draw a link between two very tragic figures in popular literature,

His Father's Eyes

Rosemary spent a horrible night curled up on her miserable cot. She almost thought she could hear the vermin writhe inside the filthy mattress that she had found in the least damp corner of the shack. She could barely sleep and the night went on, endless, suffocating. With an implacable regularity, tiny drops of water dripped between the timbers of the roof and fell on the wet muddy floor of her prison, marking time like a grandfather clock. Outside, the Scottish wind howled. A storm was approaching from the North Sea and the wailing of the wind managed to whistle its way through the maladjusted wooden planks of the walls, bringing the girl what seemed in her nightmares to be the echoes of ancient curses.

She turned and turned on her cot in fits of impatient anguish. Even though she was wracked by exhaustion and fear, she could not find a merciful refuge in sleep. After a couple of hours of slow combustion, the torch *he* had left in its holder by the door fizzled out, and she was plunged into total darkness. She thought she would go mad from the faint rustling sounds—field mice or a rat, or perhaps, more horrible yet, the labor of the spiders who infested the beams above her.

Rosemary could not guess how much time elapsed before she again heard the sound of *his* footsteps. It was not yet dawn, for no light struck through the thin wooden walls. Her senses, finely attuned to everything that happened inside or outside the shack, felt *his* presence before she heard the steps.

He had returned.

Rosemary's breath sped up. Her heart thumped in her chest. She heard *him* remove the beam that kept the door secured. She steeled herself to once more face *his* terrifying presence and his evil yellow eyes.

The beam fell to the ground. The door, which only hung by one hinge, was pushed open.

He appeared on the threshold, holding a new torch, with which he replaced the one that had burned out. His face was inscrutable, but a tiny detail managed to extract a small whimper of fear from Rosemary in spite of her resolution to be brave. There was a small trickle of blood at the corner of *his* mouth.

He remained completely still, a ghastly living waxwork, looking at *his* captive, perhaps pondering her fate.

Long minutes passed.

Suddenly, without showing any emotion, *he* turned around and vanished into the darkness—without closing the door.

Dawn came and with it a day of new terrors. Rosemary did not dare cross the open threshold for fear of being confronted by her awful jailer. She occasionally heard *his* footsteps outside and knew that *he* was close by.

Was *he* playing with her? Like *he* had "played" with Maggie before... She shook her head, not wanting to remember the awful moments when *he* had come out of nowhere during her peaceful afternoon walk on the Scottish Highlands and seized her after brutally killing her brave Shetland collie who had tried to protect her mistress from the assault of her attacker.

The blood on the corner of *his* mouth was a sign of some other atrocity that he had no doubt perpetrated during the night.

She thought she too would end up like Maggie, her throat slit by his razor-sharp teeth, her bloody carcass dismantled and thrown away.

But despite the fear that gripped her entrails, the cold sweat and the shaking she could not stop, she was still alive. So there was still some hope left, wasn't there?

Her head hurt. Why had *he* spared her? Why not kill her and put an end to the hellish torments that she had endured? She welcomed the death that *he* seemed to refuse her...

Hours went by. Rosemary lay on her cot, exhausted. She finally mustered all her remaining strength to take some cautious steps towards the open threshold. Could she walk out of this shack that otherwise might become her coffin?

Why had *he* left the door open? Was *he* so sure that she would not try to escape?

During the last hour, Rosemary had not heard any footsteps or other sounds to indicate that *he* was nearby. The torch on the wall was starting to flicker.

She strained to hear as far as she could. There was no sound.

Perhaps *he* had gone at last.

She had not had any food since the day before and she felt light-headed. The cold and the damp gnawed at her body more efficiently than the rats would have done. She knew that soon she would have no strength left.

If she were to act, it had to be now.

She thought of running away, very fast, running through the moors towards her father's house and the safety of the village...

But could there be any safety with one such as *he*? What if *he* followed her? Didn't she risk bringing *his* awesome wrath down the heads of those she loved? How could her aging father ever prevail against one such as *he*? What about the innocent folk of the village...

With a deep sigh, she stepped back, away from the beguiling opening and again lay down on her cot, her eyes closed.

She fell into a near-comatose state of almost complete apathy. She could not move. She could only see and hear—and wait for *him*.

And then she heard *his* footsteps again.

He stepped inside the shack and approached the cot. Rosemary closed her eyes even tighter and held her breath. She had no intention of screaming or struggling. She prayed for a quick, merciful death.

Through her eyes were closed, she felt *his* almost supernatural presence close to her, the burning of *his* evil yellow eyes upon every inch of her body.

He was there... so close. Seething with rage and yet totally still. What was *he* waiting for to finish his foul job? she thought.

In her mind, she silently begged for *him* to kill her as she could no longer stand this torture. Her eyes tightly shut, she imagined that she felt *his* breath near her throat... Something rustled gently past her breast... Was it *his* hand?

Suddenly, with blinding clarity, a revelation appeared in her fevered mind. Why had she not thought of it before?

He didn't want to kill her. *He* wanted her to stay with *him*.

He wanted her to be *his* mate.

When *he* had first seized her, *he* had mentioned in his ramblings the island of Cround, one of the Orkneys off the mainland. *He* had been raging, almost like a madman. Something had happened to *him* there that had upset *him* greatly. *He* muttered dark, murderous promises of revenge on someone close to *him*. Rosemary shuddered, and thought that, even though she had reached the bottom of despair, she still would not trade places with that other man, for if *he* could do to her, a complete stranger, what he had done, what even more horrible fate had he in store for the other?

She feared *his* foul touch, she was sure that would be next. Her eyes were still closed, her eyelids ached from being held so tightly shut. She strained to hear *his* every move over the wild beatings of her heart. She heard the creaking of the floorboards. She guessed that *he* had just kneeled down next to the cot.

Then she again felt *his* breath upon her face. It smelt like withered flowers, old, decaying, but not unpleasant. *His* lipless mouth, a mere slit in his taunt, corpse-like face, moved inexorably towards hers. She was trapped.

Rosemary's fingers contracted, gripped the cot nervously, then balled up into fists. She could no longer bear the horror. It was pointless to feign unconsciousness.

Abruptly, she pulled her legs up and sprang forth. She found herself upright, standing up breathlessly, hey eyes wide open, next to *his* terrifying figure. As she had guessed, *he* had been kneeling by the cot. With a speed defying imagination, however, *his* hand had grabbed a corner of her dress when she got up and *he* now held a piece of torn fabric in *his* hand. Her left shoulder was bare.

He sprang to his feet and, with a couple of steps, moved between her and the door.

She stood facing *his* ghastly, dead face where only the evil yellow eyes shone forth, and the dirty strands of long, black, matted hair quivered under the outside wind.

Any animal would have lunged forward. But *he* merely opened his arms to block her way and waited.

Then, he began to slowly step forward, all too slowly, fixing her with his evil yellow eyes.

A low growl came out of nowhere. It may have been an unconscious manifestation of triumph. For she was entirely at *his* mercy. Far from the eyes of God and Men, *he* would at last satisfy his vile desires.

She stood paralyzed, less than two yards away from *him*, reflecting that if she could have, at this very moment, found a way to kill herself, she would have done so, even at the cost of eternal damnation.

He took another step and seized her with *his* hands. *His* fingers dug painfully into her delicate shoulders. Rosemary tried to scream but found she could not. She still had the strength to cry, however, and tears silently ran down her face.

His image grew fuzzy. Only the burning amber flames of *his* evil yellow eyes shone before her. She perceived, more than heard, another, louder growl. Then, she felt her dress torn from her body. Purely by instinct, she brought her arms up to cover her chest. She heard a rhythmic sound and realized it was her teeth chattering.

She suddenly felt herself pulled forward by *his* unshakeable grip, crushed against *his* powerful chest and, finally, all her senses obliterated by horror, she slipped into merciful oblivion.

When Rosemary woke up, she was in her bed, at home. Her father was by her side and, after the doctor had gone, he told her that she had been found naked, bloodied and mud-covered in an abandoned shack at the western end of the moors. Of *him*, there was no trace.

She recovered in time, somewhat, taking comfort in the notion that her sacrifice had saved her family, and perhaps the entire village as well, from *his* anger.

But the horror began again, first a fleeting dark thought, quickly banished, then a horrible premonition, too dreadful to face, and finally an inescapable truth...

She discovered that she was pregnant.

Her faith was too strong for her to take her own life, and she would never have sacrificed the innocent she now bore. However, due to her father's position in the village, she could no longer remain when her situation would become known to all.

Her father sent her to live with his brother, who was a mason in the city of Rouen in Normandy. Being childless, Rosemary's uncle and his wife had agreed to raise the child as their own.

So it came to pass that, one grey winter morning, Rosemary left Scotland and embarked for France.

Six months later, she prepared to give birth to the child.

The midwife—a robust Norman woman of considerable experience and utmost discretion—had loudly expressed her concerns over the mother's health, which had been declining throughout the pregnancy. Rosemary had been plagued by nightmares, reliving the dreaded hours she had spent in the shack, where the child had been conceived. She had told no one about the true horrors of that night, making up a story about an ordinary vagrant instead. She had tried to hide the truth, even to herself, but now it plagued her nights in the form of nightmares, each more terrifying than the last.

Finally, after long hours of painful labor, the midwife pulled the mewling infant from his mother's womb—reporting him to be a healthy baby boy—and cut the umbilical cord. Rosemary, still panting, exhausted, drenched in sweat, asked to take the baby to put him to her breast. The midwife, concerned about the mother's excessive bleeding, did as requested and handed her the child.

When Rosemary grabbed the newborn, she looked at his face, his taut, pallid skin, and she shuddered. She began to shake violently. Then the baby, for the first time, opened his eyes and looked at his mother.

Rosemary lifted up her head. Two tears ran slowly down her livid cheeks. Then she screamed the scream of the damned and her very life essence seemed to drain from her body as she exclaimed:

"He's got *his* father's eyes! *His* evil yellow eyes!"

Rosemary was buried at the Cemetery of Saint-Sever near Rouen. They named the baby Erik, after his grandfather. On his mother's side, naturally.

"Shall each man find a wife for his bosom, and each beast have his mate, and I be alone? I had feelings of affection, and they were requited by detestation and scorn."
The Monster. Mary Shelley, *Frankenstein*, Chapter XX.

Published in *The Phantom of the Opera*, 2005

Doc Ardan is a French proto-Doc Savage created by the mysterious "Guy d'Armen" for the magazine Sciences & Voyages *in the 1920s. The title character needs no introduction...*

The Star Prince

"If you please, draw me a dinosaur!"

Francis Ardan looked at the golden-haired boy. He was dressed in an operetta-style costume, wearing a long blue coat, white shirt, pants and shiny boots. The aviator had been forced to make an emergency landing in this deserted part of the Western Sahara and was busy repairing the engine when, suddenly, the boy had appeared out of nowhere.

"What are you doing here?" asked Ardan.

"If you please, draw me a dinosaur," asked the boy.

It seemed churlish to refuse. Ardan took out his logbook and pencil and began drawing.

"Who are you?" he asked.

"I come from above," said the boy, pointing at the starry sky. "I am so bored up there."

"How did you come here?"

"It is difficult. And very painful. When I leave, I die a little. So I only come when someone is around. I can only come here because that's where they are. The machines."

"The machines?"

"They're buried deep in the sand. There used to be a sea here, and dinosaurs and other children with whom I could play. But everything is gone now. And I am all alone."

Ardan had finished the drawing. He gave it to the boy.

"It is very beautiful," he said. "Just as I remember them. Thank you. I will treasure it forever. It was worth it."

"Can't you come more often? Reach other people?" asked Ardan. "There is so much we could learn from you."

"I don't have enough power. I'm sorry. I'm only a very little star," said the boy, as his made-up body slowly began to crumble into dust, mingling with the sand that covered the ancient machines.

Published in *Tales of the Shadowmen* Vol. 2, 2006

Randy's first contribution to Tales of the Shadowmen *involved bringing together Doc Ardan and a character from a fairy tale. This has since become a continuing series.*

The Reluctant Princess

Doctor Francis Ardan (as he was known in France) was hacking his way through a massive forest of thorns on the side of a mountain in the Pyrenees. He felt as if he had no sooner chopped a pathway than a new batch was growing almost before his eyes. He would never get to the other side of the forest at the rate he was going. He was starting to feel discouraged.

He sat down to take a breather and to think about what had brought him on his strange quest. He had returned from his travels in the Far East, planning to take a well-deserved rest while doing some research on the Cathars of Montségur. But that research had awakened a curiosity he could not quench.

While reading about legends of lost treasures in France, he had come across a strange story. It was said that a young Noblewoman had been enchanted more than 400 years earlier in a village named Perceforest, somewhere in the mountains along the border between Spain and France. The legend had it that she would sleep forever, unless awakened by a stranger willing to brave the many enchantments which held her prisoner.

At first, Ardan had dismissed it all as mere fantasy; after all, it had to be a fairy tale. But something about the legend continued to eat away at him and he began to do further research. In the end, it seemed that there was clearly some truth to the whole thing. He was unable to let it rest and decided he had no choice but to set off to find the answer.

The difficulty of his quest had at least helped him to decide that it was true; but he was still unable to reach what he presumed was his goal: the other side of the enchanted forest.

192

The explorer was no quitter; he knew there had to be an answer. If this was a "magic" forest, perhaps he needed to fight his way through it by unconventional means. Rather than using brute force, he decided to use some of the eastern methods he had learned on his journey through Tibet. He centered his thoughts and tried to feel himself becoming one with the forces of nature; in his mind's eye, he pictured a path opening up through the tangle of plants, leading him to his goal. As he gently breathed in and out, he felt a change in the air around him. Cautiously, he opened his eyes and saw that a path had mysteriously appeared directly in front of him.

Still breathing in a set pattern, he began to walk through the forest of thorns.

The path curved and twisted until Ardan no longer had a sense of the direction he traveled. But his meditative breathing enabled him to remain calm and not focus on his fear of becoming lost. Eventually, after walking for what seemed like hours, but which had in reality only been mere minutes, the young adventurer found himself standing in front of a stone tower in the midst of a clearing. As he circled it, he was unable to see any opening in its rough surface. Without a doubt, this was another challenge.

He again tried Eastern meditation, but this time it had no effect. He thought about the legends he had read and tried to recall if there was anything in them that might give him an answer to how to enter the tower. Then he remembered a passage he had read that had talked about an event said to occur just before the mysterious enchantment had overtaken the young noblewoman. He looked at the tower and repeated a phrase supposedly spoken by her.

Immediately, a wooden door appeared in the wall right before his eyes. He turned the massive iron handle that held it closed, and as if it had been oiled the day before, it gently swung open on its hinges.

To Ardan's surprise, the corridors inside the tower were brightly lit with glowing torches. He had no idea where to find the object of his search, but simply walked forward, certain that he would find her as this was now clearly meant to be.

The corridor spiraled around like the shell of a snail, and eventually the adventurer reached a chamber in what he perceived was its center. There, in a large canopied bed, was a beautiful young woman. She had cascading, golden hair and alabaster skin. Ardan felt mesmerized by her beauty. She lay motionless on the bed, but it was clear that she was not dead, merely in some state of suspended animation.

The young man circled the chamber, looking at the young woman from every angle as he tried to determine what he needed to do to awaken her. Finally, he decided that he would follow the blueprint laid out in every fairy story he had ever read or studied; he approached the beautiful Princess (for he was sure she must be a Princess) and bent over her to kiss her.

As his warm breath touched her face, her dark golden eyelashes fluttered and she opened her astonishingly beautiful sapphire-colored eyes. Ardan was shocked when she reached up a delicate hand and slapped him in the face!

He stepped back as the Princess sat up in her bed. "How dare you!" she exclaimed. "Just what do you think you're doing?"

"I... I..." Ardan felt himself at a loss for words, something unusual for the sophisticated scientist. Finally, he was able to speak, "I'm sorry, your Highness. But you have been under a charm for many centuries. I have fought my way through a series of enchantments to come here to awaken you. I thought I would use a method that has been written about in many stories, and that meant I needed to kiss you for the spell to be broken."

"I don't care about you kissing me, sir," said the beautiful young woman. "I want to know what gives you the right to disturb my peace and quiet!"

"I don't understand. I simply wanted to help you. Weren't you placed under this spell by an evil enchantress?"

"Of course not! I chose to enter this state. It is my sanctuary."

"What reason could you have for such a bizarre thing?"

"You say that centuries have gone by, so perhaps you do not know what life was like for a young woman when I was born, sir. You cannot imagine how hard it was to be a woman with a mind of her own. I wanted to study and walk freely in the forests. I had no desire to be married off to some ugly, old horror of a man because it would gain my family lands and power. Indeed, I am not sure I desired to marry at all.

"If I did not marry, then my only choice was to wall myself off in a convent, and I fear I am not better made for the life of a religious, as I have a rebellious soul and do not take well to being told what to do by anyone, man nor woman.

"Thus, I chose to ask a sorceress of my acquaintance to place me in a state of peace and happiness to forever escape a life I could not bear to contemplate," she looked at Ardan in sadness for what she had lost.

"My Princess," said the explorer, taking her hand, "I think you will find a changed world awaits you! You no longer have to belong to any man if that's your wish."

"Will I be totally free?"

"No. No one is totally free, but I think you will approve of the world outside this place."

"I suppose I can give it a try. But first, tell me how you managed to get inside my tower? I had thought that I was quite clear it was to be a puzzle that no one could solve."

"Ah, that... It was something I read you had said on the day before the enchantment took hold of you."

"And what was that?"

"No day is so bad that it can't be fixed with a nap!"

Paris — Yet again we were astonished by an amazing feat of derring-do, as the latest flying ace on the Parisian scene, the amazing Phantom Angel, flew her bi-plane over the Eiffel Tower and climbed down a rope ladder (while somehow managing to keep the plane circling overhead!) to disarm the no-

torious anarchist Azzef who was threatening to blow up the radio transmitter at the top. Our City is certainly a better place for having a heroine of her caliber watching over us.

Joseph Rouletabille writing in *L'Epoque.*

Published in *Tales of the Shadowmen* Vol. 4, 2008

Randy revisits yet another of Charles Perrault's classic fairy tales, spinning a new yarn featuring a surprising cast of characters...

The English Gentleman's Ball

Once upon a time, she had been called Beauty and had slept for a thousand years. But ever since being awoken, not by a handsome prince, but by a dashing scientist, she was used to being referred to as "The Phantom Angel."

This new, modern world in which she found herself pleased her most of the time. Certainly she realized that the role of women had undergone a drastic change from when she had last been awake in a time of darkness and ignorance.

As the Phantom Angel, she was free to do as she pleased. Go where she desired. Dress as the mood took her. The world was far from a paradise, but it was a vast improvement on what she had known before, even if she had been a princess in those days.

But Angel was not satisfied with her adventures of derring-do; she felt that there should be more to her life on some level, but could not quite put her finger on what that might be. Part of it was the awareness that she was still privileged in comparison to many in this brave new world. Poverty, ignorance and darkness were still out there, but the rich pretended not to see the ugliness in the corner.

Because of her own past, Angel was particularly aware that the lot of women and children still needed great improvement. She knew that she could not save them all, but hoped that she could at least aid a few individuals. Thus she kept her ears open for cases where she could intervene.

Her sources in the *Société Secrète des Aventuriers* had told her that a Gregor Mac Dhul, a wealthy man with a daughter, had lost his wife in childbirth. He had hired a housekeeper to look after the child, and in the course of time, this woman,

Simone Desroches, had become his new wife. What he didn't know was that Simone was in reality the notorious masked criminal known as Belphegor. She had targeted the industrialist to gain access to his fortune.

Because Gregor Mac Dhul traveled frequently, his new wife was often left alone with his daughter, Sylvie. But Simone was not a good mother, nor even a kind woman, and treated the girl as little more than a servant.

To keep Sylvie from telling her father of her treatment, Simone told her young charge that she would kill the Professor if ever he heard a word of the truth.

The Phantom Angel decided that this would be her next "project;" to save Sylvie from her evil stepmother and allow her to step out into the sunlight once again.

Angel tracked down the mansion where Sylvie practically had to clean the cinders from the fireplace in order to earn a meal while her father was away. It was clear that Simone ruled with an iron hand.

The woman once known as Beauty decided to use her contacts to gain an introduction to the household and to see the situation first hand. Because of Simone's desire to flaunt her wealth, it proved an easy task to be invited one afternoon for tea.

Once there, it was clear that the rumors about Sylvie's treatment were accurate. The 17-year-old girl was forced to wait on Simone and Angel, and was barely introduced as "my wretched stepdaughter" before being dismissed back to the kitchens to scrub out pots and pans. Poor Sylvie dared a pleading gaze at Angel, as if begging her for help.

The Phantom Angel was quickly able to turn the conversation to the subject of a lavish ball that was soon to be held by a visiting English aristocrat who had taken up temporary residence in a *hôtel particulier* in the fashionable *Marais* district of Paris. Word had it that his family was eager for him to wed, and had sent him to France to find a suitable candidate; thus all of Paris—the part that counted, at least—had been invited.

Simone was clearly interested in this new "opportunity" to enhance her own wealth. It was obvious to Angel that the evil stepmother was suddenly aware that she had a powerful trump card in Sylvie; for although she treated the girl as a scullery maid, underneath the hand-me-down clothes and ashes was a stunning beauty.

Clearly wanting to get rid of her visitor so that she could further her plot, Simone suddenly claimed a headache and called Sylvie to show her visitor out. Taking advantage of the short time they were able to spend alone, the Phantom Angel whispered: "Don't worry, I'm here to help. Think of me as your fairy Godmother!"

Our heroine was satisfied with the turning of events and began her own plot to save her new-found friend from the clutches of the evil woman who controlled her. Indeed, she immediately went to the very same *hôtel* and knocked at the entrance, where a truly British Gentleman's Gentleman opened the door with great courtesy.

"Are you Monsieur Jeeves?" she asked.

"Indeed I am, Madam," he replied.

"Then it is you I am here to see."

The door closed behind her.

The night of the grand ball arrived, and Simone had worked hard on Sylvie to make sure that the "prize" was secured by her and no other. The young girl looked nothing like a scullery maid and could have been a fairy princess in her exquisite gown and jewels. But her eyes were still sad and she had the air of a rabbit in the snare of a hunter in her manner.

The Phantom Angel, of course, was also at the ball. She nodded towards Sylvie and received a nod of acknowledgment from that most distinguished of valets, Jeeves. What she knew from him, and what no one else present realized, was that Bertram Wilberforce Wooster, the aristocrat in question, had no intention of marrying anyone at the ball, no matter what his family desired. However, as always, he was up for a good time, and the Phantom Angel's plot as recounted to him by his "man" Jeeves sounded as if it would be the highlight of his Parisian visit.

As the evening wore on, the wheels began to turn. Belphegor tried her best to put Sylvie into Bertie's path, but each time something was contrived to interfere. The evil stepmother became more and more frustrated as she had visions of the Woosters' fortune slipping ever farther away. Each time her plot failed she reached for another glass of champagne. Soon it was clear that she was more than a little drunk and she was having trouble controlling her temper. She grabbed hold of Sylvie's arm, her scarlet claws leaving marks on the porcelain flesh and hissed, "Get over there and dance with that man or you'll be sorry!"

That was the moment for the plan to reach its climax. Standing directly behind Simone had been her husband, Gregor Mac Dhul, whom she had been told was on business far, far away. The Phantom Angel had flown her plane to fetch him and Jeeves and Wooster had sequestered him in the house, making sure that each time his wife had threatened or abused his daughter during the evening, he had been in a perfect position to observe her.

"That's enough, Simone!" Gregor cried in anger. "It's clear you're not the woman you pretended to be and it's over. You'll not get another penny from me and you will never come near me or my daughter again!"

Belphegor stared at him in drunken astonishment, then turned to see the Phantom Angel, Jeeves and Wooster watching her in triumph.

Sylvie ran into her father's arms and began to cry tears of happiness as she realized that she was at least free of the evil woman who had ruled her life so cruelly.

Angel turned to her allies, "Gentlemen, you've done a fine thing tonight. I'm afraid, Mr. Wooster, that if word of this gets out, you're reputation as a drone may be damaged forever."

"No fear of that, Madam," said Jeeves. "Mr. Wooster knows precisely how to tell a story so that he is able to continue in his life of pointless pleasure."

"What ho, Jeeves," said Bertie.

And they all lived happily ever after.

Published in *Tales of the Shadowmen* Vol. 5, 2009

Arsène Lupin, Maurice Leblanc's famous gentleman-burglar, is another of our favorite characters. After translating his two fateful encounters with Sherlock Holmes, we wrote a few more pastiches, included later in this collection. This one is part of an informal suite of Christmas stories...

Arsène Lupin's Christmas

Arsène Lupin was always early. He had often found it useful in his career. But this time, the girl, perhaps wiser, had not shown up for the hastily arranged rendezvous on the Grands Boulevards.

"Bah," said Lupin. Since he had a couple of hours to spare, he entered the children's theater. It was the week before Christmas and they were presenting a traditional puppet show. In the dark, among his own people, Lupin felt safe. Suddenly, just as Père Noël—Santa Claus—was shown coming down the chimney, he noticed that the child next to him, a little girl of ten, had begun to cry.

"Excuse me, Monsieur," said a woman who turned out to be the child's aunt. "I thought the show would help take her mind off of things, but you, see, the Police arrested her father last night..."

It turned out that the child's father, Monsieur Dubois, had been the *homme à tout faire*, handyman, employed, or rather exploited, by Baron d'H***. The heartless nobleman had fired Dubois, a widowed father, the week before Christmas, refusing to pay him his final month's wages. When Dubois had returned during the night through the chimney to steal something in exchange for what he was owed, the wily Baron, who had anticipated the move, was waiting with the Police.

The next day, a man impersonating Chief Inspector Ganimard signed for Dubois' release at the Prison de la Santé.

That same night, Baron d'H*** was the victim of a daring burglary which robbed him of nearly half-a-million francs.

And in Canada, there would soon be a newly-emigrated French family whose little girl never cried again when she saw Santa Claus slide down a chimney.

Published in *Tales of the Shadowmen* Vol. 2, 2006

The next three stories feature Arsène Lupin and Sherlock Holmes and were written to accompany our new translations of The Blonde Phantom *and* The Hollow Needle, *purely to fill gaps left by Leblanc. For instance, the following story, which takes place in 1904, explains the identity of Lady Strongborough, mentioned at the end of* The Jewish Lamp, *and why she is indebted to Lupin.*

Arsène Lupin Arrives Too Late

Excerpt of a letter from Jeanne Darcieux to Paul Daubreuil, Tuesday, January 12, 1904:

Dear Paul,

As you have surely heard, the Belgian Police arrested my step-father, Paul Darcieux, in Brussels. Last week, I received a communication from a Belgian policeman named Poirot, who confirmed that he would soon be extradited to France. Oh, how I shudder when I remember the horrible events that took place at Maupertuis. I still see my stepfather's evil face as he prepared to plunge his dagger into my body that terrible night. I don't think I shall ever be able to banish that image from my mind... I will never have the right words to thank you for all that you did for me, my dearest friend. (...) I have followed Dr. Gueroult's sage advice and come to London to start my life afresh. Thank you for recommending a good solicitor in Versailles to oversee the management of the Maupertuis estate, but all that is now a part of the life that I left behind...

Excerpt of a letter from Jeanne Darcieux to Paul Daubreuil, Monday, February 1, 1904:

Dear Paul,

Your letter filled me with joy. Since you were kind enough to inquire as to my progress here, I shall report news that, I am sure, will please you greatly. Yesterday, I found a position as a tutor teaching French to Lord Strongborough's 12-year-old son, Anthony. Lord Strongborough is a charming widower who is very much involved with the Jockey Club, of which I understand he is one of the stewards. I am expected to live in his beautiful estate in Surrey. My duties will include...

Excerpt of a letter from Jeanne Darcieux to Paul Daubreuil, Friday, May 6, 1904:
Dear Paul,
Edward and I are just back from the Riviera, where he has a house near Saint Paul de Vence. We had the grandest time. Upon our return, Edward decided to announce our formal engagement. A wonderful party was held at the Manor. I so wish that you could have been there. The entire Jockey Club attended. Dr. Taylor regaled us with stories of when he and Edward used to race horses in America, in Kentucky, I believe. Major Roland told us of his service in India...

Announcement published in The Times *of London, Friday, July 1, 1904:*
The forthcoming marriage is announced between Sir Edward, 31st Lord Strongborough, Baron of Cuthbert, and Mademoiselle Jeanne Darcieux de Maupertuis of Vendôme, France. The ceremony will take place at Strongborough Hall, Surrey, later this month.

Excerpt of a letter from Jeanne Darcieux to Paul Daubreuil, Thursday, September 8, 1904:
Dear Paul,
I cannot believe that I am writing this to you, but the nightmare has returned. Death again surrounds me, creeping over me, casting an invisible shroud over my life. As I wrote to you in my last letter, young Anthony passed away of gastric fever two weeks ago. Edward was, understandably, devastated by the death of his only son, who was the light of both our lives. Major Roland, Dr. Taylor and the other stewards of the Jockey Club have all tried to console him and shake him out of his dark mood, but nothing seems to work. He had the most terri-

ble row with Dr. Taylor, and has simply refused to see Major Roland. He now spends most of his time alone, barricaded in his room, just like my stepfather once did. That is a most horrible reminder of the evil days at Maupertuis...

Excerpt of a letter from Jeanne Darcieux to Paul Daubreuil, Tuesday, September 20, 1904:
Dear Paul,
My life is now worse than it has ever been, if such a thing is possible. There have been foul words spread about Anthony's death. Hushed whispers about poison. I see the way the staff now looks at me. I am the foreign Jezebel who has taken the place of their beloved mistress...

Excerpt of a letter from Jeanne Darcieux to Paul Daubreuil, Monday, October 3, 1904:
Dear Paul,
Last night, Major Roland called to see Edward. They spent some time together in his office. The Major looked quite unhappy when he left. We talked a bit afterwards. He mentioned that Mister Sherlock Holmes himself had agreed to come out of retirement and travel to Paris to tackle the affair of the Blue Diamond and give a sound thrashing to "that wretched braggart, Lupin," as he called you. He does not know what happened between us at Maupertuis, of course. I am so worried about you, my dearest friend. They say that Mister Holmes has no equal. Please, be careful. Here, even Edward, when I do see him, which is not often these days, has started to regard me with suspicion. I do not know to whom to turn. I feel as if an invisible noose is tightening around my neck and I am utterly powerless to stop it...

Excerpt of a letter from Jeanne Darcieux to Paul Daubreuil, Tuesday, November 1, 1904:
Dear Paul,
The news is too horrible for words. Edward died last night. He succumbed to the same gastric fever as Anthony. He had been

complaining of stomach pains, then fell prey to nausea and much vomiting. He was taken to the hospital yesterday. Dr. Taylor rushed to his side but it was too late.

Excerpt of a letter from Jeanne Darcieux to Paul Daubreuil, Thursday, November 17, 1904:
Dear Paul,
There is now talk of an inquest. The Police were here and questioned me and the staff... That man of yours whom you mentioned in your last letter never arrived. I hope nothing befell him. I feel as if I am being watched. In your last letter, you said you were *en route* to Uruguay. I so wish you could be here. I am certain you would untangle the mystery of what happened in no time. I have made a note of the lawyer you recommended, Sir Edward Leithen, should the need arise...

Article published in The Times *of London, Tuesday, December 6, 1904:*
Lady Strongborough was arrested today on suspicion of having poisoned her husband. The Home Secretary ordered that the bodies of Lord Strongborough and that of his son, Anthony, deceased August 25 last, be exhumed and checked for poison...

Excerpt of a letter from Jeanne Darcieux to Paul Daubreuil, Monday, December 12, 1904:
Dear Paul,
Dr. Taylor does not trust the Police; he insisted on supervising the removal of the organs for analysis. I think he is afraid of the scandal. I am being treated as if I had the plague. No one will see me or talk to me. I have written to Sir Edward to retain his counsel, although I pray every day that his assistance will not be required and I will awaken from this nightmare...

Article published in The Times *of London, Thursday, December 15, 1904:*

Traces of a poison called cadmium were found in both bodies. Cadmium is soluble in acid foods and the Police suspect it was administered to the victims in lemonade prepared by Lady Strongborough. Traces of cadmium were also found in medicine being taken by Lord Strongborough...

Article published in The Times *of London, Monday, December 19, 1904:*
Today, at the inquest into the death of Lord Strongborough, Constable Barnaby presented evidence that bottles containing cadmium compounds were found in the photographic laboratory set up for Lady Strongborough by her late husband in what used to be the conservatory...

Article published in The Times *of London, Wednesday, December 21, 1904:*
Today, at the inquest into the death of Lord Strongborough, the jury recorded a verdict of willful murder against person or persons unknown...

Excerpt of a letter from Jeanne Darcieux to Paul Daubreuil, Thursday, January 12, 1905:
Dear Paul,
It has now been two months since your last letter and I am still without news of you. I continue to write to the safe address you gave me in Paris, hoping that my letters are reaching you, wherever you might be. I pray every day for your safe return, for I believe you, and you alone, can put an end to this awful nightmare I am living. I did not poison my husband, Paul, upon my soul, and neither did I poison young Anthony, who was as dear to me as if he had been my own son. The Press has reported that serious irregularities have been discovered in the accounts of the Jockey Club. Apparently, Edward had a secret life about which I knew nothing. They say I killed him because I wanted to get my hands on his fortune before he was irremediably disgraced and ruined, but this is ridiculous, for I am wealthy too in my own right. I have property in France and

I could have helped poor Edward had he but asked. They also say that I was the only one who could have poisoned him because I have access to cadmium, even though I was always careful to lock up my laboratory and none of the chemicals were ever missing...

Article published in The Times *of London, Wednesday, Febuary 1, 1905:*
Lady Strongborough's trial began today at the Old Bailey. As the prosecuting counsel, Mister Erskine-Brown, laid out his case, everyone present was silent and somber. Lady Strongborough appeared vulnerable, seemingly on the verge of tears and, at one stage, she shook her head in grief as she heard some of the agonizing details of her husband's last moments. Sir Edward Leithen, counsel for the defense, made a remarkable opening statement in which he urged the jury to look beyond the circumstantial evidence that he called a "web of deceit." Right from the outset, the jury was left in no doubts as to the magnitude of the case. The judge, Mister Justice Wargrave, warned them that a case of this length, lasting possibly up to three months, was physically strenuous and advised them not to be swayed by the oratorical tricks of the defense and to look at "nothing but the facts"...

Excerpt of a letter from Jeanne Darcieux to Paul Daubreuil, Tuesday, March 14, 1905
Dear Paul,
I am still without news of you. I fear the worst. Sir Edward Leithen is mounting what I believe they call a "vigorous defense," yet the autopsy results speak against me. No one, certainly not I, can explain the presence of the fatal cadmium in the bodies. The Judge seems prejudiced against me. They call him a "hanging judge." I fear the worst...

Article published in The Times *of London, Monday, April 3, 1905:*

Lady Strongborough Found Guilty... Lady Strongborough burst into tears as Mister Justice Wargrave delivered the ritual sentence: "The sentence of the court upon you is that you be taken from this place to a lawful place of execution and that you be hanged by the neck until you are dead. And may God have mercy on your soul."

Excerpt of a letter from Jeanne Darcieux to Paul Daubreuil, Wednesday, April 5, 1905:
Dear Paul,
This is my last letter to you and I can only pray that it will find you in good health, even if comes too late to alter my fate, which now seems sealed. I am innocent, but I have reconciled myself to my destiny. Tomorrow, I shall walk to the gallows praying only that nothing evil has befallen you, my dearest friend...

Report from Lt. Colonel Venables, Governor of the Prison of Pentonville, Thursday, April 6, 1905:
The execution was set for 8 a.m. The night before, Lady Strongborough was visited by her counsel, Sir Edward Leithen. I was told that she had accepted her fate and that, apart from a slight nervous twitch at the corner of her mouth, she was calm. After Sir Edward had left, she was given brandy and water and at 11 p.m. she slept. She was awakened at 5 a.m. to prepare herself for a visit from the Prison Chaplin, Reverend Fergusson. The Reverend stayed with Lady Strongborough until 7 a.m. and tried to get her to confess that she was guilty, but she steadfastly denied that she had poisoned either her husband or his son and categorically maintained her innocence. At 7:30 a.m., Lady Strongborough was given a cup of tea with more brandy and water. At 7:40 a.m., she was joined in the condemned's cell by Under Sheriff Regan and myself. We told her that the time had come to carry out the sentence and she was quietly led to courtyard where the gallows had been erected the day before. Here, we were joined by William Billington, the hangman, who was introduced to Lady

Strongborough, who showed no emotion. Mister Billington tied her hands and she asked that he not draw the rope too tight before the drop. She was extremely calm at this point. She was then taken to the chapel where she received the final sacraments. At 7:55 a.m., the prison's death bell tolled, which marked the start of the procession to the gallows. Reverend Fergusson read extracts from the burial service. We were joined by the Head Turnkey, Mister Daley, and two warders, George Bulman and Derek Willis. As we walked across the yard to the gallows, a man was suddenly ushered in by warder Kavanagh. He shouted that the execution be stopped and indicated that he was holding a reprieve signed by Mister Akers-Douglas, the Home Secretary himself. "It's him!" screamed Lady Strongborough. "I knew he would not abandon me. I knew he would not be too late! It's Arsène Lupin!" "Shut up, you little git," said Mister Daley. "Don't you recognize Mister Sherlock Holmes?"

Excerpt from the Private Notebooks of John H. Watson, M.D., undated, but likely written in late April 1905:
My friend Mister Sherlock Holmes asked me to pen a few notes on the strange case of Lady Strongborough in which he was so fortunate as to be able to save her from the hangman's noose with but minutes to spare.

For reasons that will become clear to my reader, I seriously doubt that I will ever write, even less publish, a full account of this case, but it is sufficiently worthy for me to record some of the bare facts in this Journal.

As I have recorded in my account entitled "The Reigate Puzzle," Holmes had already crossed the path of, and thwarted Paul Darcieux, Baron Maupertuis, in the Spring of 1887. It was, therefore, the most amazing coincidence that he was called upon to save the life of the man's stepdaughter 18 years later, during his retirement in the South Downs.

On referring to my notes, I see that I made a copy of the cable which Holmes received on March 22, and that started his investigation. It came from some God-forsaken city called

Malatya, deep inside the Ottoman Empire, and had been re-layed through the British Embassy in Constantinople. It mere-ly read: "STRONGBOROUGH MURDER STOP DEADLY COURT STOP SIGNED AL."

Under normal circumstances, Holmes would have ig-nored the message, as he receives many such nonsensical cor-respondences from various benighted souls all around England and even from other parts of the Empire. But there was the signatory: "AL."

At Holmes' request, his brother, Mycroft, called on some of his associates in Turkey and, two days later, we learned that Malatya was deep inside hostile territory held by a mad war-lord known locally as the "Red Sultan." As the report went, a single westerner, a man in his thirties, had fought and defeated 40 of the Red Sultan's warriors to invade a telegram office and, there, had held a small army at bay during the time it took to relay that cable via Constantinople. Apparently, no more could be sent. The report labeled the man "clearly insane" while praising his bravery. When he read this, Holmes no longer had any doubts as to the identity of "AL."

Of all the enemies Holmes has fought during his tumul-tuous career, none, not even the nefarious Professor Moriarty or Charles-Augustus Milverton, have ever been able to get under my friend's skin as much as the Frenchman. "The Fren-chman" or *He* or *Him* was, in fact, how he most often referred to *him* when we discussed *him*, which was a rare occurrence at best. Perhaps it was a habit unconsciously borrowed from Chief Inspector Ganimard. All of Holmes' other foes had, in effect, played the game according to the same rules. But with *him*, there were no rules. It was like grappling with quicksilv-er.

Having ascertained that the cable from Malatya came from *him*, my friend set to work immediately.

In just under a week, he had untangled the mystery. However, it took all of his considerable influence to convince the Home Secretary of Lady Strongborough's innocence and get him to sign the reprieve which, thank God, he was able to deliver just in time to spare the poor woman's life.

I shall now jot down the conversation that ensued later that selfsame day between Sherlock Holmes and Lady Strongborough, which I had the privilege of attending.

"I owe you my life, Mister Holmes," said Lady Strongborough, who was still understandably shaken by her ordeal.

At that point, my friend pulled out the cablegram and showed it to her.

"This is not entirely true, Madam," said Holmes, thoughtfully. "Your guardian angel came through, I believe."

Lady Strongborough read the cable and began crying, silently, without sobs; tears rolled gently down her cheeks as if the weight of the grim fate she had just been spared had suddenly crushed her gentle soul. We gave her time to recover. Then, she said:

"I am most grateful that you showed me this, Mister Holmes. And naturally thrilled that it made sense to you. But I confess that I do not understand. What does 'deadly court' mean? Is it a reference to Judge Wargrave?..."

"It is not 'deadly court,' Lady Strongborough—that was likely an error in the transmission—but 'deadly cort,' also known as deadly galerina or *cortinarius speciosissimus*, one of the deadliest brown-capped fungi, found commonly throughout the American Northwest, and the symptoms of which could easily be mistaken for cadmium poisoning."

"But the autopsy said..."

"This was a most unusual case. The man who strived to engineer your doom had a diabolical mind. Your husband, Lady Strongborough, was in fact murdered after all of you thought he had been poisoned. The evidence was then retroactively tampered with to make the facts fit the theory formulated by the Police."

"So cadmium is not what killed Edward?"

"No. I will tell you the story as I reconstructed it. Your husband, I am sorry to say, Lady Strongborough, had been involved in some unpleasant business while in America 20

213

years ago. The sins of youth, some would say. A woman died in childbirth and so did the child. Much cause for scandal, if it were revealed publicly. Two years ago, the man whom you knew as Dr. Taylor appeared in London. He had known your husband in America and was well-acquainted with his past. He blackmailed him, first to get a position on the board of the Jockey Club, then to embezzle funds. But after his marriage to you, Lord Strongborough began to rebel; I believe he threatened to report Taylor to the Police.

"I have no doubt that Taylor decided to murder your husband at once, but I believe what gave him the idea on how to do it was young Anthony's death, which was, in fact, completely natural and due to gastric fever, as had been correctly diagnosed at the time.

"Taylor knew of your photographic laboratory and saw how Anthony's death could retroactively be made to look like cadmium poisoning. The criminal carried with him some finely ground deadly cort that, no doubt, he had collected while in America. He merely waited for Lord Strongborough to be afflicted with gastroenteritis, as Anthony had been, and perhaps did as much he could to inflame the condition. When your husband was taken to the hospital, he rushed to his side and there, he administered the poison. Deadly cort is instantly fatal and would mimic the symptoms of cadmium poisoning, which is slower and more painful. Since everyone later assumed that your husband had been poisoned at the Manor, when he was initially taken ill, no one bothered to look at the hospital records.

"Then, the only thing left for Taylor to do was to fool the medical examiners by lacing the samples with carefully measured traces of cadmium. If you recall, he insisted on supervising the autopsies. All the evidence against you was retroactively fabricated to fit the case that he wanted the Police to make against you. As I said, it was one of the most diabolically ingenious murder schemes I have ever come across."

"Have they arrested Dr. Taylor?" asked Lady Strongborough.

"I'm afraid that, as soon as he got wind of my involvement, he fled the country. That was, in fact, how I was able to persuade the Home Secretary that he was the murderer and that he should immediately grant your reprieve. I heard he's fled back to France."

"Fled back to France?"

"My investigation showed that he arrived from Paris in 1902. But I could find no more about him. He obviously is a most remarkable criminal. Perhaps *he*, I mean, your friend, will be able to shed more light on this... But, at least, you no longer have anything to fear, Lady Strongborough."

And thus did my friend Sherlock Holmes solve the murder of Lord Strongborough and save the life of a most gracious Lady. I have recorded this as an appendix to the case of Baron Maupertuis in the event that I ever decide to write it in full. But as Holmes mentioned, the case still contains some loose ends, and besides I know that my friend does not like me to write about *him*, so it is probably best to let it lie for the time being...

The village of Saint Paul de Vence in Provence was a jewel located in the hills above Nice. It was bright and beautiful this sunny afternoon of June. The sky was a deep penetrating blue and the quality of the light made every object stand out in sharp relief.

Lady Strongborough waited at the terrace of the single café that serviced the village, sipping on a *grenadine*. He had told her that he would be there precisely at 5 p.m. and she knew that he would not betray his word.

The village clock in the church tower tolled five.

"I deeply apologize for not being able to make it back in time," said a voice from behind her.

He had appeared as if by magic. She had seen no car, heard no engine, yet there he was, looking very much like the Paul Dubreuil she had met 18 months earlier. He pulled out a chair and sat down. He gestured to the *garçon* to bring him a *pastis*.

"When did you get back?" she asked.

"Two months ago. I lost the lives of a couple of good men trying to reach Constantinople in time, but the Red Sultan barred my way. I knew, however, that if I could send that cable to Sherlock Holmes, he, of all people, would have both the mental abilities and the power to rescue you. I was thrilled to discover upon my return to Marseilles that I hadn't been mistaken. I never would have forgiven myself if..."

She put her hand on his to dispel the ghastly image of the fate that they knew had almost been hers.

"Mister Holmes said that you knew more about this case than he had uncovered," Lady Strongborough said.

"How perceptive of him," he smiled. "His mind is as penetrating as ever. Yes, the trick that the so-called Dr. Taylor used, that bit of misdirection, of sleight of hand, reminded me of another case, one that was much covered in the Press, three years ago. *The Affair of Glandier. The Mystery of the Yellow Room*. The murderer was exposed as Ballmeyer, an international criminal of the first order. We never met but I like to keep an eye on the competition. I knew that he had been in America, at the same time as your late husband, and that he would have been familiar with poisons found on that Continent. He also had been in London in 1901 and was implicated in a murky business of stolen bonds... But more to the point, when he was finally unmasked by a young reporter from *L'Epoque* at the end of the Yellow Room case, we discovered that Ballmeyer had had the prodigious idea of masquerading as an Inspector of the Sûreté, Frédéric Larsan! What a stroke of genius! Ballmeyer, a man wanted by half the police forces of Europe and America, was hiding in plain sight in the French Sûreté! You have to admire that inventiveness! Why, I was almost jealous!"

"So Dr. Taylor was Ballmeyer?"

"Yes. And Ballmeyer was Frédéric Larsan, and I knew that Larsan had been involved in the famous case of the gold bar robbery of the Hôtel de la Monnaie, in which, if you recall, your stepfather, Paul Darcieux, Baron Maupertuis, was one of the suspects."

"Yes, that's true... I remember. He was one of the Trustees, but was cleared of all suspicion."

"By Frédéric Larsan, his accomplice, the man who likely devised the whole scheme and used his position as Inspector of the Sûreté to frame an innocent man. You see, it all ties together. So, I asked myself, what if Ballmeyer-Larsan was up to his old tricks again, seeking to kill two birds with one stone: he murders your husband to cover his tracks with the Jockey Club, and he pins the blame on you to have you hung afterwards. If Lord Strongborough had been the only intended victim, I have no doubt that Ballmeyer could have dispatched him quickly and easily. Why resort to such a complicated scheme? Because he wanted you dead as well. Why? Ask yourself: who would have profited from your death?"

"My stepfather! He's the only family I have."

"Indeed. We're drawn back to the Ballmeyer-Darcieux connection. So, one of the first things I did upon my return to this country was to check your stepfather's fate. And I wasn't surprised to discover that someone had organized his escape soon after his extradition to France."

"Oh my God! He's free?"

"Don't fear, Jeanne. I would have taken steps, but I had no need. They say there's no honor among thieves, you know... They found an unidentified body not far from here, which I know to be Paul Darcieux. There is no doubt in my mind that when Holmes exposed Ballmeyer, and his plans to have you hung failed, Ballmeyer killed your stepfather."

"And Ballmeyer?"

"My inquiries lead me to believe that the same young journalist who exposed him the first time is back on his case. He has a brilliant mind, almost as good as Sherlock Holmes, to tell the truth. And he can be quite ruthless, under his college boy manners. I hope we never cross swords. I have no doubt he'll deal with Ballmeyer—definitively."

"You see, Sainclair, I had only condemned Larsan to life in prison, but he killed himself! It was God's will. May God have mercy on his soul!"

Joseph Rouletabille revealing Ballmeyer's fate to his friend Sainclair at the conclusion of *The Perfume of the Lady in Black*, Summer 1905.

Published in *Arsene Lupin vs Sherlock Holmes* Vol. 2, 2005

This story is meant to explain why Holmes, who left Lupin on relatively friendly terms at the end of The Jewish Lamp, *feels such anger towards the gentleman-burglar in* The Hollow Needle, *barely a year later...*

The Unkindest Cut

It is only with deep reluctance that I take up my pen to explain the prodigious well of anger and extraordinary circumstances that drove my friend, Sherlock Holmes, to accidentally take the life of Raymonde de Saint-Veran, who almost became Arsène Lupin's second wife, on that tragic night in the Pays de Caux in December 1909.

After I was wounded during that wretched business of the Jewish Lamp in June of the preceding year, I spent three weeks in Paris recovering. I was often visited by my fellow biographer, Monsieur Maurice Leblanc, and we enjoyed exchanging notes and confidences about our respective illustrious companions. We have since kept up a secret correspondence, and it is only at his behest and to satisfy his curiosity that I am writing this account.

As those who have read Monsieur Leblanc's account of the remarkable case of the Jewish Lamp know, Holmes and Lupin had separated on courteous, if not friendly, terms aboard the ferry that was taking them both to London.

In Paris, Lupin was king. In London, things were much different. Holmes, of course, could not let an opportunity to arrest his rival pass. Immediately upon his return to Baker Street, he devoted all his efforts to discovering why Lupin had come to England.

Perhaps, some day, Monsieur Leblanc and I will get together, gather our notes and try to piece together the formidable adventure of the Silver Knight that occupied both our friends during the fall of 1908. Lupin was after a young madman named Flax, who had just killed Sonia Krichnoff, one of his paramours. Holmes was after Lupin. In the end, the monster managed to slip through the net, but much bloodshed was averted. Indeed, the death toll of the Great War might have been even more horrendous had Flax successfully accomplished his evil plan.

When I returned from France, fully recovered, I found Holmes in an exultant mood. He had finally managed to trap Lupin, and a new female accomplice of his who had also been pursuing Flax across the Balkans, at the Bertram's, where they were staying under assumed identities. This time, my friend left nothing to chance and even enlisted the assistance of Lestrade and his men.

The following day, however, I saw Holmes return in the darkest mood in which I have ever seen him. He locked himself in his rooms and I heard incessant violin music for the following day and night. He refused all of Mrs. Hudson's entreaties to eat something, anything.

When I asked him what had happened, he muttered something about that "infernal Frenchman" and almost slammed the door in my face. I never got a straight answer. I finally went to Monsieur Leblanc to learn the truth. It turned out that Lupin had pulled another of his amazing escapes. He had used the corpse of a recently deceased guest to fool the police, while at the same time impersonating the crippled brother of Grafin Von Schwarzburg, a Prussian aristocrat who, of course, turned out to be his new paramour. Still, Lupin had escaped from Holmes' clutches before and I could not see why this time was so different as to send my friend into virtual seclusion.

It was only by accident that I learned the secret that drove my friend to such a degree of hatred towards Lupin that he was driven to do what he did on that night of December 1909 near that deserted farmhouse at Neuvillette. It was a hatred that I am confident he never felt towards any of his adversaries before. Not even Professor Moriarty could invoke such cold-blooded fury as Holmes felt that winter when the name of "that infernal Frenchman" was mentioned in his presence.

As do all great discoveries, this one occurred virtually by happenstance. I was invited to the Christmas Ball at the Spanish Embassy. There, I was introduced to the notorious explorer Hubert d'Andresy who had just returned from Tibet. Not being gifted with Holmes' prodigious powers of observation, I naturally did not recognize Lupin. At least, not at once. But during the evening, he let something slip that echoed a confidence that Monsieur Leblanc had shared with me. No one else could have known, of course. I thought d'Andresy was Lupin, but to be frank, I wasn't sure. I then pondered what to do next. Should I call Holmes? Should I summon Lestrade and his men, at the risk of being wrong and causing a major diplomatic incident?

Then, when I saw who Lupin's companion was, I finally understood the real cause of Holmes' rage. She was older, but as beautiful as ever. Together, they made a dashing couple as they danced to the admiring whispers of all the guests. To my friend, she had always been *The* Woman. Irene Adler.

I went home that night. I never mentioned this encounter to Holmes, nor do I know if he ever learned of it. I simply never said a word about it.

It would truly have been the unkindest cut of all.

Published in *Arsene Lupin vs Sherlock Holmes* Vol. 2, 2005

The scene of the last reconciliation between Lupin and Holmes had to written; also it was a good excuse to get rid of the burdensome Florence, whom Lupin had married at the end of The Teeth of the Tiger...

Escape Not the Thunderbolt

To David McDonnell.

Some innocents escape not the thunderbolt.
William Shakespeare
Antony and Cleopatra, Act ii, Sc. 5

"Let us speak honestly," said the Beekeeper. "That is why you have come."

"To bare my heart, rejecting the masks and lies I once hid behind, yes," replied the Distinguished Gentleman.

The pale and misty light of this bleak afternoon of December 1922 bleached the normally vibrant colors of the prim cottage and its well-tendered grounds. The Distinguished Gentleman thought he was looking at a watercolor of the English Countryside, not the thing itself.

He had not had to ask many people for directions, because the Beekeeper was well-known in the South Downs. Everyone was aware that he occasionally entertained visitors from London, the Continent and even from locales as far away and exotic as America or India.

Upon his arrival in a sparkling, white limousine, the Distinguished Gentleman had ordered his chauffeur to wait and had stood outside, gazing at the Beekeeper's house. It was located on a southern slope and commanded a grand view of the British Channel. The air was brisk, but not cold. The visitor judged that it would likely rain that night.

The sight of the white cliffs, known locally as the Seven Sisters, seemed to evoke an old and painful memory in the

Distinguished Gentleman's breast, for he sighed deeply before stepping forward past the small fence, and onto the grounds of the property.

"You are extraordinary," said the Beekeeper, when he first saw the visitor. "You have completely transformed your physical appearance. No one would recognize you."

"You have."

"I'm a very poor host. Let's go inside and share some refreshments."

They shared a cup of Darjeeling in a small study, which directly faced the sea. The Beekeeper's desk stood by the window so that he had a clear and uninterrupted view straight across the Channel.

"How long has it been?" asked the Beekeeper, after they had enjoyed a quiet, intimate moment of silence.

"Thirteen years."

"I read that you'd married again... And retired too... After the Cosmo Mornington Affair..."

"Ah. You've followed it?"

The Distinguished Gentleman pulled a gold cigarette case from his pocket, and made a typical Gallic gesture of the head to inquire if he could smoke. The Beekeeper nodded his approval.

"Only what I read in the papers... The murderer was Vernocq, wasn't it?"

"Yes." After a pause, the Distinguished Gentleman continued, "I thought you'd retired too."

"I have."

"That's not what I've heard."

"Let's say that I am occasionally my brother's keeper, and leave it at that," said the Beekeeper with a thin smile.

"Your successor, the young American, he's good. Not as good as you, but very good."

"Yes, he shows promise..."

There was another long pause. Then, without displaying any more emotion than he would have shown studying the intricate mating patterns of a queen bee, the Beekeeper asked, "Did you hate me?"

The Distinguished Gentleman took another sip of tea.

"It's heartening when two men of equal worth can, this once at least, speak to each other with their hearts instead of their pride, don't you think?" he said to the Beekeeper. "Frankly, I had my doubts you and I could ever do it... And yes, I did hate you."

"Did you want to kill me?"

"To kill you—or to kill myself. Either would have done the job. But I couldn't. Just before the War, I also tried jumping off a cliff. Then, I chased after a Berber's bullet in the South Sahara. But it seems that Death really doesn't want me. You've had your share of close calls too, I suppose, so you must know how it is."

"Yes, I have."

They rested, enjoying the quasi-divine depth of silence and the descending darkness. Neither felt like asking for a light to be turned on, not wanting to break the spell that had been laid upon this room, at this time.

"Sometimes I see their faces in my dreams," said the Distinguished Gentleman. "Clarisse, my first love... The terrible Dolores Kesselbach... and Raymonde, whom you shot that night, on a cliff not far from here, as the bird flies, on the other side of the water." He gestured at the window. "Do you sometimes think of that night?"

"Often. It was a meaningless death... I regret... I deeply regret..." began the Beekeeper, his voice filled with so much emotion that the Distinguished Gentleman bent forward and placed his hand on the older man's arm.

"Don't. Do you ever wonder what might have happened had Raymonde lived? Yes, the Gentleman Burglar would have vanished like a phantom at the cock's crow. And you, not I, likely would have solved the mystery of '813.' But Dolores and her lover would have redrawn the map of Europe. Perhaps the Great War could have been averted? Once, I almost had the Alsace-Lorraine in the palm of my hands... Or maybe

Vorski would have delivered the God-Stone of Sarek to the Kaiser, and both our countries would suffer today under the Germans' yoke... Raymonde's death was *not* meaningless, Detective. It served a greater purpose. *You* served a purpose that night on the lonely farm at Neuvillette..."

"Does it help that her death had a purpose?"

"It does me. Don't you find the notion of a divine plan somehow reassuring?"

"No."

"In that we differ, too. I do. At first, I blamed you for Raymonde's death, but I understood later that if anyone was to blame, I was. As I was in Clarisse's death. Those deaths were preordained from the moment I embarked on the road that led to what I became. They were all logical consequences of that initial choice I made when I was not yet seven years of age and stole the Queen's Necklace at the Dreux-Soubizes... You can't become what I am and be burdened with a wife; it would be preposterous. Those deaths were the price I had to pay and I've paid it... What price did *you* pay, Detective?... No, don't tell me, I see it in your eyes..."

"The fewer people who are close to me, the better..."

"Indeed. Too many deaths, too many dead... I know that road well. But even if I wanted to be Raoul again now, I couldn't go back. The dead would not return to life. The only path left to me is that upon which I tread, now and until the end."

"But you're married again..."

"Florence died last September, Detective."

"Ah. I didn't know. I'm so sorry."

"I was away on a secret mission for Poincaré, our new Premier who has replaced my good friend Valenglay... I can tell you, it concerned the easing of the German Reparations... There are ill winds blowing in that country... But now, without Florence... I've closed the *Clos des Lupins* which she and I had lovingly built together, burying the last shreds of a life I wasn't meant to have, and sent Poincaré packing... Let *him* reshape the Map of Europe for a change! I'll slip away...

Maybe return to Morocco and see how my little Kingdom is faring... But I didn't want to leave without telling you I had forgiven you."

"I knew it as soon as I saw you. It was... elementary."

It rained into the night, and the whole of the following day.

On January 11, 1923, when Germany was unable to pay the Reparations owed under the Treaty of Versailles, France's new Premier, Raymond Poincaré, against the advice of the British Government, sent French troops to occupy the Ruhr. The miners went on strike and Germany printed more money and allowed inflation to spiral completely out of control. This, as well as the psychological impact of this new humiliation, was directly responsible for Adolf Hitler's accession to power.

Published in *Arsene Lupin vs Sherlock Holmes* Vol. 1, 2004

Between 2002 and 2005, we wrote a trilogy of French graphic novels (beautifully drawn by Gil Formosa), translated in Heavy Metal, *starring a more dynamic version of Jules Verne's notorious science-pirate, Robur the Conqueror. It is that Robur whom we have reused in the story that follows...*

Journey to the Center of Chaos

Even though the Monsoon hadn't yet come to the Nepalese border, the streets of Gezing were already hot and muggy. In this corner of the western district of Sikkim in the late 1920s, westerners were still a relatively rare occurrence, and the presence of Professor Alexander Whateley of the Miskatonic University of Arkham, Mass., and his companion, John Green, could only attract attention.

Green alone would have been noticed in any crowd, anywhere. He was a tank of a man, one eighth of a metric ton of bone and muscle; he could go through anything on Earth and come out wondering mildly why other people were so excited. Whateley, on the other hand, was thin, almost skeletal, and bookish. Unlike his companion, he was visibly more at ease locating a rare dusty tome in an ancient library than he was horse-trading with the merchants of Northern India, as he was presently attempting to do.

Only the most inept observer would have failed to notice that the two foreigners were watched intently by a small posse of natives, one peeking out from behind a doorway, another slithering behind a bead curtain, others peering from a neighboring windowsill. Whateley was blissfully unaware of the spies—but not so Green, whose hard-edged, clean-shaven face began to show some concern.

"Dahoor... Dahoor," repeated Whateley, addressing a merchant trying to sell him a vase that was such an obvious forgery it would not have fooled even a first year archeology student at the Louvre. "Surely you must know who he is? I've come all the way from America to see him..."

But the merchant remained obdurately dense. He kept trying to shove the vase in Whateley's hands. "Beautiful vase. From the Gupta period. Very rare."

Green, increasingly concerned about the attention they were getting, tugged at his companion's arm.

"Come on, Professor. We're wasting our time here."

The archeologist, resigned to not getting the information he sought, dejectedly walked away from the merchant's stall.

"He was lying to me, Mr. Green. Dahoor is one of the biggest antique dealers in Northern India. He's been selling to us for years. If anyone can help me put together an expedition to K'n-yan, he can."

"If you don't mind my saying so, Professor, I think you're chasing after one of those demented heathens' opium dreams. There is no lost city of the Mi-go. It just doesn't exist. This is a wild goose chase."

Whateley pulled a small carved cylinder from his belt.

"My map says you're wrong, Mr. Green."

"It's got to be a forgery. I've seen dozens of fake maps sold by unscrupulous babus in the back streets of Benares. Why should this one different from the others?"

"You insisted on joining me, remember?"

"Not quite. Meldrum Strange, who financed this expedition, asked me to do it. And he was right, too. It's not safe for someone like you to travel alone in this part of the world. He's only protecting his investment."

"Please, Mr. Green! This is just as safe as Harvard Square!"

While the two westerners were crossing the souk market, the mysterious figures that had been shadowing them had gathered into a dangerous-looking mob.

Suddenly, the thuggees—for that is what they were—pounced on the two explorers. Three of them tried to wrest the map away from Whateley.

But Green had already detected the threat. His massive fist crashed into the face of one of the men, and with a kick, he sent two of the other would-be thieves flying into the stall of a nearby merchant.

Green knew what he was doing. The merchant, who looked like a Punjabi, was understandably irate, and better yet, he had five surly brothers ready to rush to his aid.

Rush they did, and in seconds, a fierce melee had erupted between the Punjabi and the thuggees.

Judging that there was still not enough chaos for them to make a discreet exit, Green took a handful of copper coins from his pocket and threw them into the air, shouting, "Gold!"

At that point, real pandemonium broke loose.

"I think you've just started a riot," said Whateley.

"Good! That'll make it harder for them to catch us."

Grabbing Whateley by the arm, Green began running away through the narrow aisles of the street market, looking for the convenient refuge of the houses beyond.

"I bet that never happened to you in Harvard Square," he said.

"I accept that you were correct, but we'd better save our breath for running. Some of them seem to still be after us."

This time, Whateley was right. Two of the thieves had not lost sight of their prey despite the commotion. They had managed to slip by unscathed and were now running after the two westerners. In their hands were long kris knives, and the expressions on their faces plainly showed that if, before, their intent had been to get the map from Whateley dead or alive, that had now been updated to simply dead.

Green grabbed a rather vulgar statue of the god Ganesha from a stall.

"*Isakii kyaa kimat hai*? (How much does this cost?)" he asked the seller, who quoted him a wildly inflated figure. The strong man did not haggle and told Whateley, "Pay him!"

Then, using the statue as a club, he waited for the two thuggees. He quickly disposed of one of them with a massive swing of the statue, but the other managed to avoid the blow.

229

While Whateley was paying the merchant ("*Dhanya-vaad*!" said the grateful man who had never dreamed he would ever get his asking price), the other thug approached him with murderous intentions.

Whateley escaped the deadly swish of the native blade by stepping aside with a dancer's grace, and kicked the man hard in the crotch. The thug fell to the ground, writhing in agony. Green temporarily put him out of his misery by hitting him on the head with the statue, which he then gave back to the merchant, who blessed the gods for having put these two generous strangers on his path that day.

"That's a side of you I've never seen before, Professor, and I have to say it surprises me."

"It comes from growing up in a rough neighborhood, Mr. Green."

"Let's go before the others come," said Green.

"But I need a receipt!"

Taking a number of detours through the small, grimy streets to mislead any followers, Whateley and Green finally reached their hotel, or rather what passed for a hotel in Gezing. In reality, it was more of an inn, a rest stop for caravans en route northward to Mongolia and beyond. The place was managed by an old couple and their two boys; it had seen better days in the 6th century.

"Those thuggees coming after my map proves that it's authentic," said Whateley.

"What makes you think that's what they want? Maybe they're common thieves."

"You don't believe that yourself, Mr. Green. In any event, we're not any closer to finding Dahoor, and it will probably make our job more difficult."

"If you'd let me organize a proper expedition back in Bombay instead of rushing to get here, I could have found as many reliable guides as we wanted."

"Yes. Sometime next year."

"What's the big hurry? If K'n-yan exists, it isn't going anywhere. Let's have a drink and figure out our next move."

The inn came with its own bar attached, where locals and travelers mixed and dealt in various commodities in its suitably smoky and darkened atmosphere. As the archeologist and his companion sat at a table, one of the innkeeper's sons came to take their order.

"Any messages for me? Professor Whateley?" Whateley expected a letter from the University and had left the inn as a forwarding address in Bombay.

The boy did not answer. A look of total, uncomprehending blankness washed over him.

"Professor..." said Green, tugging at the archeologist, who had his back to him.

"A minute, Mr. Green. I'm trying to ask this boy if I've got a message."

"It can wait," said Green, forcing his colleague to turn around.

Whateley then saw what had caused such stupor in the waiter. The six thuggees who had chased the two men in the souk were framed within the doorway. Some of them exhibited nasty bruises and their clothes were partially torn. Consequently, they were all in a particularly foul mood. They looked like a pack of hungry wolves. Their daggers were out, and only God knew what else they had hidden within the folds of their kaftans.

The boy vanished as if by magic. The few other patrons meticulously absorbed themselves in the contemplation of the bottoms of their glasses.

The thug leader stepped forward, grinning evilly, his hand extended.

"Map, now!"

Green sighed. There was going to be a massacre. It could no longer be avoided as he had hoped. The question remained, whose? The odds were far from good and he now wished he had enlisted several of his friends to come with him on this trip. Still, it was too late for regrets.

One of his hands lie deceptively quietly on the chair in front of him. He calculated that he could swing it to hit the first man, then use the pieces to keep the others at bay, until he could reach for his gun...

Before he could move, there was a sudden and amazing change of expression on the thug's face. The sneer of rapacious savagery was replaced by pure, unadulterated fear as quickly as the tide erases a drawing in the sand.

Green immediately saw the cause of such an astonishing metamorphosis.

A Herculean figure, dressed in an incongruous white tuxedo, had just stepped out of the backroom of the tavern, undoubtedly summoned by the servant boy.

"Well well if it isn't my old friend, Ali. Come here, you son of a dyspeptic camel!" said the newcomer.

Ali—no fool he—stayed rooted in place, but the stranger stepped forward and proceeded to grab him in what is appropriately called a bear hug. Green looked up in admiration. Whateley, on the other hand, could not prevent himself from wincing when he heard an ominous crunching sound.

Ali, to his credit, remained silent, but after being released, collapsed on the floor like a rag doll. The other thuggees looked properly impressed—and properly scared.

"I think my business with Ali is done for today," said the newcomer amicably. Then he barked an order: "Take him away and don't come back!"

The thuggees nodded as one as fast as they could. They scurried away, carrying the body of their unfortunate comrade.

The huge man, beaming a cheerful smile, grabbed a chair and sat at the table.

"I understand you were looking for me. I am Dahoor. I believe you've received my map and seek the lost city of K'n-yan, hmm?"

High in the skies above Tibet flew the *Albatross*. The prodigious craft was a true clipper of the clouds, with its 37 masts, each equipped with two propellers driven at prodigious speed by powerful engines, the secret of which was known only to its captain—and inventor.

That man was presently going by the name of Robur. He was of middle height and weight, with a surprisingly large round head. At the least opposition, his grey eyes would glow like coals of fire. He was dressed in a leather aviator's uniform, including gloves and boots. He sat in the luxuriously furnished control room, comfortably ensconced in a leather armchair, sipping a cup of Darjeeling tea while engaged in conversation with another man.

His guest had soulful, ageless eyes, green with specks of gold. He was dressed in an odd mixture of European and Oriental clothing. His high forehead was partially covered by a white silk turban. His name was Sâr Dubnotal.

"No one else but you could have successfully guided me to this spot," said Robur.

"I'm happy to be of service to such a distinguished friend of our mutual acquaintance, Mr. Strange. I trust he is well?"

"Meldrum's under a great deal of pressure these days. Apparently the Kun Yin are staging a comeback. I thought the British had wiped them all out, but you know what they say, the bad penny always turns up. One of his agents stumbled across a survivor of the Iron Temple in London. Even though he was half out of his mind, what he said was enough for Strange to ask me to come here and, er, take care of the rest, if you see my meaning."

"I assume you're referring to the Crown of Genghis?"

"Yes. But Strange didn't have time to fully brief me. He said you'd fill me in."

"Cast your mind back seven centuries. The Great Khan has come out of the desert and used the Crown's powers to conquer China. Afterwards, he chose to cast it aside and entrusted it to Marco Polo to be delivered into the protective hands of the Yian Ho, the Wise Men of K'n-yan. There was no better place to keep it safe, away from the evil ones who would use it for their own ends. And in K'n-yan it has remained ever since."

"Strange believes that the Kun Yin are after it."

"I wouldn't be surprised. The Hour of the Scythe approaches. If they get their hands on the Crown before then, they will travel to the Heart of Chaos and release the Guardian of the Gate."

Robur stood up and pressed a button. Seconds later, his first mate, a burly American named Tom Turner arrived on the bridge.

"I'm going to leave the Sâr in charge, Mr. Turner. You will obey his every order, in every respect, no matter how... draconian, you understand?"

"Completely, sir."

Robur walked to a cabinet, pulled out a harness attached to a backpack and began strapping it on.

"I know I can trust you to do what's necessary if I fail to stop them, Sâr Dubnotal."

"The Abyss is dangerous only for those who look into it, Robur."

"If you say so." Then, he addressed Tom, who now stood at the controls.

"Release the hatch, Mr. Turner."

With a whooshing sound, a circular shaft slid open in the metal walls of the *Albatross*, letting in a gust of frigid air and a streak of bright blue-white light.

"The rest is up to me," said Robur.

He jumped into the shaft.

A couple of hundred feet down, his pack opened, releasing a delicate, origami-like structure that grew into an ingenious, ultralight glider.

The scientist-adventurer began his safe descent towards the ground.

If Robur had been able to scan the far side of the peak over which he currently flew, he might have seen a small, ant-trail line of people slogging laboriously through the eternal snows of the Himalayas. The expedition was comprised of Dahoor, closely followed by Professor Whateley and Mr. Green, while four sherpas hired in Gezing closed up the rear.

"Without you, Dahoor, we wouldn't have been able to mount this expedition on such a short notice," said Whateley.

"Your gratitude is greatly appreciated but sadly misplaced, Professor Whateley. Indeed, it is I who an indebted to you. In exchange for my miserable find, your munificent American Museum has provided me with ample funds to pay for all of this. And believe me when I say that I expect to earn a handsome profit from your discoveries."

"But, surely, anything that we uncover belongs to science," said Whateley with a certain intensity.

"Certainly, certainly, but how it gets to the scientists is where I make my money. After all, you will not be able to take everything away with you, eh? There will be enough wealth from this expedition to last me a lifetime. So you see, Professor, the gods indeed smiled upon me when I sent you that map."

The expedition began a slow and perilous descent into a sharp, craggy ice canyon. Green thought that the ice itself appeared to be sculpted in sinister forms, but he attributed that to the same human reflex which makes us see animal shapes in the clouds. He did notice, however, that the four sherpas looked increasingly anxious.

"It all seems so—mercenary." The Professor and Dahoor, seemingly unaware of the eerie decor, continued their discussion on the professional ethics of archeology.

"Well, wealth is good," said Dahoor laughing. "What else is there?"

"Knowledge. The origins of man. Life. Everything."

"Words don't fill hungry bellies, Professor."

"So you would loot Ubar or Ys?"

"Just so. If I knew where they were."

"But the knowledge of K'n-yan could lift your country to new heights... It could be your Holy Grail..."

Suddenly, the sherpas became extremely agitated and gestured for Dahoor's attention.

"*Shahajjo! Rakkhosh! Mi-Go Khokkosh!*" they shouted.

The lead guide walked back to confer with his anxious men.

"What is it? *Ki? Ki?*" he asked.

The sherpas all began talking at the same time while gesticulating wildly. Dahoor's face became a worrisome shade of purple as he began screaming at the men. More shouting followed, until finally, the big man pulled rolls of coins from his bag.

"What's going on?" asked Whateley.

"One of them claims to have seen a Mi-go," replied Green. "A Yeti. They're scared. They want to turn back."

"What? They can't do that!"

"Actually, they can. But Dahoor is taking care of it. He's offering them more money. It's going to cost you an arm and a leg."

"Hmf. He should have talked to me first."

"Stop it, Professor! He's only doing what's necessary."

After the labor unrest had been successfully dealt with by the transfer of cash from Dahoor's pockets into those of the reluctant sherpas, the expedition continued its arduous trek, deeper into the grim, windswept, icy canyons. It finally came to a stop when it reached the bottom and came face-to-face with what looked like a barren wall of ice.

"We seem to have come to a dead end," said Green. "With all due respect, have you been reading that map correctly, Professor?"

Whateley walked to the wall of ice on his right and began attacking it with his knife. He kept chopping away until he uncovered an ancient sculpted post that had been buried under the ice and was barely visible from the surface.

"Yes. We're where we should be. Look."

Green helped Whateley finish excavating the post.

"What are those symbols?" he inquired.

"They're Yian-Ho gate markers," replied Whateley.

"Good luck signs?"

"No. More the 'abandon all hope, ye who enter here' type."

After excavating an identical post on the left, the men were directed to use their picks to dig between the two. Soon, a crack appeared in the ice wall, between the two posts. With a thundering sound, the remaining ice collapsed, revealing gaping darkness behind it.

"The entrance to K'n-yan," whispered Whateley.

"Congratulations, Professor," said Green. "You've led us where no modern man has been before."

For hours, the expedition had traversed a maze of underground caverns, deep inside the Tibetan peaks. Without the map, which enabled Whateley to locate and decipher the sculpted posts that acted as markers, they would have been hopelessly lost in the Stygian complex of caves. As it was, finding their way was not their only challenge, they had to remain vigilant for chasms that suddenly appeared unexpectedly beneath their unwary feet or sudden rockfalls from above.

Green felt his hackles rise several times. A mysterious sixth sense told him they were not alone in the dark. He peered through the darkness every time he heard—or thought he heard—a distant shuffling. It was a sound that reminded him of the silken, deadly tread of a jungle cat before he pounces, a noise that few explorers lived long enough to recognize more than once.

Suddenly, a gut-wrenching scream tore the darkness like the slash of a razor. More terrifying was that the scream had been cut short, as if by a guillotine putting an abrupt end to its victim's suffering.

The scream was followed by a gunshot and a series of curses. Green recognized Dahoor's voice.

"What happened?" he asked.

Dahoor, his gun raised, squinted into the darkness. "A Mi-Go I think. He got Cibi. But I hit him..."

Unexpectedly, a pair of red eyes shone in the dark.

"Or maybe not..."

Without warning, several pairs of red eyes flashed in the night, accompanied by low, feral noises, intermingled with bits of what could best be described as an inhuman tongue.

"Or maybe he has friends," said Green.

Whateley was starting to panic. "We can't retreat now," he said stubbornly. "We're so close."

"Then let's make a run for it," exclaimed Green.

The six men began running through the caverns. They could hear the distant sounds of their pursuers. Except for the blood-red eyes and the occasional, spectral sight of a clawed hand that briefly emerged from the obscurity, as it tried to grab them, their attackers remained cloaked in darkness. Dahoor covered the rear, stopping several times to fire at the ravening creatures, but with no apparent effect.

"I'm sure I'm hitting them, but it doesn't seem to stop them," he said, frustrated.

Out of breath, one of the sherpas stumbled and fell. Before any of the others could even think of coming to his aid, something indescribably hideous had already fallen upon the man, whose screams of terror were mercifully brief. Green tried hard to not hear the awful sounds of chewing that followed.

"The exit should be just around the next bend," said Whateley, panting.

Indeed, they had reached the proverbial light at the end of the tunnel, although it was only a pallid, wan light that cast bleak shadows on the carved rocks surrounding them.

They emerged into a small, circular valley surrounded by the snowy peaks of the Himalayas. On its opposite side, carved into the very side of the mountain, was a strange, intricate, portal. The valley itself was a giant graveyard, littered with bones, human, animal and possibly other creatures' as well. It was almost sunset and the light was fading.

"K'n-yan! I've found it!" Whateley exclaimed, pointing to the sculpted entrance at the far end of the circle.

"Somehow, from reading the Veda, I pictured a more pleasant setting," said Green, looking at the bones.

The howl of the Mi-Go behind them reminded them that, although they had reached their goal, their survival was still very much in doubt and their bones might be the next ones to join those that littered the valley floor.

"We can't stand here and gape," said Dahoor. "Those—things—are still after us!"

The men began running again. The ancient bones crumbled into dust beneath their feet. Green cleared the way before them, hacking away at the remains with a machete.

Suddenly, they heard howls coming from the right. Then, from the left.

Then, the Mi-Go stood front of them as well, blocking their path.

Their bodies were stocky, apelike in shape, but with a distinctly human quality. They were six feet tall and covered with shaggy, coarse, snow-white hair, some with dark patches on their chests. Their faces were sturdy, with wide mouths featuring large teeth and prominent fangs. Their heads were conical, with a pointed crown. Their arms were long, reaching almost to the knees, and their hands sported fierce-looking claws.

The five men formed a small circle, guns ready, prepared to defend their lives.

"I regret that our short but eventful association had to come such a miserable end, Professor Whateley, Mr. Green," said Dahoor, sounding almost apologetic.

Whateley was almost hysterical. "I can't die here! Not when I'm so close!"

"You're not the only one with a problem, Professor!" rebuffed Green.

The Mi-Go slowly started moving towards them.

Suddenly, flares of all colors erupted in the sunset skies. Thundering noises echoed throughout the valley, its circular structure magnifying the rumble into a near-apocalyptic din.

The Mi-Go ran, terrified by this unprecedented display of man-made thunder and lightning.

Robur, flare gun in hand, stood on top of a huge masto-don skull and gestured at them.

"Quick! Follow me!"

As the hidden valley of K'n-yan was wrapped ever more tightly in a mantle of darkness, a small campfire burned bright inside the temple, its magnificent sculpted entrance standing as the last remains of a once mighty culture. Statues of long-vanished gods came to life in the flickering light. Robur and the surviving members of the expedition finished a meal that had been hastily cooked by the two remaining sherpas.

"Dahoor," said Robur. "I should have known you'd find your way here sooner or later. You're drawn to treasure like a fly to rotting meat."

"One is always pleased to see one's skills recognized, My Prince."

"I'm not your Prince anymore. Just Robur."

"Yes, of course, My Prince."

"You know this man?" Green asked Dahoor.

"We've met once or twice, yes," the guide replied.

"You haven't yet told us what you are doing here, Mr. Robur," Whateley interjected. Green noted that the Professor seemed rather ungracious towards the man whose sudden ar-rival from above had, after all, saved their lives.

"There's only one thing I want. You're welcome to eve-rything else, including fame. In fact, I'd rather that my pres-ence wasn't even mentioned..."

"And that one thing is?"

"It's known as the Crown of Genghis."

Whateley sniffed contemptuously. "So, you're a traffick-er in antiques too, no different than your friend Dahoor here?"

Robur smiled. "Oh no! I've come to destroy it."

Whateley reacted in shock, almost as if the newcomer had punched him. "What!? You can't do that. It's a priceless artifact. You can't be serious!"

"Deadly so, I'm afraid."

"But why?"

"I could tell you that it's none of your business, but I've heard of Miskatonic University, Professor Whateley, and I believe you deserve an honest answer. The cosmos is not unlike a tapestry. Scientists like you study its patterns, trying to fathom its meaning. But there are those who have peered behind the tapestry and know what lurks there. A long time ago, K'n-yan was home to a race of wise, civilized men..."

"Yes, the Yian Ho."

"Well, they became those shaggy things that almost killed you. The Mi-go are what's left of the Yian Ho. That's what the Crown did to them, and why it must be destroyed."

The next day, they began their exploration of the Temple. From the outer hall where they had spent the night, a beautifully-decorated corridor, meant to represent a descent into the underworld, took them deeper within the mountain. Its walls were painted with images of the Djad and the forgotten gods of the Yian Ho.

Lower down, they reached another hall, this one leading into a sacred chamber where mysterious ceremonies were conducted. It was a relatively large, rectangular room with four square pillars supporting the ceiling. Two side rooms and a small inner room were accessible from it. The entry walls were adorned with representations of the gods, while the pillars were mostly decorated with scenes from the Book of the Dead. The King of the Yian Ho was represented passing through nine gates guarded by statues representing the dreadful Rakashas, demons from the underworld.

Whateley studied the inscriptions in the light of his torch. "Amazing. It's all here. The entire history of the Yian Ho, and before them, the Dzyan..."

"Interesting indeed, Professor," said Dahoor, "but where is the gold?"

Robur smiled. "You're slipping, old friend. Those carvings are made of orichalcum."

The Hindu's eyes burned bright and he developed a sudden interest in the wall decorations. Green could see him already totaling up figures in his mind.

241

Whateley looked at the map. "It says the Crown was kept in the next chamber, the one guarded by the Rakashas..."

They entered a smaller chamber, walking past a short corridor lined on both sides with giant statues representing demon-like creatures with claws, sharp beaks and bat-like wings.

"There are your Rakashas," said Green.

"When I was a boy, the holy man told me demons would get me if I wasn't good. Now I wish I had believed him," remarked Dahoor.

Inside the chamber was an altar and on it lay a simple gold band, just large enough to fit a human head.

"The Crown of Genghis!" exclaimed Whateley. He ran towards the altar, grabbed the Crown and placed it on his head.

"Mine, at last!"

His face began changing, twisting, as if some powerful force was intent on remodeling his features. His eyes rolled back into their orbits, then returned to normal but the irises had gone white and the expression contained in them was distant. It was as if he was not gazing upon the room where they stood, but rather the unfathomable vision of another dimension.

"Whateley, what's happening to you?" asked Green.

"You fool! Whateley is dead!" said the spectral voice which issued from the archeologist's mouth.

"The Hour of the Scythe is almost upon us and I, the Servant of the Crawling Chaos, will at last unleash His Hideous Strength upon the Earth!"

Whatever force had taken possession of Whateley, Robur was ready. The Master of the *Albatross* reacted instantly by starting an incantation.

"Nosmo Cobis... Holo Erasma Rabis..."

Whateley raised his hand, eyes blazing with unholy energies.

"That pathetic spell has been out of fashion since the Monks of Montsegur in 1244, and even they were better at it than you are."

Robur was thrown to the ground.

"We the Kun Yin have served the Old Ones since Man, and those who came before, emerged from the primordial muck. We know you, Robur and your friend the Sâr Dubnotal, and all your other allies. Come the Hour of the Scythe, you will all die."

Whateley began to advance towards Robur, his hands extended forward. Dark tendrils of force seeped from his palms.

"But you—the Dark can't wait that long!"

Green was skeptical by nature about what he usually called the "fakir tricks" of India, but was open-minded enough to not question what he saw. He had beheld the previous scene with the dawning realization that far more than the possession of an invaluable ancient treasure was at stake. He grabbed his gun and shot Whateley, twice, aiming for the legs.

The archeologist staggered from the shots, halted, but did not fall. He turned towards Green, his face filled with so much pure hatred that the adventurer could not help but take a step back.

"For that, your pain will be increased a thousand-fold, mortal!"

Whateley gestured at the demon statues in the corridor.

"You who have slumbered for millennia, now by the Crown I wear—awake!"

Dahoor let out a bellowing scream of terror as the statues of the Rakashas—statues no longer—began to shake like a man waking up after a long slumber. Their stone eyes blazed open.

Almost faster than the eyes could see, the Rakashas leapt on the two hapless sherpas who had thought it safer to stay behind, closer to the chamber entrance. The two men fell screaming beneath the monsters' razor-sharp claws. Their eviscerated bodies collapsed to the floor like deflated balloons.

Green blasted one of the Rakashas into rubble with his rifle. Dahoor also shot at the advancing creatures. But the rubble, including the claws and beaks, continued to live and crawled towards its human prey.

"Sotheby's would have paid a king's ransom for that statue. Ah, Dahoor! Why does fortune always slip through your fingers?" bemoaned the guide.

Whateley, seeing the two men's powerlessness, gloated. "The Heart of Chaos awaits! The time has come for me to release the Guardian of the Gate. The Rakashas will soon feast upon your brains. I understand those are a delicacy. Ha! Ha!"

Believing his three remaining adversaries to be almost as good as dead, the late archeologist left the chamber with a Rakasha in tow.

Upon hearing the familiar clicking sound, Dahoor realized his gun was out of ammunition. If the Rakashas had been alive, they would have whetted their beaks in anticipation of the slaughter. As they were, they just continued their lumbering progression, stepping ever closer, claws extended, beaks hungry for the blood of their victims.

"I'm sorry I won't be able to get you that Chandela chess set we discussed last night, Mr. Green," said the Hindu.

"Where we're going, I doubt I'll have much opportunity to practice my game," replied the adventurer, realizing that it was only a matter of seconds before he, too, ran out of bullets.

Suddenly, Robur stood up and confronted the Rakashas, addressing them directly, barking orders as one would to a pack of wild dogs. Before Green and Dahoor's unbelieving eyes, the creatures stopped and appeared to heed what the mysterious man was saying.

Robur rubbed a sore muscle in his right shoulder, which had borne the brunt of his fall. Dahoor looked at him with effusive gratitude.

"My Prince! You are a man of many wonders!"

"That was authentic Yian Ho, wasn't it?" asked Green.

"Yes. Professor Whateley isn't the only one to speak it." He then pointed at the motionless Rakashas. "I told them that we were dead already. Lucky for us, their ability to tell the difference between life and death isn't very good. I doubt we have much time before they realize I lied."

They ran out of the chamber and into the great corridor—and almost straight into a pack of hostile Mi-Go! The ape-men, having recovered from their terrors of the previous evening, had followed the scent of the explorers all the way to inside the temple.

"Can these truly be what's left of the Yian Ho?" whispered Green.

"Yes," said Robur. "That's what Chaos will do to you, give or take a few centuries. But despite it, they're still fulfilling their duty. They're trying to protect the Crown. It's in their blood."

However, instead of pouncing on the strangers, the ape-men remained still. Then, a younger and particularly fierce-looking Mi-Go stepped forward and began uttering a few words which Green recognized as the same Yian Ho tongue Robur had used with the Rakashas.

"My Prince, I believe he's speaking to you," said Dahoor with a wan smile.

Robur began a dialogue with the Mi-Go. Whatever was said must have been convincing for the Hindu noticed that the ape-men had begun to look if not more friendly, at least as if they weren't planning to slaughter them all in the next few seconds.

Meanwhile, Green had kept an eye in the direction from which they had come. His face grew concerned.

"I hope you've convinced them that we're the good guys," he told Robur, "because it looks to me like the Rakashas have finally figured out that we're not really dead yet are intent on remedying the situation."

As soon as the Mi-Go saw the Rakashas, it was as if a dam had erupted. Nothing could contain the unbridled fury of the ape-men. The guardians of the Crown had recognized their ancient enemies and plunged into battle. Though the Rakashas were made of stone, even that could be pulverized, ground into fine particles, with unrelenting fangs and claws. The Mi-Go seemed to feel no pain from the many injuries the revived demons inflicted upon them. Their bodies appeared to regenerate at amazing speed and nothing short of decapitation seemed able to stop them.

During the combat, Robur grabbed Green and Dahoor. "We've got to stop Whateley from reaching the Heart of Chaos. He can't...."

"We, My Prince?" interrupted Dahoor. "With all due respect, I am very sorry but this humble tradesman has more than fulfilled his obligations..." The guide picked up bits of green orichalcum rocks that had broken loose during the battle and put them in his bag. "These scraps of orichalcum will be compensation enough. You two are great heroes but you must continue without me. These matters are beyond the powers of simple souls such as I..."

"I expected better from you, Dahoor," said Robur. "You stood by my side at Sinkuderam."

"That was long ago, My Prince. Besides it involved fighting the British. No, it's time for Dahoor to move on."

Robur made a gesture, as if to grab Dahoor, but Green stopped him.

"Let him go. He's right. This is no business for someone like him. Now I understand why Meldrum Strange wanted me to accompany Whateley on this expedition. The man tricked us all, but I'll see him and his damned Crown destroyed before I leave this god-forsaken place!"

Having said his farewells, Dahoor left, vanishing into the darkness of the corridor leading to the upper hall and the hidden valley.

As he stepped outside, he looked at the sky and the sculpted entrance behind him. For a minute, he stood still, undecided. Then he shrugged, muttered a short prayer and walked away, beginning the long and arduous trek that would lead him back to civilization.

Inside the holy chamber, the Mi-Go had defeated the Raka-shas. Chunks of broken statue littered the floor, where it was stomped into dust by the ape-men. The young Mi-Go who had spoken with Robur, looking bloodied but pleased with him-self, stepped forward and again addressed the Master of the Albatross.

"If we're going to beat Whateley to the Heart of Chaos, we're going to need a guide," said Robur. "This one seems to have a good idea of why we're here..."

"Then, let's follow him," said Green.

Robur answered the Mi-Go in Yian Ho, and all three continued their descent. The temple had been built over miles of natural tunnels and shafts, some as old as 40 million years. There were huge underground spaces, vast enough to house a cathedral, waterfalls, crystalline formations in hues of amber, white, blue and grey. Green thought they were now more than 500 feet below ground.

Following their Mi-Go friend, they continued ever downward, climbing acrobatically through a series of perilous shafts, jumping from cliff to cliff, holding their bodies at im-possible angles and positioning their weight before figuring out their way down the naked rock.

At one point, the two men stopped to take a breather on a ledge. "He says it's a shortcut," Robur said, pointing towards the Mi-Go, who was impatient to continue the descent.

"For him, maybe," said Green with a smile. Then, the explorer added: "Since you know so much, how about filling me in. Where are we going?"

"K'n-yan was built around a natural phenomenon the Old Ones called the Heart of Chaos. The magnetic power of the Earth is concentrated into one tight beam to the Heavens. My friend Seaton thinks it's like a beacon to other worlds. Me, I don't have an opinion. When the stars align to form a confi-guration known as the Scythe, the beam appears to cut through the very fabric of space. With the power of the Crown, Whate-ley can manipulate the phenomenon to open a gateway that will release, whatever you call it, the Hideous Strength, the

Creeping Chaos, the Guardian of the Gate, Yog-Sothoth... It's not pretty and it's usually hungry."

After an hour of arduous descent, they finally reached the bottom of the shaft. An opening allowed an odd greenish light to enter it.

As they emerged, they stepped onto a jutting stone platform overlooking a vast subterranean realm, a savage land filled with a primeval forest of giant trees, inhabited by giant insects and strange flying reptiles, lit only by that eerie greenish light. At its center was a green beam reaching up towards the Heavens—the Heart of Chaos.

Still led by their Mi-Go ally, Robur and Green ran briskly through the jungle towards the beam's point of origin.

Despite the urgency of their mission, neither man could stop themselves from occasionally taking a closer look at some extraordinary natural—or rather unnatural—wonder revealed by this amazing environment, like an oyster revealing the pearl inside.

Robur was fascinated by a giant white mushroom with oddly shaped red spots on its top, which appeared to inflate like a balloon, then explode softly, spreading its spores in the wind. Green saw giant flowers which attracted giant butterflies, which in turn met their ends in the webs of giant spiders.

But the Mi-Go waved them ever on, shouting at them in his strange language.

"I don't need you to tell me that he wants us to hurry," said Green, who had been entranced by the sight of a black lotus.

Finally, they spied Whateley, escorted by a Rakasha, barely ahead of them despite his considerable advance. The "shortcut" had paid off. He was making his way towards the beam that was the Heart of Time.

"It looks like we're still in time," said Robur.

Whateley was only a few hundred feet away from the beam when he saw Robur and Green. The face of the archeologist, or rather the thing that had been the archeologist, became contorted with rage.

"You?! This time, you won't stop us, Robur! Not when we're so close."

Whateley sent the Rakasha to attack the two men, thinking it would dispose of them easily. But the Mi-go who, at Robur's instructions, had remained hidden to encourage Whateley to waste his strongest weapon, sprang out of the jungle and met the challenge head on. Roaring his defiance, the ape-man savagely fought the demon statue.

Realizing that he had been tricked, Whateley shook his fist angrily. When he opened it, he released a blast of energy that hit Green, who was the closest to him.

Robur seized the opportunity to jump on the former archeologist and, wrestling with him, tried to wrest the crown from his head.

Whateley grabbed Robur by the neck and stared into his face as energy poured from his fiery eyes.

The Master of the *Albatross* collapsed screaming to the ground, smoke drifting from his face.

Then, Whateley blasted the Mi-Go who had just defeated the Rakasha.

"And now there is no one left to stand in the way of destiny," he said as he stepped into the beam.

The crown... Whateley's entire figure... began radiating a shimmer of strange energies, and coruscating waves of unearthly power that mingled with the beam. The column of light began pulsating to the rhythm of an alien song that the archeologist started to sing—a song written before the birth of galaxies, that no human larynx could possibly utter, and yet which fed the phenomenon.

Above, a black tear opened up in the very structure of space itself.

Darkness began to fill the cavern. Inside the fracture, one could see the phantoms of alien stars, bizarre shapes, other worlds and other galaxies... Horrible abysses of radiance... *Yog-Sothoth*.

Outside, the phenomenon spilled out over the mountain peak. The tear in space was weirdly omnipresent throughout the celestial axis that the beam followed.

In the hidden valley, the remaining Mi-Go howled in terror.

Plowing through the snows of the icy canyon, just outside the secret passages under the mountain, Dahoor, too, saw the fracture and addressed another, more fervent, prayer to the gods..

Aboard the *Albatross*, Tom Turner by his side, Sâr Dubnotal had been using his own mysterious powers to monitor the events and his face grew somber.

"Chaos is rising, Mr. Turner. Stand by to release the Void That Consumes, but not yet. The plan that Meldrum Strange and I designed still has one last chance to succeed. But if not..."

His hand moved ominously near a red switch.

In the cavern, near the Heart of Time, Green stood up, battered and bruised, and prepared to step forward into the beam where Whateley was still chanting.

Lying on the ground, Robur, his face badly burned and charred, shouted after him: "Don't do it! He'll fry you alive!"

"Like he tried to do to you?"

"I have protection against that kind of thing—you don't!"

"I've got something better..."

Green boldly stepped into the beam.

As he embraced Whateley and held him close with his left arm, he pulled a blood-red jewel from his pocket.

Immediately, the Crown changed colors, turning from its white-gold radiance to a sickly reddish-brown shade. Whateley screamed as the metal liquefied on his head, leaving charred marks on his forehead and dripping into his eye sockets, burning his eyes to cinders.

Above, Chaos flickered.

The loss of his eyes and the pain that would have incapacitated any human did not seem to stop the archeologist. "Where did you get that jewel? Who are you?" he snarled, looking with sightless orbits at the man who had defeated him.

"My name is James Schuyler Grim. In this part of the world, they call me JimGrim. Meldrum Strange hired me to keep an eye on you and he was right. And he gave me this trinket—the Heart of Ahriman—or of Azathoth—for just such an occasion."

Whateley's entire body had begun to liquefy and melt away, forming a putrescent puddle at Grim's feet.

Grim cast his eyes above. Chaos, while still flickering, was not gone—and showed signs of breaking through.

The adventurer extended his hand to Robur, inviting him to join him inside the Beam.

"The rift needs to be repaired but I can't do it alone," he said. "I don't have your expertise."

"I've done this before," said Robur with a wry smile. "Let me show you."

They held hands, both grasping the blood-red jewel. Sweat, tears, pain, even thin rivulets of blood seeped from their faces as they strained to repair the damage, close the breach...

"It's too strong," said Robur.

"No, we can win. We must win!" said JimGrim.

Aboard the *Albatross*, Dubnotal's hand rested on the red switch. The time had almost come. Only a few seconds remained before he would do what had to be done.

Suddenly, a third, bronzed hand joined Robur and Grim's.

"Maybe even great heroes can occasionally use simple souls such as me," said Dahoor.

And on that day, Chaos rested.

Robur, Dubnotal, JimGrim and Dahoor stood on the bridge of the *Albatross*, watching the snowy peaks of the Himalayas below them.

"You and Meldrum Strange cut it rather close this time, didn't you?" said Grim to Dubnotal. "The Heart of Ahriman... My role in all this..."

"We didn't know exactly what the Kun Yin plan was... If Robur had managed to get to the Crown before their pawn— Whateley—got his hands on it... You were there mostly as a back-up precaution, Mr. Grim. One that turned out to have been a bit of enlightened forethought, I'm happy to say."

"I haven't thanked you enough for coming back," said Robur to Dahoor.

"The orichalcum from the K'n-yan are thanks enough, My Prince. I'll be the richest man in Gezing."

"But you will keep the location of the Hidden Valley a secret?"

"My lips are forever sealed. After all, I am but a simple soul..."

Published in *Tales of the Shadowmen* Vol. 1, 2005

This (hopefully) funny pastiche in the styles of Agatha Christie and H. P. Lovecraft was originally written for a French book devoted to Hercule Poirot put together by Xavier Mauméjean and André-François Ruaud.

The Murder of Randolph Carter

My friend Hercule Poirot had come to spend a few days in Ghent to relax and reacquaint himself with the warm atmosphere of a town he had often visited during his youth.

Acting upon my recommendation, he had booked a room at the Pension Doucedame, Rue du Vieux Chantier, an old but respectable lodging house.

Alas, as increasingly happened to him these days, the horrible specter of crime haunted his every step, even in our beautiful city.

An American tourist named Randolph Carter was found murdered in the library one grey morning. And what a murder it was! The victim's body appeared to have been torn apart by some unfathomable monster who had vented its anger on him; his face reflected only unspeakable terror.

My friend's reputation preceded him; his crime-solving exploits during the Great War were still fresh in the minds of the Belgian Police; the investigation was entrusted to him in the hope he would quickly find the murderer and thus help calm the protests of the American Consulate.

After a week of arduous investigation, often thwarted by the lies and contradictory statements of the suspects—three other Americans who had arrived at the Pension soon after Mr. Carter—Poirot gathered us all in the library in the presence of Inspector Owen to inform us of his conclusions.

Everyone's attention was focused upon the detective as we all waited for his definitive solution to the murder of Randolph Carter.

"*Ph'nglui mglw'nafh Cthulhu R'lyeh*, n'est-ce-pas, *wagn'nagl fhtegn! Aaaaiiiiii!*" said Poirot, holding in his hand a copy of Quentin Moretus Cassave's renowned Flemish translation of the *Necronomicon*.

"*Fhtagn*," corrected Charles Dexter Ward.

"*Pardon?*" said Poirot.

"*Fhtagn*," said Dexter Ward. "It's pronounced *Fhtagn*. I can't understand you with your damned French accent."

Poirot shook his head in irritation.

"*Fhtegn*. That is just what I said, Monsieur Ward. Please, pay attention. This book, a 17th century edition, once part of the Comte d'Erlette's collection, a fine example of Belgian engraving, it is one of your obsessions, *non*? You can recite entire passages from memory. You and Monsieur Carter had both come to Ghent to negotiate the purchase of this rare book. But Monsieur Carter, he arrives a few days early and he buys the book before you. You are upset, *naturellement*, but you repress your anger and you go and talk to Monsieur Carter in this very room where we stand. You offer to buy the book from him for twice the amount he paid. He refuses. The anger, it becomes very strong. Then, you suggest that you should combine your expertise and exploit the book together. He turns you down again. And then, you learn that Monsieur Carter, he has bought the book with only one purpose: to burn it!"

The audience shivered with palpable surprise.

"I found a *briquet à amadou* in Monsieur Carter's pocket, a lighter powerful enough to produce a strong flame. Look at the corner of the book, here. The binding is charred. So Monsieur Carter, he was trying to burn the book, but he did not succeed. Why? I blame the damp that pervades this house," he said, throwing an unkind glance at Monsieur Doucedame, our hotelier. "Still, one fact leads to another. When you find out his purpose, you become furious. I made inquiries about you, Monsieur Ward. It seems you are afflicted with a serious personality disorder. You are subject to violent episodes during which even your friends, they say they do not recognize you..."

"I suffer from some gastric problems, yes," said Ward dismissively. "I have a sensitive stomach. What has that to do with this case?"

"*Eh bien*, when Monsieur Carter, he reveals his intentions to you, you become overpowered by your insane passion and you grab the first thing at hand, this Arumbaya fetish, and then, you strike!"

"You have no proof of that!"

"*Au contraire*! In your rage, you break a piece of the ear of the fetish, a piece that I found in your coat pocket later."

"You dirty, lying, Belgian weasel," screamed Ward, while being dragged away by Inspector Owen's men.

I thought that, because of his political connections, he would be quickly extradited and would not have to suffer Belgian jails for long.

"This nightmare is finally over," said Lavinia Whateley. "Thank you, Monsieur Poirot."

"I fear, Madame, that it has only begun."

The young woman blanched, if that was at all possible considering her extremely pale complexion. She was seven months pregnant and had told the Police she had come to Ghent for the waters. When apprised of the fact that there was no thermal source in our beautiful town, she had merely replied she had been misinformed.

I was no MD but her belly seemed abnormally large. I also could have sworn—but no doubt it was a trick of the light caused by the dimness of the *lampes à quinquet* that lit the Pension—that I'd seen it tremble and quiver, as if under a pressure exerted by some inhuman thing incubating inside.

"The nightmare of a young mother alone, pregnant with a child whose father is unknown," continued Poirot. "Please note, Madame, that I do not judge the scandalous behavior of a certain depraved American youth. Undoubtedly, you were the victim of some fiendish Oriental drug. A man, most evil, took advantage of your passivity... Your body barely conscious, pliant, supple, ready to yield to his bestial transports..."

Poirot's eyes glazed over, becoming lost in the distance. No doubt, his little grey cells were actively gathering clues, working to solve this baffling mystery.

"Poirot!" said Inspector Owen.

"*Ah oui, je m'excuse*," he said, batting his eyes. "The nightmare, as I was saying, of a young mother alone, pregnant, who fears to lose the inheritance she is counting on to provide for herself and her child!"

"Heavens! How did you know this?"

"*Très simple, Chère Madame.* Your cousin, Wilbur Whateley, he dies recently in a hunting accident. Normally, you would inherit his vast fortune. But then, you receive a letter from Monsieur Carter informing you that he, too, is a cousin of Wilbur. And according to the antiquated laws of the State of Massachusetts, it is the male cousin who inherits! So you take the first ship for Belgium where you know Monsieur Carter is going—I checked the passengers manifest of the *John Flanders*—because you want to plead your cause in person. At first, Monsieur Carter, he seems reasonable. He is ready to abandon the inheritance. *Mais voila*: he puts a condition to his offer. A horrible condition. I do not dare to repeat it here, but you know what I am talking about, do you not, Madame Whateley?"

The gesture of the young woman, clutching her hands over her stomach to protect her unborn child, answered more clearly than any of Poirot's remarks might have. I even thought I heard a hiss of rage that sent Murr, the Pension cat, slithering out of the room, but it was more likely the wind gusting through the fireplace.

"That night, your decision is taken," continued my friend. "You know that Monsieur Carter, he likes to nap alone in the library after dinner. You walk down very softly, armed with this three-pronged garden weeder that I later found hidden in the tropical fish aquarium. There, you find Monsieur

Carter, battered by Monsieur Ward, but still breathing. And you strike, with all the ferocity of a mother seeking to protect her child!"

Inspector Owen's men took Lavinia Whateley down to the station. The woman was in tears and I knew that no jury, be it Flemish or Walloon, would have the heart to condemn the poor child after such an ordeal. No doubt her child would grow up to become an outstanding citizen that would help Belgium project its pacifying influence abroad; a fearless reporter with a tuft of hair, for example...

"Congratulations for a fine piece of crime-solving, Monsieur Poiret."

"*Mais non*, I am not yet finished, Monsieur Marsh. And my name is Poirot, not Poiret or Popeau."

That David Marsh was a strange and repulsive man. A native of the small town of Innsmouth, he had a narrow head, bulging, watery-blue eyes that seemed never to wink, a flat nose, a receding forehead and chin, and singularly undeveloped ears. His skin was rough and scabby, indications that he either suffered from a rare firm of Ichtyosis, or that he was allergic to the *carbonade* drink served by Monsieur Doucedame.

"I had you investigated, Monsieur Marsh," said Poirot gravely. "You and your family are smugglers, pirates, the leaders of a town of pirates and smugglers. Your ships, they bring back drugs, slaves, pagan idols and God knows what else from the Southern Seas. But one man knew of your nefarious traffics: Monsieur Carter, who had gathered in the taverns of Antwerp enough evidence to have you all put under lock and key. Evidence which he was preparing to give to the Federal investigators. You were sent by your accomplices to insure his silence, in the most definitive fashion."

"I protest!"

"Do not interrupt me, Monsieur Marsh. You arrive in the library after Madame Whateley has left. The twin shadow of the Manneken Pis which so puzzled me, it was you! That detail, it confuses me, until I remember how much water you drink with each meal. You come into the library and there, you find Monsieur Carter, writhing in agony but not quite yet dead. Madame Whateley, she is a weak woman. So you see an opportunity to have someone else accused of your crime. You put your hands, your vile, slimy, viscous, strangling hands, around the neck of Monsieur Carter and you squeeze, squeeze, squeeze..."

"Poirot?"

"*Ah oui*, excuse me again, Inspector. Once your sinister task, it is concluded, you go back to the dining room and order your favorite dish, a plate of mussels. But instead of asking for them *à la crème*, as you usually do, you ask for *moules provençales*, a recipe that contains much garlic. Why? Because Monsieur Ward, he has told you of his stomach problems and you are trying to divert the attention, but Poirot, he isn't so easily fooled, *oh non, mon ami*."

"Please, listen to me," said Marsh. "It's true, I did come here to kill Carter, but when I saw the job the other two had done on him, I decided to leave things alone. I didn't lay a finger on him. He was still alive when I left the room."

"You lie, Monsieur Marsh. Only your face—you will excuse me for speaking frankly, your repulsively, obscenely hideous face—can explain the expression of unspeakable horror on the dying Monsieur Carter."

"I'm not hideous! Ask Pht-thyar-l'yi!"

"He is delirious. A typical sign of dissociative personality common amongst murderers. Take him away, Inspector."

"Do you really think he killed Carter?" I asked Poirot after the Police had removed the suspects and we prepared to leave the Pension Doucedame. "He seemed sincere."

"The little grey cells, they do not lie," said Poirot, lightly tapping his forehead. "Once we have eliminated the impossible, then whatever remains is bound to be the truth, even if, as was the case here, it is very strange. Because, if Monsieur Marsh is not the murderer, then the only hypothesis left is that the house itself killed Monsieur Carter; but houses, they do not kill people, *n'est-ce pas*, Monsieur de Kremer?"

Poirot shut the front door of Malpertuis behind him and together we stepped into the darkened street.

Published in *Tales of the Shadowmen* Vol. 3, 2007

CLUB VAN HELSING

To accompany The Katrina Protocol, *the English translation of my French novel* Crépuscule Vaudou, *published as part of the* Club Van Helsing *imprint, I wrote four additional short stories taking place within the framework of the Van Helsing family as imagined by Xavier Mauméjean and Guillaume Lebeau.*

The first of these stories was the prose adaptation of a comic-book story we wrote for The Forbidden Book, *a 2001 anthology put out by Renaissance Press. Exquisitely drawn by Philippe Xavier, it features the character of Hogun Temu, a wizard-judge of a long-lost African civilization. The story is framed within a narrative by Marie Laveau, the Witch-Queen of New Orleans, telling it to young Hugo Van Helsing. Marie and Hugo are among the protagonists of* The Katrina Protocol.

The Clay Dogs

To Philippe Xavier.

"Marie, please tell me a story!"

Marie Laveau looked at young Hugo Van Helsing. The rambunctious eight-year-old liked to come to play in the vast shady park of her mansion in Bayou St. John, and his uncle Ohisver was happy to let him enjoy the company of the great *mambo*. After a few hours spent running and hiding amongst the majestic cypresses encrusted with Spanish moss, Hugo would generally retreat from the sweltering heat and humidity and rush back inside the house, to enjoy its refreshing coolness. There, he would while away the rest of the afternoon reading *Doctor Strange* comics or listening to Marie's stories.

Marie, whom some still called the "Voodoo Queen of New Orleans," liked the boy. She had immediately detected great potential in him and had used her wiles to persuade Ohisver to entrust part of his education to her. She hadn't had to argue much. She knew that, properly raised, young Hugo might grow up to become a great *houngan*, one who, one day, could tip the scales in the eternal combat.

"Marie, please tell me a story!" repeated the boy.

The *mambo* smiled.

"What kind of story would you like today, Hugo?" she asked.

"Something with lots of black magic," he replied enthusiastically, still clutching one of his favorite *Doctor Strange* comics.

"Show me," said Marie, gesturing for Hugo to give her the book.

"This is the one where Doc fights Dormammu after he's returned to the Dark Dimension and Umar..."

"I see. Well, would you like me to tell you about another man who was also a great and wise magician, who fought evil in all its guises?"

"Yes, please! Was he a superhero?"

"After a fashion, I suppose. His name was *houngan* Temu... Do you know what a *houngan* was?"

"No."

"A *houngan* was many things in those days: a justice of the peace, a law-giver, a cop on the beat, if you will, endowed with great magical powers."

"Cool."

"This story takes place a long, long time ago, thousands of years ago, in Africa. Not the poor and wretched continent that we know today, but a mighty land, proud and powerful, home to vast empires which are less than dust today. One of these Empires was that of the Dogon, a wonderful people who lived in Western Africa. It was ruled by the wise Lébé Serou from his capital of Ife, which is remembered today by less than a handful of men. Keeping the peace throughout the Empire were the *houngans*, a group of learned and powerful beings who..."

"Like the *Green Lantern Corps*, you mean?" interrupted Hugo.

Marie smiled. She had seen his comic book collection and understood the reference.

"Yes, like the *Green Lantern Corps*," she nodded. "And Temu, the man whose story I'm about to tell you, was the wisest and kindest of all the *houngans*." She smiled wistfully. "Now sit down and listen..."

Houngan *Temu and the Clay Dogs*

Once upon a time, *began Marie, houngan* Temu was returning from a long journey beyond the great savanna that lay east of the Empire's farthest border. What he had done there is a tale for another day. Suffice it to say that he and his great mount and companion, Agna, were tired, hungry and thirsty.

"Praise Amma! We have finally crossed the desert," said Temu, as he spied the village of Dogul. "There we shall find food and water."

Dogul was one of the poor settlements which eked a meager subsistence from the waters of the Nyambeenge River, whose periodic floods helped keep the local fields fertile. It consisted of no more than 30 houses made of mud and brick, encircled by a semi-fortified wall that had seen better days.

"Yes, I know you've done all the work, Agna, and I'm grateful," continued Temu, speaking to his mount. "But think, our long journey is almost over and soon we'll again see my brother!"

Now, you may think that the *houngan* was addressing his beast in the way we talk to horses and dogs. Not so! In those days, other species shared the land with the sons of man. One of these was the *tô*, great reptilian creatures who were gifted with intelligence and great sensitivity.

The village gates were open, as befitted this time of peace, so Temu rode through them. The rays of the sun were still beating down as mercilessly as ever, even though the afternoon was already half-over. As the *houngan* approached the town square, with its sacred baobab tree growing in the center, providing shade and comfort for all, he beheld an appalling sight. A group of villagers had gathered and begun to stone a half-naked man who lie at the foot of the tree, his blood staining the dirt.

"Stone him!" "Kill the *puru*!" screamed the crowd, *puru* meaning abomination.

The Emperor had long banished the practice of public stoning and Temu thought that the man must have been accused of some particularly abominable crime to provoke such anger. Note that I said "accused" and not "guilty," for he was a wise *houngan* and did not presume guilt on the basis of appearances alone.

"Stop!" he shouted, stepping into the middle of the crowd. In his right hand, he proudly held the intricately-carved staff that was both the vessel of a *houngan*'s power and an indication of his rank. The villagers immediately recognized him for who he was, and separated to let him pass. None wished to incur the wrath of a *houngan*, especially one as tall and powerful-looking as this one.

"What is going on? What has this man done?" inquired Temu in the sternest tone.

The villagers looked at each other, fearful of facing the penalties for having broken the Law of the Empire. Finally, one of them, either bolder or more foolish than the others, stepped out and confronted Temu.

"He is a murderer!" he said, pointing at the victim. "He killed our beloved *Olubaru*!" The Olubaru was the chief and the elder of the village. "He deserves to die!"

Some in the back of the crowd began barking, "Yes! Stone him! Kill him!"

Temu banged his staff on the ground and the shouts stopped at once.

"Silence! I am Temu, *houngan* of the Dogon. Has this man been properly judged, as prescribed by the laws of Lébé Serou?"

No one answered. They looked at each other, or at the ground, mute with shame and fear. As the realization of their guilt spread, some began to shuffle away meekly. Others, their heads bent down in sign of atonement, approached the *houngan* to place themselves at his disposal.

"Give some water and food to my *tô* and keep the accused under guard," ordered Temu. "I will conduct an inquiry into the crime according to the Law."

The man who had narrowly escaped being stoned to death stood up and wiped the blood from his arms and his face.

"Thank you, mighty *houngan*," he said. "My name is Kemenem. I am innocent."

"We shall see," said Temu. Then, he turned towards the villagers and asked: "Where is your *Baru*?" If the Olubaru is like the Mayor of a town, the *Baru* is like its Sheriff.

A man wearing the traditional green hat of the *Baru* stepped forward. He stood a good head taller than the other villagers. His face showed pride and determination. He, too, held a staff, although its carvings were fewer and less complex than Temu's.

"I am Ginu, *Baru* of Dogul," he said, introducing himself.

"And I, *houngan* Temu of the Dogon, Master of the Old Speech. I salute you, worthy Ginu." The two men exchanged a ritual salute, lowering their staffs and holding them parallel to the ground. Then Temu continued: "So you have found this man Kemenem to be guilty of murder?"

As two of the villagers took Kemenem away, and others were bringing a bucket of water for Temu's mount, the *houngan* and the *Baru* walked away from the square and into the narrow streets of the village.

"Kemenem is of the Binu Yoma clan," Ginu explained. "They hated the late *Olubaru* because they said that he cast a spell to entice the waters of the Nyambeenge to flow towards our fields, which they claim made their own fields barren... It is a lie, of course. We never took more water than the Law allows. It is not magic, but the Gods of the river who gave us more water. No one can say otherwise."

"I see," said Temu. "So you think that Kemenem came to kill your *Olubaru* to repay the harm he supposedly did to his clan?"

"Yes, I do."

"May I ask what other evidence you have?"

"After his wife found the *Olubaru*'s body," said Ginu, "we searched the house and found Kemenem hiding in a closet."

"A compelling case, it seems," said Temu, after a moment of reflection. The *houngan* then sensed an almost imperceptible easing in the *Baru*'s body. Ginu was trying to hide his relief from Temu, but had failed. The *houngan* thought that there was much here that remained hidden. So he said: "I would like to visit the home of the deceased." And at once, he sensed Ginu tensing again, confirming his suspicions.

"Very well. Follow me," said the *Baru*, barely concealing his displeasure.

They took a turn to the right and soon arrived before a house that was much larger than the others and more richly-decorated. Temu noticed the ceremonial markings above the threshold and nodded in approval. The *Olubaru* had obviously been a devout man, highly respectful of the Law of the Dogon, and had strictly followed all of the Emperor's orders.

Ginu knocked on the door. It soon opened, revealing a beautiful young woman dressed in a rich purple gown that made her look like the loveliest of orchids. Her eyes shone brightly, like black pearls. She wore the stone of widowhood on her forehead.

"This is Yapilu, the *Olubaru*'s widow," said Ginu. "Yapilu, this is *houngan* Temu."

"*Amma Inu*, Yapilu!" said Temu, bowing slightly.

"The *houngan* is investigating the death of your husband," explained Ginu once they had stepped inside. The air was fresh, smelling of rare perfumes. The walls has been painted white and the floor was stone-tiled, all signs of a modest but comfortable household.

The young woman's eyes betrayed her surprise. "But I thought that Kemenem had killed the *Olubaru*?" she said.

"I regret to inflict further pain on you, honorable Yapilu," said Temu, "but the Laws of Lébé Serou are clear. May I see the place where the noble *Olubaru*'s body was found?"

The young widow nodded and silently took them to a round adobe room decorated with many sacred paintings and carvings. On a shelf, next to a closet, were small jars, sculpted stones and a pile of scrolls and tablets. Several sacred masks stood on ornate stands, apparently undisturbed. At the center of the room was the traditional ritualistic brazier inside a tripod made of orichalcum, and a small altar sculpted in a block of dark granite.

"This is where my husband worked his spells at night," explained Yapilu, somewhat unnecessarily.

Temu made a slow tour of the room, examining every item carefully. As he expected, there were no other entrances or exits, no windows, no skylights, not even a single crack in the wall. The *Olubaru* had been a most conscientious man.

"How did Kemenem get in?" he finally asked Yapilu.

"He'd come to beg my husband for work, and been allowed to stay on the property, in exchange for tending the gardens..."

"Obviously a pretext to do his dirty work," interrupted Ginu.

"The *Olubaru* was too generous," agreed Yapilu, with an undercurrent of raw emotion that Temu construed to be spite. "Kemenem slipped out of his shed last night, came into the house and killed the *Olubaru*. Then, when he heard me coming, he sought refuge in that closet where my husband kept his sacred herbs."

She pointed at the closet located next to the shelves. Its door, a simply decorated wood panel with an ordinary latch, was still half-open.

"I see," said Temu. Then, the *houngan* pointed his staff towards the three statuettes that stood on the altar next to the brazier.

"These clay dogs are?..."

"They are meant to draw the backlash of the spells cast by my husband," answered Yapilu.

"Ah yes. I am familiar with the practice." Temu raised his staff, clearly intending to smash the statuettes. "Let's see what magic the noble *Olubaru* has been casting recently..." Seeing Yapilu step back in panic, he added: "Have no fear. I am a *houngan*."

The staff hit the clay dogs. Small, white butterflies made of light briefly floated in the space over the broken statuettes, then, one by one, vanished. Temu watched them attentively. They did not convey a feeling of bad magic, only of good.

Then the *houngan* walked to the herb closet and pointed at the unlatched door.

"This is the closet where you found Kemenem?" he asked.

"Yes," said Yapilu. "I summoned Ginu immediately. Kemenem didn't have time to escape."

"He was inside? With the door locked?"

"Yes."

Temu made another tour of the room to give himself time to think, but he had seen enough.

"I would like to talk to Kemenem now," he said.

Ginu looked none too pleased, but went out and promptly returned with the accused in tow. Some salve had been used on his wounds and he was no longer bleeding. Temu instructed the man to sit down and began his interrogation by repeating the charges against him.

"Yes, it is true that our fields had grown fallow, and many of us blamed the *Olubaru*, but I did not," replied Kemenem. "When I came asking for work, he let me tend his garden and sleep in the shed outside. He was a kind and noble man. I grieve for his death as much as anyone else."

"What happened last night?" asked the *houngan*.

"I worked all day. The Sun was very hot. After Yapilu served dinner, I went back to my shed as I always do. I fell asleep, I did not go out. I don't know how I ended up in that closet, but I know I did not kill the *Olubaru*." Then, he repeated again, more forcefully: "He was a kind man!"

Temu stepped back and now addressed Ginu and Yapilu.

"When you want to cure a mad bull, seek the small thorn that drives him crazy," he began. "When seeking the truth of a murder, always search for the smallest *nyama*, for it is there that the greater evil hides..." A *nyama* is an evil stain, an ill-omened blot, a perfidious lie.

The *houngan* continued: "Ginu tried to hint at me that the *Olubaru* had cast black magic, yet none of the clay dogs showed any such thing. Yapilu accused Kemenem of having hidden in the closet after murdering her husband, a closet whose door, by her own admission, was locked, *even though it clearly locks only from the outside.*"

The crestfallen faces of Ginu and Yapilu as they looked at the latch on the outside of the closet's paneled door was all the confession that any Imperial Magistrate would have required, but Temu relentlessly pursued his discourse.

"Since Kemenem could not have locked himself in, someone else had to do it, someone who had drugged his evening meal so that he would sleep and could be moved to the closet without awakening..." Then, the *houngan* directly confronted the two whom he had just accused of murder. "The *Olubaru* was old, and perhaps too generous with his wealth. You are both young and wanted him out of the way, but you had learned the lesson of the clay dogs. Someone else was needed to draw the backlash of your own evil actions. When Kemenem moved in, you saw the perfect opportunity and the deed was done."

Ginu had quickly recovered from the shock of having been so casually exposed. His hands gripped his staff tightly. *Too tightly*, thought Temu.

"An admirable deduction, worthy *houngan*; what do you intend to do now?" asked the *Baru*.

"The law of Lébé Serou is clear," replied Temu. "You and Yapilu will be taken to Ife to face the justice of the Emperor."

"I believe you have just returned from a long journey from the Lands Beyond?"

"That is true."

"So no one in Ife yet knows of your return?"

"Also true," said Temu, calmly. "Sadly, I have been unlucky in my efforts to communicate with the Empire."

"Then I can foresee a more pleasant alternative for Yapilu and me," said Ginu, grinning evilly.

The renegade *Baru* pointed his staff at Temu, murmuring some words in the Old Speech. A hideous, powerful *Ifrit* rose from within the wood and grew in size, until it loomed gigantically over the silent *houngan*, encircling the man's impassive form within its fleshy coils.

Temu, unfazed by the demon who was preparing to devour him, tapped his staff on the ground. An even greater *Ifrit* suddenly arose, a mighty horned beast bellowing as if all the circles of Hell itself could no longer hold him captive. Growing to truly colossal size, it briefly stood silhouetted against the evening sky, towering over the village itself. Then, swifter than the eyes could follow, it appeared to shrink and then swooped down, devouring Ginu's own demon, chewing it to pieces and swallowing it in a single, mighty gulp.

Then, the *Ifrit* turned towards the evil *Baru* and, almost as an afterthought, plucked him off the ground with its clawed hand as casually as a boy plucks a daisy from a field to hand to his girlfriend.

The *Baru*'s scream of horror and pain was soon cut short.

"Ginu!" cried Yapilu in anguish as she saw her lover being consumed by the demon.

His grisly task finished, the *Ifrit* evaporated into a foul-smelling miasmic cloud which coalesced around the *houngan*'s staff before being slowly reabsorbed into it.

"I am *houngan* Temu, Master of the Old Speech," said Temu to the few villagers who had dared enter the house. "This is the Law of the Dogon. I will appoint a new *Baru* and Yapilu will go to Ife to face the justice of the Dogon."

Temu stepped outside the house. Agna, his *tô*, was already waiting for him, having sensed that his master's business was done and that the time had come for them to depart. The *houngan* mounted his faithful companion and left Dogul, riding north.

"As for me, my road is still long before I gaze again upon the face of Emperor Lébé Serou—my brother."

Published in *The Katrina Protocol*, 2008

Buccaneer Izak Van Helsing was one of my creations, to flesh out Hugo's family tree, but his companion, the beautiful pirate lady Scarlet Lips comes from the Hexagon Comics series Dragut *and was created by Guido Zamperoni*

Women, Fools and Serpents

> *"We should always deal cautiously with fire, water, women, fools, serpents and members of a royal family; for they may at once bring about our death."*
> Chanakya
> (Indian politician, 350 BC-275 BC)

"I seek the human Van Helsing, who claims to be hunting monsters," said the Sea Serpent.

The creature had suddenly burst out of the water and towered over the ship, terrifying the sailors who were already signing themselves and confessing a vast litany of sins.

"Van Helsing, you say? Never heard the name," said Izak Van Helsing, Captain of the *Sémillante*, without losing his cool. He turned towards his second in command, first mate and not-so-secret lover, the beautiful Scarlet Lips. "Does that name ring a bell, darling?" he asked her

"I can't say that it does," replied the blonde woman.

"Sorry, can't help you there, mate," said Izak to the Serpent, flashing what he hoped would look like a convincingly sincere, warm smile.

"What a bother," said the Serpent. "If you could help me find that pesky mortal, I might be prepared to be generous..." The Monster tried, but utterly failed, to look sympathetic.

"Generous, how so? asked Izak Van Helsing, raising an eyebrow.

"I will promise you a quick and painless death instead of chewing on the marrow of your outer appendages," suggested the Serpent.

"A tempting offer, indeed, but I still find myself oddly unmotivated," said Izak Van Helsing. "Perhaps if I were to know more about your quest... Why exactly do you seek that Van...? Van...?"

"Van Helsing. It has come to my attention that that wretched little man has had the temerity to stalk some of this world's greatest denizens."

"Ah!—you mean Monsters."

"Watch your tongue, manling. I mean creatures such as me, who are ancient, learned and beautiful..."

"Sorry to interrupt," interjected Scarlet Lips, "but we've just met the Zombie King in Saint-Domingue and, Lord, he was *uuuugly*!"

"Well, perhaps not zombies then," said the Serpent.

"And what about that mangy Kroatoan wolf-monster, flea-ridden and slobbering like a dog in heat," said Izak Van Helsing, snapping his fingers. "Have you ever seen anything more pathetic?"

"...Or werewolves..."

"And what about the fish-men of..."

"Enough!" shouted the Sea Serpent, causing the ship to almost capsize. "I'll grant you that not all of our races are truly beautiful..."

"Or learned," said Izak Van Helsing. "You should have tried talking to the Last Ghoul of Lemuria. He could barely spell his name in Sanskrit."

"...Or learned," grudgingly admitted the Serpent, gritting his teeth, producing a noise not unlike the screech of chalk on a blackboard. "But we *are* ancient!" he finished in a triumphant tone.

"Yes, you are that. Can't argue about that, can we, darling?" said Izak Van Helsing to Scarlet Lips.

"Nope. Some of these monsters are really really old," she replied. "In fact, I've heard—but no, it would hardly be polite to mention this before our towering scaly guest here."

"What have you heard, female?" roared the Serpent. "And be careful. I have a mind to end this most annoying of conversations right now and consign you all to Davy Jones' locker."

"But then, you wouldn't find out what she knows," pointed Izak Van Helsing.

"If you insist..." said Scarlet Lips.

"I do, I do," said the Serpent.

"Well, it's been said that some of you elder creatures are so old that... that... well, you know..."

"No, I don't," said the Serpent.

Scarlet Lips tapped her forehead slightly in an unmistakable gesture.

"...That you've all gone a little ga-ga," she finished.

"Ga-ga?" roared the Sea Serpent, causing a tear in the mizzen sail.

"Senile. Doddering. Feeble-minded."

"I know what 'ga-ga' means, female! I mastered your inane language 300 years ago!"

"Sorry," said Scarlet Lips, looking properly apologetic.

"She's right, you know," interjected Izak Van Helsing. "I've even heard some no doubt misguided souls claim that you can't even remember your own name."

"Of all the stupid things!... That's absurd! I am Jörmungandr, also known by the secret name of Uroborus and..."

Suddenly, there was a long silence. The Sea Serpent had realized that it had said too much, for his name was his secret, his secret was his name, and there was much power in both.

Izak Van Helsing smiled. It was an ugly, triumphant smile, nothing like the smile with which he had first greeted the Serpent.

From his pocket, he produced a bottle made of a substance that might have been glass, except that it was totally dark and did not reflect light.

It was a matter of mere seconds to incorporate the true name of the Sea Serpent into the eight conjurations of the Saaamaaa Ritual, recite them aloud, and thus force the creature inside the bottle.

"So much for the Sea Serpent," said Izak Van Helsing to Scarlet Lips. "He was much easier than I thought. They may be ancient and learned, but they sure are stupid. What's next on the list?"

"Something about a giant white whale, I think..."

Published in *The Katrina Protocol*, 2008

Ohisver Van Helsing, Hugo's uncle, is also my creation for The Katrina Protocol. *The fanatical Jesuit, Father Rodin, was created by Eugene Sue for* The Wandering Jew, *and is one of the most chillingly cunning villains in the history of popular literature. It was Rodin's secret plan which, after several plagiarized versions, ended up being the inspiration for the hateful* Protocols of the Elders of Zion.

Sacred Monster

December 13, 1968. A Friday.

Inside the empty hangar was a cross. It was made of wood, ancient wood, and it had been lovingly erected by the two monks.

On that cross was the Monster.

He was whimpering softly and occasionally tried to shake himself free, but the blood-encrusted leather bonds with which the monks had tied him to the cross would neither break nor slip. Besides, he had been drugged.

Two men entered.

"This is the Monster," said Father Rodin. "You know what to do."

"Yes," said Ohisver Van Helsing. "Damn you, yes, I do."

The Jesuit ignored his companion's angry outburst. From a leather pouch he carried over his shoulder, he pulled a dagger that was made of a spear's head mounted on a bronze handle. He offered it to his companion.

"This is Longinus' weapon. Go!"

Ohisver took the knife and walked slowly towards the cross. Towards the Monster.

The two monks silently stepped aside to let him pass.

"I'm sorry, I'm really sorry" said Van Helsing softly to the Monster. Then, with all his strength, he plunged the blade deep into the creature's chest.

The Monster screamed.

The Day Before...

When Ohisver Van Helsing returned from Tokyo, Zaka told him that he had a visitor waiting for him—a man who had simply introduced himself as "Father Rodin."

"So, you've come to collect, priest," said Ohisver to the Jesuit, coming straight to the point, without any words of welcome.

Father Rodin was a tall, almost ascetic man, with steel-grey hair. He was dressed in an ordinary black clergyman's suit. His face was that of an Inquisitor and in his eyes burned a fanatical flame. This was a man used to power, used to command, who brooked no disagreements.

"Yes, I have, Mr. Van Helsing," he replied. "A life for a life, a soul for a soul. It is the Eternal Covenant, isn't it?"

Ohisver poured himself a stiff drink from the liquor cabinet and drank it quickly. He did not bother to offer one to Rodin, for he knew the Jesuit didn't drink.

"Yes," he said. "I will honor our agreement. What do you want me to do?"

"I'll tell you in a moment," said the Jesuit. "You may find some comfort in knowing that you will perform a great deed in the service of our Holy Mother the Church."

"I care little for the Church."

"You will see the error of your ways in time, I'm sure. The Church has been generous towards your family over the centuries."

"Old stories. What do you want from me today?"

"Why, I want you to slay a Monster, of course," said Rodin with a mirthless smile.

"I don't understand."

Now, it was suddenly Father Rodin's turn to hesitate. Ohisver Van Helsing noticed that, for the time, the Jesuit avoided his eyes. The priest licked his thin lips then said:

"Throughout history, God has occasionally chosen to incarnate a portion of Himself into human form, a man whom we call His Son..."

"You mean, Jesus."

"Yes, Jesus—and perhaps a few others, whom we have failed to identify and destroy in time."

"Destroy the Son of God?" said Ohisver Van Helsing, surprised. "But isn't that against your faith?" Now he understood the Jesuit's reluctance to speak.

Father Rodin's nostrils flared. Van Helsing had never seen him this upset.

"We already have a Messiah. We already have a Church, Mr. Van Helsing," said the Jesuit, curtly. "We don't need any more."

"So you want me to slay the Son of God who apparently has returned. I get it. You don't want the competition."

"No!" shouted Rodin. Then, the priest composed himself. Calmly, he continued: "No, it's not just that. Think of the millions who have died during the crusades, all the *jihads*... Do we want God's word to be misinterpreted again, to start new faiths, to launch new armies of fanatics who will soon be wading in blood through our cities?"

"I see your point, I suppose. It's an interesting philosophical debate, anyway. I always wondered what your Church would do if Jesus were to come back. Now, I know. But you haven't really answered my original question. Why can't you do the job yourself? God knows you've slain your hundreds over the years, Rodin. Why choose *me* to be your executioner?"

"Because you slay monsters and the man we seek *is* a monster. A profanation of the Divine incarnated as mortal flesh; what could be more monstrous? He is what our French brethren call a *Monstre Sacré*, a Sacred Monster..."

"Still, you wouldn't invoke the pact we made 16 years ago in Brazil when you saved Maria's life..."

"Her soul."

"Yes, Maria's *soul*, if you only needed my expertise as a Van Helsing. Tell me the truth."

"It is a matter of doctrine..." Rodin began.

"Cut to the chase," said Ohisver Van Helsing.

"Very well. Our, er, spiritual investigations have led some of us to believe that the man who slays the Sacred Monster himself becomes cursed, loses his soul and, even after death, will not find eternal peace."

"Ha! Now the truth comes out. You're too chicken to do the job yourself and lose your precious immortality, so you want me to do it."

"A soul for a soul. You owe us."

"Very well, I'll do your dirty job, Rodin. It isn't everyday that one kills the Son of God, after all. And you can take your curse and stuff it, too. I'm a Van Helsing. We *are* the curse!"

Back to scene...

...The Monster screamed.

Then his body appeared to undergo a mysterious transformation. Before, he had seemed almost angelic, radiating a unique power, a divine charisma.

Now, he was just a man, a worn-out, tired-looking man—and yet, he lived—and yet, he breathed. The two monks carefully undid the straps, bandaged his wound, which, oddly, had stopped bleeding, and helped him back to his feet.

Ohisver Van Helsing, still clutching the bloodied dagger, turned towards Father Rodin.

"I don't understand. Didn't I just kill him?" he asked.

"Yes, you killed the Divine Essence that resided within him, but the Mortal Host lives on. Now he's just a poor, wretched, soulless man, doomed to die."

The Jesuit took the blade of Longinus from Ohisver Van Helsing's hand without a protest.

"We have refined our methods over the ages," the priest added. "Our spells no longer kill the mortal half of the Monster."

"So I am not...?"

"Oh, yes, I'm sorry to say, you are still most definitely damned. You *have* just killed His Son after all."

Outside, the monks helped the man into a cab. Las Vegas

278

sparkled in the distance, like a Christmas tree incongruously deposited in the middle of the Nevada desert.

"You will remember nothing, Mr. Presley," said one of the monks, completing the spell of amnesia.

"Just... call me... Elvis," said the Man Who No Longer Was A Monster, slurring his words.

He needed a drink.

Published in *The Katrina Protocol*, 2008

The last story included The Katrina Protocol *was translated from the French and featured the character of the indomitable and resourceful Sydney Gordon, created by French science fiction writer Richard Bessiere. The Gordon story is framed in a conversation between Hugo Van Helsing and his attorney, Zigor Side, both created by Xavier Mauméjean and Guillaume Lebeau.*

Don't Throw Granny to the Xhlingniarf

"Why don't you use something from your vault as extra protection?" asked Zigor Side.

The attorney and his client, Hugo Van Helsing, were having breakfast at the Amsterdammer Club. In a couple of hours, they were scheduled to meet at the Central Park Boathouse with Prescott Brown of the Clock Company and a representative from Morrison, Morrison & Dodd.

"What vault?" said Hugo.

Zigor burst out in a joyless laugh.

"Come on, Professor! This could just about be the most important meeting of your life—the most dangerous too, maybe. I'm doing my lawyerly duty here by suggesting that you improve your chances of getting out of it alive by having some kind of hidden ace up your sleeve, and you start going coy on me?"

"I don't know what you're talking about, Mr. Side," said Hugo, coldly.

"You're a terrible liar, you know."

Hugo was unable to repress a tight smile. "Not true. I'm an excellent liar," he said.

"For your common variety cop or immigration officer, maybe, but I'm a master of the bar. I've cross-examined some of the best liars in the world. You wouldn't stand ten minutes if I had you on the stand."

Hugo quickly finished his cup of tea, folded his napkin and then looked at his watch. "Very well, we still have some time left before we have to go. What do you want to know?" he asked.

"I've heard that you have a secret vault somewhere down here where you keep all kinds of dangerous artifacts and magical weapons, not unlike..."

Zigor lightly tapped the spot under his stained shirt where Hugo knew the Medallion of Damballah hung.

"That's true. We do have such a vault, but it would be sheer lunacy to try using any of the items we keep down there against our enemies. The catastrophes we might accidentally unleash would far exceed our current problems with Mr. Barnum."

"Well, yeah, but..."

"No ifs ands or buts, Counselor. Let me tell you the story of our last acquisition. In fact, I'll have our latest contributor tell it to you himself..."

Hugo Van Helsing got up and walked to a nearby table. There, he tapped on the shoulder of a middle-aged man with a mop of unruly brown hair and twinkling, blue eyes. After a few minutes of conversation, the man followed Hugo back to the table.

"Mr. Side, this is Sydney Gordon, features editor at *The New Sun*. Mr. Gordon, this is my attorney, Mr. Zigor Side."

Zigor had made a face when he had heard the name of the paper, something that did not escape the journalist.

"I know, I know," said Gordon, "we're a tad less reputable than the *Weekly World News*. My last headline was *Angelina Adopts Alien Baby*—and I'm proud of it. But I know you too, Counselor. You're hardly one to criticize when it comes to trawling the gutters."

"Mr. Gordon's paper and I have enjoyed a profitable and mutually-rewarding relationship over the years," interjected Hugo Van Helsing. "They have often generated information that proved crucial to us..."

"...And we, in turn, have enjoyed some of the world's juiciest exclusives. By the way, thanks for the Big B's phone number, Prof. He'll be our next featured celebrity."

"Mr. Gordon, I would like you to tell Mr. Side the story of the Xhlingniarph, in your own words. I want to convince him that whatever we bury in our vault is better left buried."

"My pleasure, Professor..." began Sydney Gordon.

Sydney Gordon's story:

They say that bad things always come in threes. I'm the living proof of that.

The first bad thing that happened to me, last Christmas, was Margaret's news that her mother Iris was coming to spend the holidays with us.

"Us" means the Gordon family, i.e.: Sydney, head of the household, at least according to the US census bureau form, Margaret, my wife, and Bud, my 20-year-old son. I'll be candid: at this point in my wretched life, I only have two dreams left. One is to see the Red Sox beat the Yankees, the other is to see Bud leave his computer and the lair that he calls his room to rejoin the human race.

So the news of Iris coming to spend the holidays with us definitely meant that I wouldn't be able to watch sports on TV and guaranteed Bud's isolation. So much for dreams.

Because, compared to Iris, Cruella deVil and the Wicked Witch of the West are like Mother Teresa, and I know what I'm talking about because I've met the Wicked Witch. Iris has buried five husbands, who probably preferred an earlier run towards their little plot of Heaven, as opposed to the continued existence in this Valley of Tears that their lives must have been like.

The second bad thing that happened—but that, I understood only later—was a letter that I received from an El Paso, Texas, attorney informing me that, during the sale of the old Gordon ancestral home, a.k.a. the shack, they had found a chest that belonged to my grandfather, the explorer Francis X. Gordon. The worthy shyster asked me if I wanted to take possession of it, which I could, as long as I paid him a hefty fee naturally, lawyers not being philanthropists. I'm a sentimental person, so I said yes. A bad mistake, as you will soon discover.

The third bad thing.... But let's not get ahead of ourselves...

On Christmas Eve, after the excellent meal cooked by Margaret, we gathered around the tree to open the presents. As we do every year, we had invited our friends, Professor Archibald Brent and his wife Gloria, to spend the evening with us. The word "presents" had even managed to convince Bud to crawl out of his lair. That boy had smelled the possibility of a new game for his PlayStation the way a starving ogre smells a virgin; his every instinct had told him that "Granny" hadn't come empty handed.

Let's talk about "Granny" for a moment. During the day, Iris had beaten her own world record in the Perfidious Statements contest, with new ground-breaking entries like: "Margaret, didn't you date a Lenny Goldberg in college? I've heard he was just appointed Ambassador to Filikistan." Or my favorite: "You know, they have pills for that sort of dysfunction nowadays," accompanied with a pointed look in my direction.

Bud's instincts had not led him astray. Granny had indeed brought with her the latest PlayStation game, *Killer Bondage Nuns IV*, and my son, who was smarter than he looked, and to my great surprise, pulled out a present wrapped in some tacky gift paper, to give to his grandmother.

"Oooh that's so sweet," cooed the Granny Monster. "This boy must take after his mother."

Once unwrapped, we discovered a small glass jar, Persian-style, with lovely painted swirls and characters on it, quite exquisite really, not at all the type of artsy present I would have expected Bud to buy. In fact, how had he bought it? If he had ordered it on line, we would have seen the delivery man. It was a mystery.

"For you, Granny," said my hypocritical son, simultaneously grabbing his videogame, then beating a quick retreat

283

to his lair, just like an Ogre who has just received a copy of *3000 Ways to Serve Virgins* from the Good Cook Book Club of the Month and is eager to try a recipe.

If you watch CNN, you already know what happened next. Iris had the bright idea of removing the glass stopper that kept the jar closed. Immediately, a *Xhlingniarph* came out, the size of which made King Kong look like a Hobbit. The creature then began roaming through the city, devouring two US Army divisions, 12 fighter jets, 24 TV news vans, 3245 persons of good will, including seven Santa Claus and two Frenchmen.

I could write a book about it, but I already sold the film rights to Ryan Entertainment, so now I don't have to and you'll have to wait for the film. I'm that smart.

Archie eventually managed to decipher the characters painted on the jar. It was some kind of ancient tongue used by a long-gone tribe from Northern Afghanistan. It explained that the jar contained the spirit of the *Xhlingniarph* (that's what it sounded like), the God of Mean, bottled up by a Holy Man whose name has been forgotten by History—that bitch!

It then came out that Bud, pressed to find some kind of present for Iris, had broken into Francis X. Gordon's chest, which I had stored in the attic. A fractured lock, some wrapping paper and presto—instant gift!

So I hear you ask, the third bad thing happened when Iris uncorked the jar and freed the Xhlingniarph?

Not at all! We New Yorkers are used to giant monsters walking down Fifth Avenue, swallowing tourists like M&Ms. No big deal.

The third bad thing actually happened when Iris said: "This is all your fault, Sydney. If you gave that boy enough money, he wouldn't have to ransack through your old garbage to find a suitable Christmas present for his dear old Granny."

At that point, I don't know what came over me, but I pushed Iris back and she fell into the jar.

Yes, you heard me right. *Into* the jar. *Inside* it.

And right there and then, the Xhlingniarph vanished. Poof! In one fell swoop. Just like that. Everyone and everything he had swallowed before found themselves back exactly where they were when the demon had grabbed them, with not even a slight headache.

Archie explained that the Xhlingniarph required a sacrifice, the gift of someone incredibly mean and nasty. Where 3425 New Yorkers had not sufficed, Iris, on the other hand, had done the job.

So I hear you say: "All's well that ends well, right?" For New York, undoubtedly. But for me, not so much. If I don't want to continue sleeping on the living room couch where Margaret has exiled me, I'd better pray that Archie finds a way to extract Iris from the jar.

And that's the third bad thing.

Published in *The Katrina Protocol*, 2008

ON THE WHITE RIVER

In addition to the story featuring Sydney Gordon, we have written a number of other stories for various books published by Rivière Blanche, *our French sister imprint. The first two feature André Caroff's* Madame Atomos, *a ruthless Japanese scientist who lost her family to the A-bomb which destroyed Nagasaki and is out for revenge. The* Madame Atomos *novels are scheduled to be translated and released by Black Coat Press.*

Madame Atomos' Christmas

Winter had come early that year and, with the approach of Thanksgiving, consumers' thoughts had already turned towards Christmas.

Dallas had hung its traditional season's decorations across its boulevards and avenues, and the department stores on Market Street had begun to decorate their windows accordingly.

There was enough of a chill in the air to easily conjure up images of turkey and roasted chestnuts.

Madame Atomos was dejectedly watching the efforts of a clumsy department store employee, promoted to decorator for the occasion, to hang a red plastic Santa Claus above an impressive pile of newly-arrived color televisions.

It was the hour of the local news broadcast.

Only a few months before, her first attack against the country she hated so much had failed miserably. However, she had succeeded in inflicting thousands of deaths upon her sworn enemy: the United States of America. Still, all that had happened on the East Coast and the few Texans who knew the truth, despite the news blackout arranged by the FBI, were used to their Eastern colleagues' exaggerations. In fact, the good citizens of the Lone Star State took the whole thing with a hefty grain of salt. Wasn't New York where a giant ape had allegedly once climbed the Empire State Building? Hadn't they been told about a flying saucer and a giant silver robot paralyzing Washington DC? And what about that bronze fella and all his gimmicks? No, really, a good Texan couldn't very well believe in all the tall tales that one read in Eastern papers.

The store employee had just failed to hook the Santa Claus for the third time. Madame Atomos sighed. She had stopped there to look at the local news to see if they reported any suspicious troop movements or special security measures being taken locally. Her next plan would start with the destruction of Texas and her latest discovery, a virtually indestructible plasmoid substance, was slowly maturing at her secret base, located not far away, near the property of a trusting rancher named Calvin Pooley.

Despite her scientific knowledge, Madame Atomos had a poor understanding of American society, much of which left her perplexed. Yet, she realized that, in order to destroy America, she had to gain a better understanding of it. That's why she forced herself, whenever she could, to watch the news—she favored CBS—and, especially, the local news which was often full of revealing details.

But today, this stupid, clumsy man was disturbing her concentration.

Madame Atomos turned the stone of her ring, which looked like a large ruby in a gold setting. It emitted a thin red beam, no thicker than a human hair, which went through the glass and pierced the employee's skull. The man's brain, suddenly subjected to incredibly high temperatures, exploded. He dropped to the floor, where he remained still. A few rivulets of bloodied brain matter began to seep from his nose and ears.

Madame Atomos sighed again and walked off into the night. As she crossed Elm Street, she realized she was bored.

Suddenly, a bit of news she had just watched on television gave her an idea. A magnificent idea. A smile appeared fleetingly on her razor-thin lips. A diabolical plan was already forming inside her prodigious mind. It wouldn't take much more than ten days to execute it, she thought. And her plasmoid wouldn't be ready, in any event, before the new year.

Ten days... Why not twelve days? As in that insipid song, *The Twelve Days of Christmas* that some stores had already begun to play.

The Twelve Days of Christmas, indeed! Why, it would be her own Christmas gift to herself!

Twelve days later exactly—Madame Atomos prided herself on punctuality!—the guinea pig whom she had personally selected and who had just been subjected to an intensive nuclear treatment, was, for the last time, sitting attached to a metal chair in an underground base located near Calvin Pooley's ranch.

Everything was ready. But Madame Atomos left nothing to chance. She had to have the man repeat her instructions one last time.

"Tell me again what you're supposed to do, Mr. Lee Harvey Oswald," whispered the deadly Madame Atomos.[7]

Published in *La Saga de Mme. Atomos,* Tome 1, 2006

---

[7] According to several reliable witnesses, Lee Harvey Oswald, during the last months of his life, when some of his whereabouts remain unknown to this day, had changed physically, experiencing unexplained hair loss and premature aging.

Bringing together Madame Atomos and Monsieur Ming, a.k.a. The Yellow Shadow, Bob Morane's nemesis (from the novels by Henri Vernes) was an old ambition of mine...

Madame Atomos' Holidays

There is no rest for the wicked.
Isaiah, 48:22

"Your problem is that you never go on holidays," said Madame Atomos.

"I beg your pardon?" replied the Yellow Shadow.

They were both relaxing in their chaises lounges on the private beach of the magnificent Xanadu Beach Resort on Grand Bahama island. The weather was perfect; the turquoise blue sea made a striking contrast with the immaculate white sand that was raked every morning by the *boys* of a palace which, once, had counted Frank Sinatra, the Rat Pack and Cary Grant amongst its guests.

A light breeze gently caressed the palm trees, which cast their shadows over the beach-goers and kept the temperature wonderfully cool for the season.

Madame Atomos delicately took a sip of her pineapple rum cocktail, which she had been nursing since she had come on to the beach to join her occasional associate. She had gestured to her usual companion, the hulking Isadori, to go and play in the water while she talked business with the Yellow Shadow. She wore a striking black bikini with as little fabric as the law allowed, which emphasized her splendid figure. But she entertained no illusion as to the power of her feminine charms over the stone-faced Mongol. Madame Atomos knew Monsieur Ming well enough to know that he was entirely invulnerable to her sex appeal.

They had agreed to meet at the Xanadu. In the past, her organization had lent assistance to the Yellow Shadow, in 1965 in San Francisco, when Ming had established his base in the underground city of Kowa, and later, in Africa, to help him spawn his deadly butterflies. In exchange, Ming had pretty much let Madame Atomos have a free rein in America and had given her financial support whenever he could.

"You're always working," explained Madame Atomos. "Constantly coming up with new schemes, which are then invariably crushed by that insolent Frenchman. This creates a permanent stress that must be very bad for your health."

"My health is fine, thank you," said the Yellow Shadow, rather testily, his robotic right hand clamping on his left to hide the slight shaking that had started to plague him recently.

"If you spent more time relaxing on holidays," continued Madame Atomos, "you would feel more rested when the time comes to launch your next offensive. Don't tell me that you don't occasionally feel like you're not as good as you used to be, or that you've been repeating yourself lately? Not that it doesn't happen to all of us eventually," she rushed to add, having noticed a quick, baleful look in her associate's amber eyes.

"So... What would you suggest?" asked Monsieur Ming after a pause.

Madame Atomos stretched like a big cat, boastfully displaying her perfect breasts and her long, smooth legs.

"Do as I do," she purred. "Find yourself a beautiful toy, a little corner of paradise and have some fun."

With a gesture of her manicured hand, she blew a kiss to Isadori who was still frolicking in the water.

"I don't think that's in my nature," sighed the Yellow Shadow with some finality. "I've come to tell you that I've experienced some financial reversals of late..."

"That Frenchman again?" inquired Madame Atomos, whose eyes pointedly stared at the Mongol's left hand which was trembling.

Monsieur Ming ignored her and continued:

"...Therefore I can no longer finance your organization. I know that you have suffered some major setbacks. However, because of my debt to you, I will give you the blueprints for a new type of quantum field generator that will enable you to build a new and better generation of transdimensional saucers."

"It's more than I would have dared to hope for," said Madame Atomos. "Thank you!"

Monsieur Ming got up. Even in black Bermuda shorts, he still looked like a dour clergyman.

"Are you sure you won't stay for dinner?" asked Madame Atomos.

"No. I'm expected in Macao."

The Yellow Shadow walked away.

Madame Atomos smiled. She had duped the Mongol, who was after all a potentially dangerous rival. Monsieur Ming had not suspected the real reason for her presence in the Bahamas.

She looked at the 13th floor penthouse of the Xanadu. For ten years, she had had various servants of hers surreptitiously administer a carefully prepared mixture of drugs to its occupant, who was also the Hotel's owner. Thanks to her efforts, he was now a full-blown lunatic, who barely weighed over 90 pounds, no longer cut his hair and his nails, and slowly agonized—but not without having discreetly transferred half of his vast wealth—$2 billion!—to her Swiss bank account.

Howard Hughes will be dead with three months, thought Madame Atomos, *and with his money, I will rebuild my organization and be even more powerful than before!*

As if she had the time to go on holidays!

Published in *La Saga de Mme. Atomos,* Tome 6, 2008

This tale features Cal de Ter, *the hero of five famous French SF novels penned by P.-J. Herault between 1975 and 1984. Sometime in the future, a bloody war has erupted between Earth and its Martian colony. During one of the battles, a military strategist named Cal is forced to go into a hiberna-tion life pod, condemned to drift forever in infinite space. However, thousands of years later, the pod lands on the planet Vaha, still in its primitive stages of evolution, Cal emerges and eventually comes across a deserted alien base, left by the long-lost, advanced race of the Loys. He uses the base's re-sources (including its giant computer HI) to make himself a squadron of sentient androids, and goes back into hibernation, from which he periodically emerges, when alerted by his an-droids, to monitor Vaha's progress and safety...*

The Artifact

The artifact had landed during the night.

HI 20314, the giant computer abandoned by the Loys on Vaha, had not detected it. Later, Cal assumed that the regular distress calls that HI broadcast into space had been responsible for the artifact's coming. Shortly before going into hiberna-tion, he had ordered the computer to stop all broadcasts into space, but the transmissions themselves would continue to cross the vast sidereal space forever.

The artifact was clearly of alien origins.

However, it had not been built by the Loys and nothing in HI's database could help determine its origin. It remained a mystery. Cal tried to communicate with the artifact, using all wavelengths of the visible and electromagnetic spectrum, but it remained stubbornly silent.

The artifact had killed Sirkou.

Cal, his face somber, rewatched the scenes captured by HI's remote exploration units. He had just returned from a

292

short journey into space, having finally made the decision to guide the evolution of Vaha, his new adopted world, when the computer had alerted him, as it had been instructed to do, to let him know that something was wrong in the Northwest Region of the Great Lake.

The first image that Cal saw was the corpse of Sirkou.

Sirkou was twelve. He was one of those Vahussi children to whom Cal had taught the breaststroke and the front crawl, before the Tocosab attack.

Cal remembered him very well: a smart little boy with wide eyes, always eager to learn new things, a gifted swimmer who, later—and if it had been in the nature of the Vahussi—could have become a champion.

Cal had subsequently learned that Sirkou's parents came from Olam, a large village of weavers, located 300 kilometers to the north. They had embarked on the ritual journey that every master weaver has to perform before reaching his fortieth year. Colu, Sirkou's father, had chosen to perform this task with his wife and son.

After the defeat of the Tocosabs, Sirkou's family had returned home and had contributed significantly to the trade relations between the different communities of the Great Lake.

Then, the Apemen had attacked Olam, and Colu, and his wife, and little Sirkou had died.

The Apemen, who had been sent by the artifact.

Cal continued to view the images on the big screen. HI 20314, ignorant of human feelings, made no distinction between an act of slaughter and a sunset, and did not spare him anything.

The Apemen were what, on Earth, would have been called Neanderthals--at least, it seemed so to Cal. Or perhaps, they were a race of anthropoid mutants, like the Mangani? They lived in the arid North, barely surviving on the products of their hunts. They were aggressive, divided into small clans, selfish, making the notion of progress virtually impossible.

The Vahussi called these primitive and brutal creatures "Lari" and avoided them whenever possible.

Then, the artifact had come and everything had changed.

The Lari had united and—inconceivably!—the artifact had taught them how to make and use weapons, primitive, but daunting, due to their immense physical strength. Cal's face broke into a bitter smile when he saw the image of the new Chief of the Lari brandishing an ax of roughly cut stone and slice open the skull of one of its rivals.

Cal had taught the manufacture and handling of the bow to the Vahussi, so what right did he have to object to what the artifact had done with the Lari? But there was a fundamental difference, he thought. The Vahussi had used their new technology solely to defend themselves, while the Lari, driven by the powerful influence of the artifact, had descended at dawn on the village of the weavers and had massacred and eaten one third of its population .

Cal understood that two competing forces were now at work on Vaha, each intending to lead it at their own discretion, controlling its development for their own purposes. He, assisted by the Loys' science, and the artifact, whose identity and resources remained a mystery.

Cal could, of course, accelerate his program. He could, for example, teach the Vahussi how to make gunpowder. With firearms, they would quickly repel the invaders. But what would be the artifact's response? What would it then teach the Apemen? What monstrous escalation might then afflict this planet?

Cal was still looking for a solution. Several times, he had tried to contact the artifact, but without results. And again, he watched the film showing the death of Sirkou.

The apeman had first killed Sirkou's mother. Colu was already dead, having perished defending his village. Then, he approached the small human, exposing his sharp teeth in a gesture which left no doubt as to his intentions.

Sirkou grabbed a large knife, sharp as a razor, which was used to cut the light fabrics, and struck a blow, a deadly blow, literally gutting the apeman from top to bottom.

Unfortunately, the long arm of the dying creature had time to grab the child and its clawed hand had smashed the child's head like a ripe fruit.

The survivors of the Lari then returned to the valley of the artifact—where it had landed—and made bloody offerings to their god.

Cal had made his decision. The future of this world weighed in the balance. The fate of the Vahussi rested on his shoulders. Cal—once a Logician of Earth—could make no other decision.

"Implementation," he said HI 20314.

The Loys had anticipated that if the accursed spores that had been responsible for the destruction of most of their race, ever found a foothold on one of their worlds, they had to have the means to cauterize the area, or risk the fate of the entire planet. A small satellite orbiting each Loys world, contained within it a microscopic granule of antimatter capable of total destruction within a radius of 100 km.

It was this weapon of Apocalypse that Cal unleashed on the valley of the Lari.

A little later, Cal asked HI 20314 to transmit the first images of the post-devastation. Nothing had survived the death from the sky. Not even the artifact, whose shape was still silhouetted against the rock now laid bare: that of a large black monolith...

Published in *Le Retour de Cal de Ter,* 2007

This second Cal de Ter *story was an excuse to reimagine some of the events of our past, projecting them on Vaha, and correcting one of the most egregious mistakes in our history...*

E Pur Su Muove...

From his cell window, Palando Palandei could see Chagar illuminating the night sky. In a few hours, the devoted henchmen of Pontiff Klari would come and drag him out of his wretched prison and onto the central square of Blirod where the stake had already been erected and was only waiting for its victim.

According to the forms of the Law of Frahal, the Pontiff would exhort him to publicly renounce his sacrilegious theories. If Palandei did so, he would then be quickly and mercifully garroted by the Brother Executioner. If not, it would be the horrible death of being burned alive before the crows, a salutary lesson for all the other heretical savantists of Blirod.

Palandei had made the decision to not renounce his research, the fruit of an entire life spent observing the stars. The Church of Frahal had tried to seize and destroy all the copies of his treatise *Sideralus Nuncia*, printed by poor Rogar, disemboweled by Klari's torturers, but some copies were bound to have survived, and might even reach the more enlightened state of Pandria. His work would survive, and that was enough to allow Palando Palandei, former High Astronomer of the Seignory of Blirod, to wait for death with serenity.

Suddenly, he heard a key turn inside the lock. The guards were not scheduled for another two hours. The hour of the execution had not yet come. Palando Palandei wondered who could thus risk his life in order to talk to a notorious heretic whose words could lead an innocent straight into the cells of the Pontiff.

Two men entered silently. At least, the astronomer thought they were men, because the newcomers were wrapped in long gray coats, hoods raised to hide their faces.

The first of the two lowered his hood, revealing an open face, with strong, energetic features, eyes filled with determination and ancient wisdom, something which seemed to the astronomer to be in contradiction with the apparent youth of the newcomer.

"It is of my sad duty to inform you that your presence here may bring upon you the wrath of the Pontifical Question," said the astronomer, referring to the ecclesiastical court of Pontiff Klari.

"Be assured, Master Palandei, that no one will learn of our visit," answered the unknown man, smiling.

"But then... why did you come?"

The man pulled out a copy of *Sideralus Nuncia* from beneath his cloak.

"Are you the author of this remarkable treatise?"

The astronomer smiled. Even at death's door, the understandable vanity of the scientist caused him to smile modestly.

"I am honored that my humble work found merit in your eyes, Lord... Lord...?" he said, trying to in vain to guess the identity of his visitor, whom he thought was of noble blood.

The other remained unaware of the question and continued:

"And it is your theory that Vaha is only one celestial body amongst others, orbiting around its star Oma, which itself is only one sun amongst billions of others, each also having their own Vahas? That is why you were condemned to burn at the stake today?"

"That is so. The Pontifical Question judged that the notion that Vaha was neither single, nor the center of the celestial world, was sacrilegious. However, my observations are irrefutable. It is enough to note..."

"No need to argue your thesis with me, Master Palandei. The Church is wrong and you are right," said the man, with such certainty in his voice that the astronomer was shaken by it.

"Really, My Lord...? But how can you...?"

"I know because I myself come from the one of these distant points of light in the sky—another sun named Sol. I was born on its third planet, Terra. Because of that, my name is Cal of Terra."

The astronomer then burst into tears. He had had, until then, faith in his observations, the product of thousands of sleepless nights spent bent over a telescope, wearying his sight as he watched the motion of the stars; faith in his calculations, made and remade thousands of times, covering entire note-books meticulously filled with rows upon rows of figures; faith, at last, in the rational organization of the cosmos. But it was something else to find himself before the massive and irrefutable proof of what he had merely believed, delivered by someone who had fallen from the very Heavens themselves.

"My Lord Cal..." he murmured at last, "you really come from another star?"

"I do."

"Are the Heavens populated with other worlds, similar to our Vaha?"

"They are."

"And do men travel between the stars like our sailors on the oceans?"

"They do."

Palandei wiped away his tears.

"My Lord Cal... I have never known greater joy in my life! I can now die in peace. The bite of the flames will be nothing compared to the celestial vision which you have just offered me... Men sailing between the stars... Thank you, My Lord Cal, thank you!"

"I did not come here to let you be devoured by the flames of Pontiff Klari, Master Palandei," said Cal, smiling.

"What do you mean?"

Cal made a gesture with his hand and the second visitor took off his hood.

The astronomer uttered a cry of horror when he saw the face of the second man.

Because it was it his!

Cal's Report recorded in HI's databanks:
I had left my android Lou with specific instructions to supervise the development of the Vahussi's scientific research. Thus the publication of *Sideralus Nuncia* immediately drew his attention, as well as the death sentence of its author, Master Palando Palandei. The injustice of the latter convinced Lou to temporarily pull me out of hibernation.

I immediately took the decision to free the astronomer, but a heuristic projection ran by HI at my request showed that, if it became known that Palandei had escaped, whatever the circumstances, it would result in discrediting his scientific theories and would delay much of Vaha's evolution.

For the astronomer's thesis to take root, his death as a martyr at the stake was necessary. Thus his defeat would become his greater victory.

Refusing to sacrifice such a noble scientist, I asked HI to manufacture a proto-android in Palandei's likeness, but with unconnected synapses, no artificial intelligence, and only primary response automatisms, whose existence would be enough to satisfy the Pontiff's torturers.

As for Palandei, he continued his research in peace under another name on the island of Psorda, after I had taken him alongside me on a shuttle into space so that he could see with his own eyes what only his mathematics and great mind had until then enabled him to imagine: the universe.

Published in *L'Epopée de Cal de Ter*, 2009